Phil Kafcaloudes is a writer, journalist and broadcaster who hosts an international breakfast show on the ABC's Radio Australia network, and regularly appears as a guest host of the evening program on ABC NewsRadio. His first book, The ABC All Media Guide to Court Reporting (ABC Books) is now a standard text in many media courses. Out of some of the cases he covered as a reporter came his collection of short stories, The Chequered Lady (Federation Press). He has written for Limelight magazine, blogs for The Drum and is correspondent for Radio New Zealand's flagship Morning Report. Phil regularly appears on the News Breakfast on ABC News 24 and ABC1. He lives with his wife in a house full of dogs and music in Melbourne, and is working on a sequel to Someone Else's War.

Someone Else's War

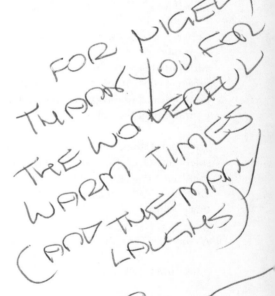

Phil Kafcaloudes

SEW Books

here be friends, here be heroes
here be sunshine, here be grey
here be life, here love lies bleeding
memories so hazy
and dreams that drove me crazy

here be doubt, here be paradise
here be starbright, here be pain

pictured within

kith and kin
pictured within

- **Jon Lord** *(Pictured Within)*

Prologue

In the satchel delivered from a city solicitor were all manner of documents: a certificate of marriage, wartime travel passes, deeds now useless.

But the eyes of the four siblings were on the parcel wrapped in greyed butcher's paper which had torn in places, showing it held some kind of manuscript.

Tina, Freda, Nicky and my mother all had the same thought, the same hope: that these pages could hold the answer to the mystery that had defined their lives.

They scrabbled, almost as one, to get into the parcel, but it was bound tightly by a length of wool that was once bright red but now faded to the colour of dried blood, its knot so locked that my Uncle Nicky had to cut it with his good bread knife. When the butcher's paper was finally pulled back, it revealed a sheaf of hundreds of pages, rough and frayed, covered in pencil hand-writing in old formal Greek.

On the first sheet there was a note in English:

My children,

I would exchange every thing, every life I have helped, for the chance to have been with you, but it was a choice I did not have. Please know that no matter where you were, I was your mother, and I was watching you.

Now I am gone, this diary is yours so you can know at last.

There was a pause in that moment when the four were frozen by the sound of these words, the tone of their mother ringing in the air, matter-of-fact, confident, perhaps stinging.

Then at once they were the children they had not been for decades, tearing through the pages for the answers to the years of questions. They tried, the four of them, to make out what they could, but the writing was very faded, and as Olga had written on both sides of each page and the lead had leaked through the transparent wartime paper, the writing often appeared to be no more than a jumble of confused forward and backward letters.

When, one by one, his sisters had given up on getting anything out of the diary, my Uncle Nicky gently put the pages back into their numbered order, lifted the bundle into a shoe box and put it away, not sure what to do with this decayed diary, but not wanting it to be thrown away. For years it stayed in that box on top of a ceiling beam in his garage, never touched, too high for the hands of his growing children, forgotten by most.

It was at a Christmas much later that he gave it to me, the last born of the next generation, the one who listened closest to the stories of Olga's war deeds, the one who asked questions. Uncle Nicky made no fuss about it, he just quietly gestured me to come to the garage with him, then got me to lean the old paint-spattered ladder up against the beam and get the box down. We touched the papers together, just my Uncle Nicky and me. We laughed a little at how impossible they were to read, and I think we cried a little too.

To my shame, the pages stayed in that box on my wardrobe for some years more. They stayed there as the box got dustier, as I wrote other people's stories, as I went to the funerals of an auntie and uncle, as I made a family of my own. It wasn't until a chance meeting with an archives researcher that I shared the story of the box, and she told me her department had just developed technology that might make the writing more legible.

So it was that I opened the box once again to see the jumble of Greek letters that was once a story. I picked one of the clearer pages and my elementary Greek could make out the faint words scratched into the paper:

… this was someone else's war, miles from my life. But I had been pulled into it. It tore me as I realised that this was now my war…

It was the way her fingers - they must have been strong - pressed into that miserable tracing paper. My grandmother's voice was jammed through the texture, as if she emphasised words by pushing harder on the pencil. I could hear her as loud as if she was there with me, across the years, oceans and the grave.

I packed the box and took the papers to the archivist. It was late on a Friday and she wanted to go home, but I begged her to at least look at the pages. Once she saw them, she couldn't leave. We stayed there in her lab for the next four hours, testing settings on her scanner, darkening, contrasting, adjusting levels, until the scratches on the paper showed up as dark lines, filling in where the pencil lead had faded, until the scribblings became words, often paragraphs, in some cases whole chapters.

Over the next weeks, as she processed the rest of the pages, I tried to find someone who could translate them. Four professional readers gave up after a page or so. An intrigued friend promised to have it done in a few days, but baulked after the first line. A university student, excited about using this translation as part of her Masters thesis, took a copy of a few pages to translate, but from that moment never answered my calls.

My godfather thought all this terribly funny. He was no learned man, but was tenacious about the history of Greece. He had been in the same resistance as Olga but never met her. To him these translators were amateurs, people who didn't care for the history of the ancient land. After I told him about the Masters student, he made an offhand promise to look at the manuscript. After only a week presented me with a handwritten translation of the entire sheaf, apologising that he wasn't quicker.

His notes showed that these papers were less of a diary than a serial letter from Olga to the oldest of her children, my mother Nellie.

I spent many nights with Olga's story, researching the history of Greece in the war and finding her place in it. Her spirit was with me every evening as I worked. Her voice, sometimes chiding, sometimes soft and cooing, pushed me on, her spirit at my shoulder, never letting me forget or delay.

In this way the story slowly came together and now, through her writings and the tales of her children, Olga's story can at last be told.

Where her own words from the diary are used, they are prefaced by 'Olga'. The rest are mine.

Preface

Olga

I am not a runner. They say I am strong, but they are being fooled by my eye. The strong of eye can fool anyone.

Never mind that though, I could run when I needed to. I surprised myself at how fast I could be.

I surprised myself about many things in fact.

Central Greece, July 1942

They are running for a fall. The two figures are running too fast. They know they are.

It's the fear. The fear of being seen. Their camouflaging black clothes and face paint are of no use tonight on that high road on the hill, where the full moon makes them silhouettes any German patrol would be able see from miles around. But they don't have the time to negotiate the rough and snaggy gullies. The high road is their only choice. So they run.

One slips, the bag in his hand coming down hard on the ground, smashing something inside.

Criticising each other serves no purpose, so they don't. There isn't even time to see what they have broken. There are still two miles to the bridge.

At night the wooden arch seems titanic, much bigger than its fifty yards.

They climb out under the supports, one on each side, their moccasins slipping and getting stuck in the tight angles of the criss-crosses. At the agreed span, they feel in the bags around their necks. There is no binding tape in the supplies. It ran out a week ago. They have to make do with pushing and jamming the cylinders in hard to the wedges of the woodwork. Then the leads, the detonators, the igniters and timer, all snatched from a crude supply, often homemade from stolen pieces. The fall on the road had broken one of the timers, so they have to hope the explosives from one side of the bridge will set off the detonators on the other, but with the bridge being a typically over-engineered British design from before the first world war, if this doesn't happen, and only one side goes off, the bridge might still support itself.

Springs are turned, time is set, and they hope.

When the explosives blow and the dust and smoke drift, they see the bridge still stands ever magnificent through the full moon haze. They dare not look at each other, knowing they have neither the material nor the time for a second attempt.

Then slowly the wooden planks of the road start to dance up and down, and a roar like a maimed animal echoes from the ravine. The bridge, with grace, collapses.

They stare for a long time, both of them thinking of the power of two against the monolith. The anchor points fall last, leaving the cliffs like they must have been back before the days of the Turks, before the days of the British, before the Italians, before the Germans, perhaps to the days of Aristotle, if he ever ventured to this dry cracked place.

Finally, with just the luxury of a slap on the back and the squeeze of a shoulder, they saunter back along the gully, in no hurry this time, like any two workers after a hard day. The Germans might catch them, but to hell with it. In these moments they don't care.

There is no other celebrating though. The German supply line may have been broken, but in doing so, Olga and her comrade have also destroyed a bit of Greece.

Theaterina

(Three years earlier: August 1938 – January 1939)

Athens, Greece

They marched into the square with a pathetic air. The first among them was a little man with baggy knees in his trousers that made him appear to be stumbling when he wasn't. Behind him was the tallest of the group, his pants far too short, making him look like either a fool or a bum. Then there was the man in the perfect suit. How easily he seemed to have no dignity, and how silly his good clothes looked here and now.

The seventy of them had been taken from a bed or a kitchen or an office by the Greek military. All had been angry, disbelieving and demanding of rights they no longer had. This was peacetime. They were simply journalists who told the truth, communists who demanded change, or pacifists who got angry when people disagreed with them.

They burned in the worst of the Athens heat but some would not give in, like the suited man who would not take off his coat or the two communists who sat, getting up slowly again when ordered by soldiers, then sitting again after a while.

This is how they waited through the midday in the dry square, some forgetting where they were, eyeing the lady workers and housewives who were doing their presiesta shopping. A cooling wind came through, and it relaxed to an afternoon that could have been pleasant.

The guarding soldiers smoked and leant against the church wall in the only shade. One of the prisoners, with the face of smiling cheekiness, jerked his head towards a smoking soldier, flicking his fingers for a cigarette. The soldier threw one to him and laughed with his comrade about how the man was going to light it. They stopped laughing when one of the other prisoners brought out a lighter. The cheeky man lit up and handed the cigarette around to the others. The police had taken cigarettes and watches, but forgot about lighters.

A rustle in the prisoners and one man broke through and walked strong past the soldiers and out of the square. It took only seconds. The soldiers saw it happen and were impotent. They could stop a running man. They could tackle him or shoot him. But this man did no running, and like fools they watched till he was no longer able to be caught. The soldiers were more vigilant for a while after that. Then they leaned and smoked once more.

After an hour, the man they all knew entered the square. That short, stocky war hero and tyrant, John Metaxas, with his brilliantine hair, perfectly pressed suit and craggy face. He stomped to the space between the soldiers and the caught ones. The noise stopped. The sitting prisoners stood. The standing prisoners stood straighter.

Prime Minister Metaxas lifted his chin to the air, a habit that made him feel taller. He swivelled a look across the prisoners, from left to right and right to left. He had meant to be disapproving and fearsome, but his shortness and thickness made him look like a father. And he spoke in a voice thin for a tyrant.

You. Men. This will be quick. Sign the paper that will be handed to you. Agree to support the Greek government. War is coming to Europe and we must be united. That is all I require of you.

He made a little nod, along with the smallest of smiles. Of course they would all sign.

No. Sir.

It was very quick, this answer from the editor of the Socialist Weekly. The 'sir' was not added because the editor wanted to be respectful. He just wasn't brought up to be rude.

No, sir. We will not sign your little piece of paper.

General Metaxas felt as though he'd been slapped. The editor sensed this.

You have taken us from our own homes. Sir. You must know that many of the people here were arrested in front of their families, in the night.

Passers-by were now stopping, feeling it was safe to hear the argument between the Prime Minister and the newspaperman.

Metaxas quivers a little and is sure the group was seeing it. He tries to be firm in his voice. To those listening, he is whispering.

You newspapermen write things, lies, about the King and the King's government. You make the people hate their own country.

No, sir. I love Greece, and will pledge loyalty to Greece at any time.

Metaxas says that loyalty to Greece and loyalty to the government are the same thing.

No sir you are wrong, the newspaperman was shouting now. Your regime is not Greece.

Then you will rot in jail.

Then I will rot in jail.

The General doesn't understand how the editor man can look so happy. How he can look like a weight has been lifted.

Then a man in the front row throws out his body as if restrained and calls out that the Prime Minister has no right. A soldier raises his rifle to his eye in the quickest of movements, pointing and cocking it at the shouter. Metaxas rocks on his heels, not discouraging the soldier.

There is a howl from the group then, from somewhere deep inside. Someone calls him a murderer, a brutal animal.

A guard runs in and pulls the man, still yelling, to the General.

They are face to face, the man screaming a demand for release and for liberty and democracy in Greece.

The General takes his pistol from his waistband, very clumsily for a soldier, points it up at the man's head, and fires.

The man drops.

The General puts his gun back shakily, and raises his chin.

The prisoners have never known words to kill so suddenly. This has always been a country of loud mouths and hard words. They stare at the dead man and move forward, not aware they are doing it. The soldiers, who are also shocked by the General's ease of killing, are slow to raise their rifles. Metaxas has to command them to do it. The mob stops.

Metaxas seemed to be pleading now.

It was his very own fault. Just sign the paper and you will all be free... stop all this treason...

He marched out of the square, arms swinging, the soldier always.

The General gone, the group seemed to lose its anger. The prisoners had seen enough, and when urged by the soldiers, they marched easily back to the jail.

The soldiers had forgotten about the body, and it was left in the square. A few minutes later a man and two women came out. There were no tears. They just took him away.

The same day in Central Athens

In the morning her shoes had a snap to their step, but it is midday now and hope has gone from these shoes that have taken her to all over Athens. Fifty-two shops she has seen, and each has been the same play: the shopkeepers are servants to her when they think her a customer, but when she asks for a job their eyes fade to look through and around her. No-one needs a cleaner, no-one needs a woman who can speak English. We regret, they all say, not regretting at all.

One place off Leoforos, a little cargo agency, does let the woman clean. No promises, the owners say, while offering a mop. No promises.

For twenty minutes the woman scrubs the linoleum under their desks and in the corners where no-one has bothered to clean before. For twenty minutes she washes and dusts every dirty place, picking away at the chewing gum, coffee spills and rat shit. For all of those twenty minutes she tries to ignore the words of the women who taught her, the women who would not imagine her ever being this poor, this needy, this desperate. She shoves those words far away from her and they fill her head even more, so that she doesn't even see that the owner has not bothered moving from his desk. She mops around his shoes without realising.

Panting and satisfied, she finishes as a mess in her good clothes, stinking of detergent.

The shopkeeper's wife looks her up and down, tuts at her state and gestures to the door. Her work is not good enough.

She offers no argument; she has none to offer. Picking up her purse, she leaves the little office with no look backward, head up, shoulders square.

Down the street, at a wall in a lane that she thinks is away from eyes, she is as a doll, blank faced and empty, not feeling angry, not feeling anything. Absently, she touches in her purse and pulls out a photograph. She stares at it, still as the air, and suddenly cries. In this city where no-one notices each other, people do look as they pass. But they don't stop. Perhaps it is that her grief is too strong, or too rudely public, or it is that they fear this woman who is tearing at herself. They are best away from her, so they leave her.

She will not remember how she got out of that lane or the hour's bus ride back to Glyfadia. She will remember the smell of tomato and garlic that wafted to her as the bus pulled away after letting her off. She will remember the warmth of the voices and the sounds of glass and plate, the sounds of life. They pull her across that little square and through the door of the taverna.

She will remember that for an hour she is with them, eating, bantering, laughing, not as a peasant, not as a woman alone and poor, but as one of them, at one with them, sharing in the wit and goodwill. Yes, this is what she needs, and she drinks it in with the retsina. One hour, ignoring that she has not enough to pay for this little snatch of life, her purse sitting by her, hot and empty but for that photograph, calling her to order, trying to remind her of this afternoon's cargo shop, and that the friends she is with are of the moment. For an hour Olga ignores her purse and wishes for nothing. Her life is this hour. She feels the joy of wearing nothing on her mind but a flirt here and there or whether to eat another piece of bread.

This joyful hour passes as it must. The taverna clears except for two old Greeks over their thirteenth game. The sounds of the streets die, for the noisy children are scrubbed and smothered in houses unseen; dogs are curled in corners somewhere, licking mange sores and flea bites; horses and carts are locked away. The world has moved a little, and it has moved towards Olga and her purse.

The waiter smiles and asks if she wants something else. No. I'm fine, she says, and stays sitting alone in the quiet. She has always thought herself courageous, but tonight she is nothing, sitting on that cushion on that bench with her little purse. A bill is laid on the table, and she pretends not to see it. The waiter pulls the windows closed. The old men look to be near the end of the game that she wishes would go on forever, one of them throwing down the last of his ouzo, and not ordering another. The light goes out in the kitchen. The front mat is pulled in. But the courage doesn't come.

In the end it is not courage that comes to her, it is the waiter asking her to please settle the bill, they want to go home.

He can't understand what she tries to say, and brings out his brother the cook, who understands all too well. She sits under them at the table that had brought her such joy, as they tear at her: she who has played with the children of Kings, she who has given birth to five beautiful children, she who has built a shop just like theirs. They don't know any of this. They can't, so they insult and sneer, and at one moment she thinks they are going to slap her, and they could have with rights, for one hour ago she was a woman with no money. Now she is a thief, a tramp.

She takes it all, in full payment, and leaves in a cower. People pass and look away.

Olga

Never get your head down girl. It need never come to that.

This was Ellie's commandment. The wisdom of a street child, a wisdom I had carried for years. When I needed it, when my head really went down, those wise words failed me. On this night my feet and a dirty footpath were all I saw on the way home, and the full stomach helped not at all; it only reminded, for in these moments there could be no sky above, only an eternity of gods and souls pressing down, the Gods of Hate hating.

They hadn't condemned me so for some time.

Once, it was not so long ago, I was as happy as any woman who had taken baby to breast. The sucking of my sweet dolls. You were the sweetest of them. Your little hands would clench and open and clench as you suckled and, when you were full, your legs would jerk out straight and I would wipe your mouth and your top lip that would stay pointed. You never cried, always happy with your lot. Never in our days did you complain of me, born so perfect as you were, and so right I was as your mother.

From a mother I became a tramp who stole food from good people. Those old men and their backgammon, they loved enough not to look as I was being shamed, those men who had faced the terrors of a war, the Turks, the Italians, a depression, yet have grown to be old men playing a game of dice and diamonds without care for time, even as their time was running out. I had faced no guns and known no poverty until now, and at this first challenge I failed. There have been times in my life when I thought this life was not for me. This night there was no Michael or Mother Hadjidaki to disagree. They wouldn't disagree, the Gods told me. You have scattered the ashes of a good life. That is why you are here.

An apartment block in Glyfadia (that night)

It is a tatty, badly built place of cracks and sloping floors, a building where nobody talks to anybody, where greetings are evaded by neighbours who pass hunched and mumbling. As she walks the landing to her room, she bitters at the closed doors of her cruel neighbours.

It would be very quick. A turn of a lever on the rattly smelly stove. Never in its long life would that stove have performed such an honourable service.

A turn of a lever.

With a deep breath, she looks through her purse for her key. A turn of a lever and debt will be paid.

Are you serious, Mother Hadjidaki asks. Is this what you want to do? She has the right, says Ellie. It is her life. Mother Hadjidaki sighs and turns away. For as long as Olga can remember, Mother Hadjidaki has been turning away.

My girls will miss me.

No they won't, says Mother Hadjidaki looking back over her shoulder. Not after what you've done.

But I had no choice, Olga cries aloud. Mother, you know I had no choice.

Choice, asks Mother Hadjidaki. You talk of choice? Like the choice I had when you were a foundling. Don't tell me about choice. Life is about choosing and living to regret that choice.

But is this the way?

You must find your own way girl, says Mother Hadjidaki.

Your own way, says Ellie.

Will I be damned?

You were never a Sunday School kind of girl. What do you care of damnation?

So, with bitter thoughts of Father John who groped her eight-year-old leg and begged for her kindness, she looks for her key. But it is not in her purse. She looks again. She empties the purse on that cold cement floor and tears through every crevice of that little bag again and again for nothing, desperate to get into this room that she hates, to turn a lever and earn her fit damnation.

As she searches again, she knows and regrets that the only person who can let her into her apartment is the landlord, an old widow in the old room next door that she knows will stink of mustiness and meals long eaten. Olga may be ready to face eternity, but the fear of seeing a living face living a dying life terrifies her.

Her knock is answered almost straight away. To a suspicious gap.

Olga explains about the key.

Yes, yes, the woman answers. Just come in and I will find the key in a minute. Stay.

There can be no arguing. The key will come when the woman wants to get it. Against all the wishes of her body, she is led towards a small table.

The apartment is small, and the smells are not of the old but of a small posy of gardenias, or are they camellias? The woman's life is told through faded blurry photos of children and yellowing greeting cards that fill the space on every table and sideboard.

From my children, the old woman says, pointing to the photos, almost offhandedly.

They are handsome, Olga answers, meaning it, drinking in the faces that are not smiling.

They never come to see me, the woman mutters, taking one of the photos. It is of her youngest son, her life light, her love. She kisses her finger and presses it to the photograph. She replaces the frame so that it fits exactly in its own groove in the dust.

Family, she says. A pride and a shame. But what is one to do? One must be a mother. Children are as children are. They never visit.

And after this unwitting invitation, Olga breaks the burden of her shame, speaking in a torrent against the hiss of the old woman's little gas flame and the creaks of their chairs. This woman is the first Greek Olga has told of that night, of how she left her family in Australia, of how she just got up from her bed and left. To be here.

Olga is crying without fear, without realising.

The woman is embarrassed. After a few uncomfortable seconds she shuffles out, escaping, promising over her shoulder to find Olga a handkerchief.

She returns with a rag and a sudden question.

How could you leave your children?

It is not meant in a harsh way. It stabs Olga.

There is too much to tell, and Olga tells only a little of it. Of that last night. Of rising before she could be missed. Of kissing her sleeping girls and passing through the little shop Michael had built, with its vats of oil and its dead chickens and its smell of dirty potatoes. Whenever she smells potatoes it breaks her heart.

But why, the old woman asks. Why did you leave your children?

She wants to tell. She wants to give this story to someone else, to pass it away. The story has been started, but the sight of the widow's interest, the interest of gossip, sobers her.

Olga shows her the photo instead.

The widow says they are very pretty, and at this Olga becomes a mother for the first time in a year. Nellie would be fifteen soon, she tells her. Then there's Freda, she's a year younger. The boys chase her already. And Tina…

She is very dark, the widow says, and seems pleased at Tina's Greekness.

Tina. She could silence grown men with a stare of those black eyes. Olga sees Tina in every Greek she passes on the street. And every time she looks in the mirror.

Yes, Olga says. She looks much more Greek than either of us. She's smart that one. Smarter than any of us. I don't know how she came to be in me.

The woman asks the boy's name.

Olga tells of how she and Nicky always knew what the other was thinking. Maybe it is because he is deaf.

She always forgets the effect Nicky's deafness has on people. The old woman's face flattens and she rubs off a fleck of something from the photo with her forefinger. She doesn't seem able to think of what to say.

My husband used to hit me, Olga lies.

And the woman, now satisfied, tuts at that. For her be-loved Michael, Olga resents her for it. But she keeps on the lie.

He hit me because he got jealous of the people I worked with. Those handsome actors. The poor singers.

This perks the widow, who forgets Nellie and Freda and the little deaf Nicky, the beating husband, the aban-doning of them.

Actress? Really? The woman drops the photo face down on the table, and starts on about her son who had wanted to be a film star, like that Robert Donat. But she proudly announces that she talked him out of it. Acting is for layabouts. Men should be building or doctoring. Women should be caring for children. Then she takes Olga's hands and asks, beaming, if she is working on a film right now.

Olga wishes just then that she could be true with this woman and kiss her wrinkled hands and rest on her long breasts and be kissed back and be looked after. She longs not to be admired; she longs to be little.

She just answers no, I have no work right now.

The woman takes the photo again, looking at Olga's babies from top to bottom without seeing. What about teaching then, she asks. Her theatre friends need a gover-ness. We mustn't be too proud to do physical work. After all, being an actress doesn't mean we are anything special.

An hour later, Olga sits at her kitchen table by that stove with the lever and picks at her thigh with a pin. The woman's very old rotting chair had put a splinter in deep. Poking at it only hurts more, but the more it hurts, the deeper the bit and the more important it is to get out now, before it goes bad. A little blood and hurt it would be over. Theatre people, the old woman had said. Of her happiest times she remembers the theatre group in Ultimo. It was a terrible group, all vaudeville and ham, but oh that time when her Nellie and Freda played the children of Corinth, they must've been only six and seven, always looking the wrong way, stepping in all the wrong places.

Never was she so proud. Never was she closer to her poor dead Mother Hadjidaki than when she was on that stage, imagining Mother in the front row watching her girls, nodding. Well done girl. Yes, look at them. You have done me proud.

She gives up on the splinter and tries the old radio for a station. There is only a news reader on, and all his news is bad. A play is banned; people die from meat poisoning; a communist is shot dead after attacking the Prime Minister.

Olga will sleep thinking of her children and of Michael with a hurt. They would be waking around this time.

The same day in Pyrmont, Sydney

The staircase is so narrow and dark that it makes the whole house feel grey. The builders of these thin terraced shops considered windows a luxury, and those little yellow light globes way overhead are hopeless.

Jean pulls her case up the stairs. She's podgy and the staircase isn't wide enough for her and the big case to be side by side, so she goes up backwards, pulling the case up after her. The case bangs on each step. The more she tries to quieten it, the louder the bangs.

Here. Let me help.

Michael is at the top of the stairs. It surprises her how old he looks. He isn't fifty yet, but his curly hair puffs out and his old man's pyjamas sag at the belly and the knees. An old man, Mrs. Minnie said. Find a younger feller, there are plenty around for gawd sake. He's still married, you know. You're right missus, Jean answers. Always agree with the biddies. If you offend them, they spread rumours. Jean is yet to learn that they will anyway.

Michael dashes down to her, awkwardly, splayfooted, and puts his hand over hers, lifting the case in a heroic way.

She follows into his room. She's been in men's bedrooms before, but only to clean. And no man had ever been in the room when she was. Her mother forbade it.

Here, he is the nervous one. While she sits on the bed, he stoops over the dresser, fiddling with a cat figurine. She likes something in that, the boy in the man.

Don't be scared Mr. Stambolis. I don't bite.

Yes, yes. Of course you don't.

He still fidgets. She waits for him to speak next. He paces and taps, starts to talk, reconsiders, waits, then begins in a flourish.

So why are you so late Jean? It's morning already. I was expecting you hours ago.

She tells him about the problem with her Uncle Stan's corn and bunion. It was a bad one…

As she explains he watches her fidgety fingers and sees the differences between Jean and Olga. This squat girl, not yet twenty, so fresh and pink with her knitted cardigan and heavy shoes, everything about her being for a reason. He remembers Olga sitting on this same bed all those years ago, probably the same age as Jean is now but erect like a woman of years, wearing the most delicate of negligees and watching him with the deepest of black eyes and a wide jaw that, even at that youth, dared to be defied. She was all the things Jean isn't. Jean is soft, even to look at. Olga's square shoulders and firm white arms led to perfect fingers never blemished, even after five babies and fifteen years as mistress of a shop. Jean's fingers are scrubbed dry and cracked. He loves Jean's fingers.

Jean has finished her story and is staring at Michael staring at her hands. They have, for the first time, space between them. She wonders how could a man get to his forties, have a house full of children, all that, and still be shy with a woman.

She asks if he wants a cup of tea.

Yes, yes, he says, relieved.

Jean bounds down the stairs before him.

At the old round table Jean listens to Michael talk about the shop's winter damp, the girls' schools, the publican next door getting drunk on his own whisky, the price of fish. She pours him more tea, and he chatters more. Eventually he'll get onto it.

When he does, it surprises her, because it's in the middle of him telling her how he breaks chicken necks.

Do you think you could love an old man like me? There's twenty years between our ages, you know.

Closer to thirty, I think.

She doesn't say it with any meaning, just in the way that she says a lot of things. Matter-of-fact. Michael crumples a little, and Jean rushes in saying she wouldn't have cared if it was fifty years difference. Or a hundred.

He nods, looking more than ever to her like an old man, and quite lovely. The lovely baby things that return with age: the jowls, the thin hair, the mouth that looks like it wants to cry.

Mr. Stambolis, I have always loved you, even back when you took me on, when I was a little skip of a girlie...

But people might treat you bad. I am still a married man.

Jean gets an Irish flash of irritation. The people here will have to get used to it, she says.

He smiles, and his eyes are wet. Instantly, it seems to her.

Well then, she had better call him Michael.

A voice comes from above, the top of the stairs.

Yes, call him Michael.

A lithe and very pretty girl jumps down the break-the-neck stairs. She wraps her arms around her father's shoulders and hugs really hard. Michael locks his arms around her just as hard and pulls her over his lap.

So you are going to stay with us again, Jean, the girl asks through the gap in his elbow.

Yes Freda. I'm staying.

The girl yelps pleasure, then looks at her suspiciously.

Where are you going to stay? You're not going to cram in with us again are you? Four is too much. Dad? Four is too much. It's too small. Tina's getting big, and Nellie's fifteen nearly. It's too small, Dad.

Michael says yes, it is a problem. What is there to do, he wonders out loud. Ah. His room. Jean could stay with him. Mother's gone away, and there's so much space. Yes, that'll fix it. Would Jean like to stay with a smelly old man?

Jean says she doesn't mind. Yes he is smelly, she agrees, but he is nice smelly. Freda laughs, but remembers that women and men shouldn't sleep together. It's all right, Jean tells her, if the man and the woman know each other really well.

This satisfies Freda. She tugs at her father's hair, her eyes shining because she was involved in the decision. Above them there's the sound of more feet coming down the stairs.

Freda bangs the table, wanting this moment all for herself.

Nellie comes first, then Tina, both sleepy. The stumbling Nellie goes to the ice box and takes out some milk. She is only a few years younger than Jean, and a child still. Tina is nine, but with a head that sees something has happened.

Michael stands like to make a formal announcement. Ladies and gentlemen. Well… ladies. May I present the newest addition to the Stambolis household, Miss Jean.

The slightly curdled milk jams in Nellie's throat. She likes Jean, but…

There is a scream.

Get off that chair. That's mummy's chair!

Freda freezes, half onto the old bentwood chair on the other side of the table, the one jammed up against the wall. She's stopped not because of Tina's order, but because she, like the others, remembers this is indeed where Olga, and only Olga, used to sit, straight as a princess holding court, shelling peas while each of them was around the table with their big mugs of tea, writing or drawing, Olga answering Nellie's homework questions between calling out to Michael in the shop that the oil smells like it's up too high. It is a memory to Freda so calm that there is no wind and no other sound in it.

Freda looks up, expecting to see everyone watching her, but they aren't. They're all looking at the chair, even Jean.

Tina, satisfied now that Freda will leave the chair alone, starts swinging happily on her father's neck.

Jean resumes as if nothing has happened.

Yes, love, she says to Nellie, it'll be like before. I'll cook and clean with you, and look after the shop. And your father too. I'll look after him.

Tina's swinging is now almost pulling him off the chair.

I want mummy back, I want mummy back, she calls in a bright ring-a-rosy chant sung for the fun, not the words.

Jean has already decided she would keep out of any discussion of Olga. She liked her and thought her a good mother. Like everyone else, Jean has no idea why she left so suddenly.

Tina keeps swinging. She is coming back, isn't she? The girls at school say she isn't. They say she left us. They say she hated us.

Freda and Nellie look at each other. Michael sees it and tells them what he couldn't know. He says they'll see their mother again. Soon, he's sure.

You promise? Tina asks, jumping up, trying to push down his shoulders.

Yes, but…

Good. I'm going to bed.

She races up the stairs, and calls out near the top.

Did Freda tell you there's no space in the room?

Yes, she told me that…

But Tina is gone.

Nellie rinses her glass, puts it back on the sink upside down and follows Tina.

Good night dad. Good night Jean. It is nice to have you back. We missed you.

Jean gets teary eyed, she can never help it. Just say something nice, and here the tears come. It's the Irish or the Scottish. The same place as the God-almighty temper.

Freda, jealous at those tears, grabs Jean and tells her she is her best friend.

Freda goes to bed happy that she made Jean cry too.

Glyfadia, Athens

The night had been hard, her sleep full of accusations and dragons and bad meals and children with skinned knees. Yet waking in that little room was no relief at all for her with the nightmares of the real outside that peeling wall. With the waking and the sleeping as paltry choices, she switched all night between the two, until woken as the sun was well in the sky by knocks on her door.

Across the threshold was the old woman in her dressing gown, the only clothes Olga knew of her. Peering in but never wanting to come in, the woman said she had telephoned her theatre people friends, and yes they did need a governess, and yes, they would see Olga tomorrow. Her hands were then taken, being rubbed and kissed. The woman eyed Olga marvellously for but a moment, then pulled her hands back and, with looks up and down the corridor, was gone.

Olga has no taxi fare. She hasn't even enough for a bus. So the next day she leaves the apartment before the sun, and walks to Athens, past Athens, to the north, to their house. She could have asked the old woman for the loan of a pittance, but she never would. The woman had done enough for her, the next good deed should be her own.

She walks and hurts in her heeled shoes through the cracked concrete and the wolf whistles of the early morning, her head clear of voices and urges.

The Diathini's house bulges with rich gardens and money. There seems to be a gardener for every tree, a servant for every room.

They had dressed for the interview, he sweating in a suit with vest; she in a neck high dress and sitting posed like a slightly moving photograph. They fidget too, she going to snatch at the cakes and thinking better of it; he picking at lint he doesn't have on his sleeve.

They banter with Olga as trained diplomats, seeming to care whether she thinks the weather clement or that Gauguin over there a touch gaudy. These are people who think anyone in good shoes a member of their society. It is simply that Olga is wearing her best shoes, the ones Michael bought her for the Christmas ball. She has no other left.

When the woman's question comes it is sudden, as if she can't fit it in anywhere else.

What if you were offered a job in a play? Would you just leave our children?

Both the woman and her husband lean forward together, faces eager and intense, as if to be able to hear better in that most quiet of rooms.

No, Olga answers quick and definite, I would never leave children who depended on me.

The Diathini's lean back, again in that perfect unison, and Mr Diathini smiles, telling her she can start on Monday.

Olga

On the bus home, with a month's wage in advance in my purse, I realised the widow must have told them of leaving you. I regretted my lie about that, but not too much. This was a good day. It was not a day for regretting. A child, a little girl, on the street was jumping, the sun flying off her hair, brightening the world. How could the world be anything but as bright as that girl's hair?

When we have, we forget the times when we have nothing. Easily, too easily, I fell into this rich home like a visiting aunt who couldn't be pushed out. I found myself checking the dust on the tables and suggesting menus for dinner. I had no right, but I had fallen.

Diathini House, Athens

It is washing day of her third week in her new job. Mrs Diathini brings a woman down in the washroom, a wide, flowered woman with an unfortunate smile that reminds of nausea. She is introduced as a Mrs Genges, one of the leading patrons of the theatre in Athens.

Mrs. Genges barely says hello and is already mentioning the names of many of her protégés who have gone on to become the greatest in the world of film and stage. Olga recognises not one name. Mrs Genges is not impressed when Olga says her most recent role was in Shaw's Pygmalion.

He is a communist, Mrs. Genges says, flatly, and with last looks at the washing, and then at Olga's thin waist, she leaves, throwing over her shoulder that auditions are tomorrow. She calls out that she should bring some knitting.

Olga has an ouzo on the way home. In that same little taverna across from the bus stop, she takes her little wage to the waiter to pay for that meal from last month. But now they know she can pay, they insist it all had been a misunderstanding, that night of horrors and old neighbours, and they refuse to take her drachma.

The next day

The theatre is an old church, like the Church of England chapel she would pass in Pyrmont and never think to go in. Small and neat, with not a piece of wood or brick more than what is needed for quick prayers and salvation. Its lead light is so cheap that one can't tell Peter from Paul. Marks on the floor show where the pews used to be, scuffs where generations of pious English scraped their shoes rising and kneeling.

Fat women sit in a line along the left wall like choristers, except that they knit, not sing. They talk, but only about grandchildren, idiot husbands and new dresses. None of them and all of them look at Olga as she enters.

Mrs. Genges is there too, hovering across the floor as the mother hen she resembles, wringing her hands and ordering children to be quiet. Of course they ignore her, and she ignores them ignoring her.

A woman on stage is reading out lines very badly to the director, who talks to a man next to him. The playwright. After a few stanzas of stutters, the director claps his hands and waves the woman off the stage.

Olga tries to sit in one of the rickety metal chairs, the good ones having been taken by the knitters. A child comes to her.

Do you have a baby?

The child has a white bow in her hair, in just the way of Nellie many years ago, when she was small and quiet and stumbly.

Yes, I have…

Mrs Genges grabs Olga's arm in excitement to say she can try out now.

The script is pushed into Olga's arms by the director who snaps out 'page twenty-seven monologue'.

In the moment she has, Olga sees only that little girl, who has moved to the edge of the stage, standing as a little girl does, legs apart, waiting, watching.

The director claps his hands. Are you going to read?

Olga's eye goes to the script. It is open to page twenty-seven, to a soliloquy from a princess explaining why she had killed her husband. She looks to the girl, but she has gone.

Read or get off the stage.

The cue words on the script. Desperate. Angry. Tearful. Alone.

Olga improvises, coming to front of the stage and playing to the director, spitting to him why she had to kill the husband who cheated on her, stole her family fortune and her pride. She races over the lines like they are the script of her own life.

At the end, the knitting needles are quiet, the fat women all looking at the director. He nods to Olga, and as if this is a cue to them too, the knitters resume their clatter, jamming needle on needle and insisting, loudly, that she must be sleeping with him.

She sees the child, who is at the other end of the hall, clapping with her palms, but Olga can't be sure if she is clapping her or some boys playing jacks.

Two weeks later

The mothers and reluctant fathers of Athens pull their loud children into the theatre, which transforms the little boys and girls into wild things who run around playing tag games to screams of fright and cries of rules broken. Their parents try, not very hard, to settle them down. In Greece on a Saturday, no-one tries to do anything very hard.

It is curtain time on this opening night, but no-one has taken their seat. The usher begs people to sit and is heard by no-one. Politicians stand in a clump organising coups that will never happen, while their wives, floralled and yet frumpy, gossip about whoever is not there.

It is only when the lights are turned down that people break off their talk and tread on toes to their seats.

Olga is to open the play, but for a moment she stands in the wing frozen, touched by the silence. Silence is so rare in this city that it seems the louder to her than any of its noises. In the silence a baby cries somewhere, and she hears the cries of baby Christopher, the cries that lasted for just one day, the last sounds he would make. She had forgotten that cry and had promised herself she never would.

Just as quickly she realises, gathers herself, and makes the entrance of a princess.

In that ebullient Greek way, the players are given a standing ovation, shared by the stagehands who bring themselves out for the bow. The loudest clapping, though, seems to be for the woman in the princess costume who refuses to believe the ovation is hers.

The supper party afterwards, organised by the knitters, is well oiled by ouzo and supplied with everything but supper. It is well attended: actors and critics; producers; bankers who had refused to invest in it; even players from the only other show in this part of town, a Gilbert and Sullivan musical in Greek.

Olga is caught between a piano and a wall by the Minister for Island Affairs who insists, several times, that she was the best thing on the stage, offering to help her into a better group, and saying all this as his hand rubs her back.

She takes the compliments, escapes the Minister, is cheered from the room, and waits alone for an hour on a street corner for the bus that will take her home.

The High and the Despised

(January - June 1939)

Pyrmont, Sydney

Jean, mouth full of pins, has already set the seam for Nellie four times. Nellie is fast developing a strong bust and over the two weeks since the last fitting the dress has become too tight across her back. But there isn't any more time, the Australia Day Ball for Greek debutantes is tonight, and it's too late to set the seam on the Singer machine. Jean promises the pins will hold it.

It looks good, love.

Nellie feels the fragility of the dress all the time, especially as she walks up the steps of the Town Hall. She turns back to the truck to see her father and Jean waving. The truck looks particularly dirty tonight.

What a lovely dress, she hears, but it isn't for her. The ticket seller at the little box table is speaking to the girl ahead of her. The woman says nothing to Nellie when it's her turn to buy a ticket.

The inside of the Town Hall is full of streamers and starers. All the tables, it seems to Nellie, are taken by groups of girls or families she doesn't know. She wishes for an empty table, or for someone to call out to her to come and join them. She settles for a chair against the wall, the middle of three empty ones, and sits with her purse on her knees, not knowing how to go for a drink. She wants to do it, to have something to do, to show herself to be busy. Should she leave her purse on the chair and just take some money? In the end it's too hard and she just sits, as the band starts playing the Greek National Anthem.

Hello, you're Nellie Stambolis aren't you?

Standing in front of her is a short, plump, dark girl with curled hair and a beautiful corsage.

They told me it was you, she says, looking over her shoulder to a table across the way. You own the fish shop don't you? Your dad is the man with the white hair.

Nellie doesn't know this girl but is pleased that someone knows of her, and that her father is important enough to be talked about. She considers asking the girl to sit with her.

Before she can, the girl asks, Is it true your mother walked out on you and your sisters in the middle of the night to go and have an affair in Greece?

The girl looks back over her shoulder again, and Nellie sees the girls at the table standing in pairs and looking at them, hiding their mouths behind hands.

Nellie knows she must be reddening, and wishes for the low light to cover it. Freda would know what to say to this girl. She would make her and her friends regret this.

But Nellie isn't Freda. She just grips her handbag and looks away until the girl gives up and leaves. Nellie stays in that seat for an hour. When the lights dim for the speeches, she sneaks out a door.

Olga

I wish I was more like Nellie. People take to her. I am like Freda, too brash, too quick to react. Like today.

I thought someone was following me. I turned to look twice, calling out for him to leave me alone. No-one was there. I wonder what would a stalker want with one such as me. A lust? An easy purse? A canvas on which to draw his hates?

Perhaps it would not be like that. He could be handsome and kind of word; a sensitive soul too afraid to speak. He should know he can talk to me if it is with an honest mouth. But I have always found men are either too loud or too shy. I have never understood men. Men have never understood me.

Michael and I were orphans of a type. That was what brought us together after months of being married. He had only a sister living, and I thought I had no one of my blood, so we made our blood with our babies. I remember it so well, your quiet face, searching us, eyes from one to the other, those eyes the crux of our lives, those beautiful eyes. You never cried in complaint; you were too interested for that. From those eyes I looked to your father and saw the same face, and we were one then. I had never loved, and suddenly at once I loved two.

I knew so little of life when your father came for me. I was sixteen and he came with a gulf much bigger than the fifteen years between our births. To him, I was a child. To me he was an old man who had nothing a budding woman craved. His talk was of his shop and the travel arrangements, his eyes were for his watch and for Mother Hadjidaki's cakes. I could see he didn't know what he was doing there in that parlour, but he was there all the same.

Too late, after it was done, after Mother Hadjidaki had turned and walked away at the church, did I know that rend that every woman must learn, the rend of letting go of one family to build another. Life is a cruel choosing, the cruellest thing being that we have no choice. It happens to us all, except for the sad spinsters we see pushing their mothers or fathers through plaka and shop. These spinsters that never smile. Does no-one notice that these spinsters never smile?

I made the choice and went with the man I didn't know to his shop on the other side of the world. Ellie had made me promise never to be beholden to a man, while betraying this promise every day herself.

Ellie had gone by the time my man came for me and I forgot that promise in a moment. In less than a moment.

Your father loved me gently in many more ways than a man bedding a woman. He allowed my indulgences in his own way, muttering when I brought home runaway children, complaining when I fed them his cakes, but we both knew he meant none of it. In the end he was the one who would be upset when fathers come to collect their waifs. Or when I fought with that damned woman across the road, the one who bemoaned the wops taking over Ultimo. Your father's mouth would have an edge of a smile when I came back to the shop, red faced and furious.

This was a man who only laughed easily after a time, once he came to know me, his new wife, and that was well after the weeks on the boats, and well after he had settled me into the cramped little shop that he announced as our home.

I wonder if your father would laugh at the irony of me being fired today. For stealing a loaf of bread.

I only took it for the rich widow next door who hides her money rather than spend it on food, hoping no doubt to win over her son with her leavings when she is in the ground. She frets away without food or friend, alone at the cemetery's gate. A stale loaf, meant for the birds, was all I could offer.

That stale loaf a stale excuse for Mrs Diathini who resented me from the first day, from the interview, when her husband eyed me over.

Touché missus. I respect that. Strike your enemies. But over a loaf of bread? Surely you could do better than this.

On the bus on the way home I saw a notice in the newspaper. Governess wanted. Must speak Greek, English and Italian. Experience living overseas. Of mature age. Reliable. Well kept.

It is time for my good shoes.

Two days later

Olga sits in the Syntagma sun, watching the children run in circles, roughing each other with laughing and squeals. Mothers and uncles and grandfathers pretend not to see the pinching and tripping, and they know it all. The rough boys are part of their blood, of their breath. Everything is known. These people are settled with their way and Olga is settled to see them so. Children are born to do this and this is how it should be.

It is not only the children who are at play. The men are here on this spring day to watch the women, and the women are here to be watched by men. For a few short weeks of good warm and breeze, the gods are letting their chosen people play.

A balding man at another table tries the game. A plump jowly girl sees him, but sees his head and chins and looks away. Only Olga sees his crumpling, so slight it is.

He turns his eye to Olga, sees she is looking, and smiles an awful leer of a flirt. She keeps watching him and he straightens, puffing his chest, palming his remaining hair, and rubbing his mouth clear of traces of cake, all the while searching her face.

He sits up further as she comes over to him and leans over his coffee. To his blinking desirous eyes, she asks him if he is Mr. Drago Stephanellis, who is to meet her here about a governess job.

The waiting room has only three seats, all taken by an Italian couple and their child. There is no Sydney courtesy in Athens, no men offer their seats for women here. So she stands, and the man doesn't notice.

The door to an office opens and four men come out, handsomely dressed in the sort of clothes that do not wear well in Athens: trousers made of silk and gathered at the ankles, and double breasted coats like they wear in the gangster films from America. One kisses the hand of the last man, who is a stocky figure with a smile on his face. The first man asks for his regards to be given to Il Duce. There is laughing and awkwardness getting around the furniture as the group move towards the stairwell, not seeing anyone but the smiley man. At the end of the pantomime, when they are gone, he loses his smile and goes back into the office.

After a few seconds his door opens again and he comes to Olga, smiling again and speaking in English, apologising. His fingertips guide her elbow, not too hard as to be pushy, not so soft as to be weak, but just as a good lead in a dance.

His office is highly decorated with books, plaques, stuffed small animals, silver goblets and photos lining the walls of this man with Clark Gable and Winston Churchill and Mussolini and other people who look like they must be famous. They smile with him and suit him. He is dapper; his almost black hair oiled and pushed back. He is not a handsome man, but Olga cannot stop looking in his eyes.

He offers a cigarette. She sits back and lets him light it for her with, of course, a silver lighter that shines almost to a cliché. It is her first cigarette for two years. Michael would be mad. Cigarettes are common, he would say, yet here she is in an embassy, sitting beneath Clark Gable, smoking, without the smell of potatoes and feathers.

The Count is saying it would be an honour to have her working in his house. He was entranced by her performance as the princess.

Olga

It was hard not to smile like a flattered idiot, still full of your father and his tuts.

The Count talked of his daughters, of how he wished they could have the bravery to do a play. They are timid. Would I teach them some acting, maybe?

Your father laughed when I told him I went to the picture studio in Maroubra to try out for a moving picture they were making. I was a wife, he said, not Theda Bara.

Lift their spirits, the Count asked. Make them happy again. They wanted to dance in the ballet once. Now they just mope.

Moping, why was I always moping, your father wanted to know, never understanding what I'd try to explain.

He would look at me blankly and ask again, why do you mope?

Why would they mope, the Count asked.

Because they have everything maybe, I stammered close to tears, and there's nothing left for them to ache for. They must be taught there are many things worth aching for. It lies before them.

Yes. Yes. That is it, he said excited.

They need to know, Count, that there is more in heaven and earth…

Horatio…

Yes, Horatio.

So with a Shakespearean quote and a night's performance as my only references, I was hired to be mother again, and with that I had a new position and place to live. Outside, away from the spell, I realised we had been swimming in each other's eyes, this Count and I, all the time he talking of his daughters, and I thinking of mine. I had forgotten how Greece was a country of eyes.

Pyrmont, Sydney

The fish frying, the potato slices stacked, the work done for a moment, he catches Tina watching him from the kitchen, but watching him as she had never before. Tina's eye is black, certain, seductive.

Michael dares to look deeper into his daughter's gaze and is caught in it.

Her head is pointing down just a bit, but her eyes, her black eyes are looking up at him with a longing.

His heart drops for a moment at this alarum.

These are Olga's eyes, the child's eye of a woman. These are the eyes that Olga had given him when he first met her in Alexandria. He had thought she wanted him, that 16-year-old girl of a seamstress. Here today he understands there was no seduction, it was just a little girl watching with the only way she knew.

What are you thinking, he asks Tina, desperate in this moment to understand what Olga could have been thinking back then, still wondering whether their whole life together was made on a wrong assumption.

I'm wondering, dear father, Tina answers, why you don't pluck the hairs from your nose.

Athens, Greece

In the back seat of the diplomatic car with her bags and clothes, she passes the bus station, past the eyes of the old women she had waited with so many times. She sees their impatience and tiredness, their edging to the pavement desperate to be the first one on the bus, hoping for a seat they will never get. These women with puffy ankles and flattened feet and slouches to the side. Only two days ago she was with them, only two days ago she was becoming one of them.

These things she dares only see out of the edge of an eye; she can't bring herself to insult them by letting them see her seeing them.

The driver's lamppost of a head in front of her has eyes only for the road. He had no small talk when he carried her cases or when he held the door for her. Everything has been in order in this: her first lesson in diplomacy. Chattering does no good to anyone. A driver is there to drive. He must do his job well. This fine lamppost is a fine first teacher.

Before she can unpack or refresh, she is to go to the Count's daughters. The Count's secretary, whose name she didn't catch, leads her past drawing rooms and libraries, reception rooms and lounges. He opens a door and introduces the girls, who curtsy suspiciously.

It takes her only minutes to see that these beauties would not have done well in Alexandria. In that place girls weren't allowed to be silly, shy or bored. Olga discovered young that there were men who fancied little girls, and to beat these men you needed be as tough as a man, not to scream like a monkey when one grabbed your arm, not to punch out or struggle, but to stare the man down. Men, she found at the age of ten, are scared of tough eyes. The Count's girls have reached the ages of fifteen and seventeen without seeing a bad thing in their lives.

In the teaching room though, they have domain. The older one, Maria, complies with Olga's kindness with reticence that is copied by her sister. Olga's raised voice brings feigned ignorance, cocky glances, whispers behind hands. Flattering them does no good. They have been flattered enough for a lifetime. The times were many on this first morning when Olga wanted to take those fresh, pink rinds of ears and twist them.

Would they like to do a play?

The older one peeks shyly and hopeful, betraying at last something.

The play would be an old one, Olga tells them, about women who stopped their husbands going to war by refusing to make love to them. The younger girl, Irene, knows nothing of love making, but when her sister laughs, she does too.

Could it stop the war that's coming now, she asks.

Maria quickly pinches her little sister's fat thigh, shushing her with scared eyes.

Olga doesn't answer her question; she thinks of the frightened eyes of a war long past and times that were so very bad. She remembers as easily as she had forgotten. The tears of the wives in Alexandria and the man with one leg laughing a brave face on his ruined life. The mumbling pickpocket, who was once a lawyer until a month in a trench of mud and blood. The stooped mother in black for her three sons who died on the same day in different countries. The war changed them all in a moment, put a black fright in them, sank their eyes into their sockets. She remembers now the rifles pointed at the Egyptian boys by the Empire soldiers, pretending to shoot them like vermin. War, Mother Hadjidaki said, it is how it is. Forget about it, she commanded, and Olga did forget so quickly for so long.

To the Count's girls, she could simply pledge not to tell of their escaped secret, and a breath is let out of the room.

Olga

I dared to look at the photo of you all again, and saw you looking at me with those eyes of women. Sometimes those eyes accuse, sometimes they love. A photo as a talisman. Are you disdaining me like your photograph, or have you forgotten me? Could your dreams be telling you of me? If they did, would you love me or hate me, being here while you are needing a breast for your tears. Your eyes pierce me from a square of silver and white, and I hope it is a liar.

Pyrmont, Sydney

The two men walk quickly up Harris street. They have an arrogant confidence that makes children clear a pathway for their sweeping overcoats and shining shoes. Everybody lets them pass.

At the fish shop they stop, smirking at each other a smirk they know so well.

Jim Casey from the refinery is leaning on the counter, eating his chips from a torn open newspaper roll, and nattering to Michael about nothing special, when he sees the two men through the window. He dashes out of the door. Michael calls out that he has forgotten his chips, and Jim's disappearing arm waves that it doesn't matter.

The two men come in.

Hey big feller, how's business?

Michael turns to the cooking trays. He never could look them in the eye.

Good Sergeant. Everybody has got to eat.

Good to hear. Hey, do you have some spare butter?

Michael turns, surprised. More butter. He tries to smile as they smile at him.

Butter, big feller, repeats the sergeant.

And a chook, his partner adds. My missus forgot to get one from the butcher's.

Nellie pulls on her father's sleeve. She had been cleaning under the counter. Dad, she whispers, we've only got a pound. Not enough for tomorrow's batter.

Michael waves her quiet. He goes into the back of the shop and brings out the whole block. He hands it to the sergeant.

Thanks, big feller. Now what about that chook?

No chickens today. I get them tomorrow.

Well then we'll come back tomorrow.

His partner glares at Michael and slaps his hands on the counter so hard that Michael feels as though he's been hit in the face. The sergeant gently pulls his partner back.

Hey Senior. The big feller's all right. He doesn't have any chickens. He'll have some tomorrow. We'll come back then.

But I promised my wife we'd be having chook.

The sergeant leads his partner towards the door, satisfied. He'd got his butter.

Something, maybe guilt, makes the sergeant come back in, leaving the senior constable outside to berate some children. The sergeant winks to Michael like a friend.

Pay no mind to him. He's young and wants everything now. No patience. Like this afternoon we saw a couple of smugglers. He wanted to go in fists and all and get them, do the old involuntary assault and battery. I had to pull him back, I tell you. Wouldn't listen to anyone, even the ol' sergeant here. Don't let him worry you eh?

Michael shrugs, feeling a little lighter.

The sergeant leans over to Michael and whispers.

But you will have a chook tomorrow, won't you? The Senior likes his chicken.

The sergeant leaves with right on his side and his conscience eased. Police look after people, and these people have to pay for it. It is how it is.

Michael turns back to the cooker, pretending, as Nellie runs through the curtain into the back room, crying at her weak father, at the wrong of it.

Athens, Greece.

Sitting at the Count's dinner table is a group of the high and the despised: condescending academics with Communist leanings; ambassadors; businessmen; and Grant, the English philosopher and troublemaker who works his bakery in Monastiraki. They sit drinking the Count's wine and breaking his bread and spitting at his country, because his Mussolini is a friend of Hitler, and Hitler is a threat to Greece. The Count allows frank talk on these nights with his friends. He agrees privately with what they say, that Italy has no right to have soldiers on the border of Albania and Greece. With Bulgaria's troops waiting to the north for the match to be lit, these nights of wine and rich food are becoming nights of suspicion and bile.

The Count's wife, who prefers not be burdened with the title of Countess, sits next to the Bulgarian ambassador, hoping her presence might make the others more likely to eat and less likely to fight. So far on this night it has been calm, all the guests spooning their soup, except the Greek army minister, who hasn't looked away from the Bulgarian.

Tell me Mr. Ambassador, he asks, are you Bulgarians gathered on our border because you plan to help your good friends the Germans take over the world?

The Bulgarian nods his approval of the soup to the Countess, and turns to the Greek minister.

Rumours are started at dinner parties by people who have drunk too much. All Germany is doing is helping other countries.

Ah, and how long will it be before you help Greece.

The Bulgarian looks down at his own soup.

I have no wish to ruin a good dinner with bad talk. And my talk will be with General Metaxas, not his minions.

The Greek minister stands and swipes towards the ambassador with such suddenness that it makes the Bulgarian drop his spoon.

The Countess cuts in, snapping that this is not a war room. It is a dinner. People are being rude.

The minister realises, and gives her an apology of sorts, but he can't hold his silence, mumbling warnings to the

Bulgarian through his considerable moustache while stirring and not actually drinking his soup.

The Count has to say something, although he'd enjoyed the scene. The Bulgarian has become cocksure ever since his country allied itself with Germany.

Carry on like this you two, he said, and you'll give the poor Japanese ambassador indigestion.

Someone laughs. The minister again stands, and bangs the table, causing the Japanese ambassador's soup to splash on his tie.

I have no quarrel with you personally, Your Excellency, but remember this is not your home. This is Greece. Withdraw from Albania and tell your Bulgarian friends to get their troops off our border too.

He pushes his chair back hard, flipping it on its back and sliding it into a pedestal that has a sculpture on it, a sculpture of the head of Artemis, that rocks, then steadies again. The minister wants to say more, but embarrassed by his clumsiness in diplomacy and the chair, leaves the room.

The Japanese ambassador spoons on through the ruckus. The Italian soup is good. Always is.

Pyrmont, Sydney

Do you think mummy's coming back?

Tina had never spoken much as a little girl, but having finally found her voice, she is always asking questions, even here in her little cot in the middle of the night, when her sisters are trying to sleep.

Freda rustles first. God I don't know Tee. Things are good here, aren't they?

I don't know.

With Jean and all. She's nice isn't she?

Yes.

If mummy comes back, Jean will have to go.

Why?

Because there's only room for one mummy in a house.

A voice comes from Nellie's still bed: Who do you want Tee, Jean or Mum?

Neither Freda nor Tina had heard Nellie sound so bitter.

Who do you want Freda? Jean or Mum?

No need to be angry Nellie. Tina was just asking. Just because you got teased by Stephen Dragopoulos. What's a little tease?

He called mum a slut!

What's a slut, Tina asks.

Ignore him. He's a dumb arse with a little pee wee.

What's a slut, Tina asks again.

Freda, you don't know anything about it. They never dare tease you.

They used to tease me all the time, Nell. But I didn't let them see me upset, so they gave up. Don't let them see, and you'll be okay. Really.

What's a slut?

They all lie down again, not sleeping, Tina's question hanging.

Athens, Greece

The Count hadn't received his usual pleasantries call from the Greek government the morning after the dinner. Nor the day after that. After two weeks he rang Rome, and the Italian foreign office told him that if the Greeks were going to be so stupid, then to hell with them. The Count tells them it is difficult to be an ambassador to Greece if he doesn't speak with the Greeks. To hell with them, he is told again.

This is not the Count's way. He rings the Greek prime minister. General, he asks, are things still good between us?

Of course, the high voice answers, we are friends are we not?

Good, it is just that there has been very little talk between us for some time.

Ah, my Italian friend, times are odd, and your Mussolini makes it no easier. He's making a lot of people get stiff necks, and mine is pretty bad. How is yours? You need to be careful of your neck, Count.

After the General hangs up, the Count runs out to the car, calling for the driver to take him home quickly.

The children meet the Count at the door, smiling and careless. Irene grabs his knee and swings off it.

You promised we could go swimming at Mr Giafis' swimming pool, remember? Can we still?

The Count laughs and gathers his hefty monkey daughter. His panic is silly. There is nothing to fear. And a promise is a promise. Of course they will have their swimming.

Pyrmont, Sydney

In the rain the grey street is greyer. The black figures of mothers dash from kerb to kerb, hands holding coat collars tight, their children trotting along, pulled by firm hands. A horse stands depressed at one of the last troughs, foot cocked, eyes blinking. Even a dog runs to get out of the weather, with a face chastened by the rain. The only man on Harris street is small and determined, carrying a bag. It is heavy today. The threat of war has brought more letters from Europe. They're full of pleas of relatives for sponsorship in Australia, or parents begging their children not to go fighting for a country that isn't theirs.

Freda races out to be the first to get the letters when the whistle blows, rain or no rain. Each day she reads the bills and proudly tells her father how much more in debt they are.

Today there is just one letter with fancy stamps. She breaks it open. It's a personal letter but that doesn't matter. As she tears it she screams to her father, who is in the kitchen plucking chickens.

Dad. There's a letter from Darwin. It must be Uncle Mick. Uncle Mick. He's sent us a letter.

It is from Mick Parrelis. A man of money who is no man of words. He made his fortune by getting his hands dirty. Some doubted whether he could write at all.

From Michael Parrelis
The Resting Place Cafe, Darwin,
Northern Territory
Australia

Dear Michael,
Thank you for your letter. Yes I accept your girls. They will be a help here in the cafe. Nellie to start with. I will be a full guardian, but as I already said I cannot pay wages. Tell me when she is coming. It would be good if it can be as soon as possible.

Your faithful,
Michael Parrelis

In this house of thundering noise it is dead quiet as Freda stands in the doorway staring out at her father. He knows she is there, and keeps on with the plucking.

It's the best thing really, he says while feeling under the tub for another chicken. He promises she will understand later. Mick is family. It will be good for them.

Please Dad, no. We need each other.

Michael swings the flaccid little chicken's body onto the top and puts a knife to its belly. He's watched the rivalry between Freda and Nellie for months. He thought they would like being apart, but in this moment he sees that their bickering, teasing and fighting for affection isn't rivalry. They are just being sisters.

Freda, with angry calmness, asks him to remember what happened last time the family split up. When Mum and the others went to Greece in 1929. Little Christopher.

Michael pushes her away with a bloody hand and the threat of a slap. Mesa. Get upstairs, and leave the letter on the block over there. And no word to the others. You shouldn't read other people's mail. Go on. Mesa.

Freda slams the letter down and stomps inside as hard as she can, past Jean, ignoring her What's the matter? Freda has no coat and she doesn't care.

She finds Nellie and Tina in the Hay Street market and spits the plan at them. Nellie says nothing, twisting a curl behind her ear. Freda looks back and sees a slight smile on her sister's mouth.

Nellie. Don't tell me!

Nellie says she thinks it will be exciting, going to Darwin and all.

Tina and Freda peck at her stupidity.

Exciting? What's exciting? We're talking about Darwin, not bloody South Africa. If we let them do it, you'll be alone up there and we'll be down here.

Nellie won't argue, and this, as always, makes Freda flop her arms and walk off. Tina goes with her and slips her hand into her sister's elbow, consoling and being consoled.

Nellie follows them back to the shop, but at a distance, through the shouts of Chinese vegetable sellers and their children who are weaving in and out of horses and trucks and the slush of the gutters.

Her only thought is that in Darwin they wouldn't know.

Olga

These girls are so very much like Nellie and Freda. They bicker with love and they deny their need for each other, but need each other they do. To rend them would be a cruel thing. I had no sister so maybe I know nothing of it, but they love so easily. In fact they said they loved me today, the words thrown out as sudden as a cat's spit. We had been rehearsing our little adaptation of Dante's Divine Comedy, chosen because I thought a little reflection on damnation could do two spoiled girls no harm.

The damnation part of it passed them by. They saw it only as a reflection on love. Both wanted to be the angel Beatrice; neither was interested in Virgil, hell's guide. I had to insist that Irene play that part for she was the softer of the sisters. I have always found that actors learn more from roles that are nothing like their own natures, like that rough butcher in the Pyrmont troupe who took to playing an angel with great imagination.

We played with Dante's simple and short rhyming stanzas, until every word was a picture, until we could see the hate and love. They learned quickly.

The moment of love came when Maria touched her sister's face in Paradiso XXX, where Dante finally sees the love in his guide…

The beauty I saw went so far beyond
Not only our capacity, but I believe
That only her maker could enjoy it perfectly

The lines were said with the knowledge of a woman who knows love as a mother and as a lover. It was a moment. The girls looked beautiful in that moment, as though they too had seen the guide to heaven. They were slower at that moment, more erect, deep of eye. They didn't look to me for approval. They knew they had done well. Irene kissed me and told me she loved me. Maria, behind her sister, said she loved me too. Then they left the room to have their lunch without a second thought for me or Dante.

To be of a family where such things are said with no reflection, as natural as the refilling of a glass of wine. For just that moment they didn't see me as a Greek fishman's wife without home or country. It was a moment made by three lines. The answer in three lines. Love, always told in truth, and complete. In a three line stanza.

I never gave anything to my girls like this. I was a poor kind of mother. I didn't offer the words my children needed to hear.

Pyrmont, Sydney

Nellie can't get the image from her mind of those scandalised faces at the dance. She sees them in the girls at school, in the street, in the customers. Her father sees it in her face and begs her to cheer up and offers her a saveloy and a pat on the hand, but she aches for that night, the night when her mother came to her without being beckoned, and held her head to her breast and let her cry.

Tell me, dear, her mother had asked in a voice softer than Nellie had ever heard. This woman was not the mother she had lived with every day, that mother of practicalities. Here at this moment of crisis she became a Demeter mother of the earth and milk.

As Nellie told of her ghosts, her mother said nothing else but, yes my love, you are not alone. I know.

And Nellie knew that her mother really did know.

For the years after, Nellie would remember this wonderful time in the tiny bedroom. She thought the glow of that night would last her all her life, but it only took a nasty girl at a dance to make it die.

The Eye of a Hurt Heart

(June 1939- Aug 1939)

Italian Residence, Athens

Olga is surprised. She thought he would laugh at the stupidity of her idea. She expected him to say how preposterous it was of her to suggest taking the girls out of the country. Doesn't she know the dangers a diplomat's family could face away from their security. Stick to teaching, woman.

But the Count says none of these things. He listens to her say she wants to take the girls to see everything Dante saw, all the places he lived, wrote, drew and breathed, all the places that smell of him, all the smells he smelled.

That would be everywhere in Florence, he laughs.

Well then, that's where we'll be going. Everywhere.

In their laughing, neither Olga nor Count see Drago Stephanellis pretending to be tending to papers at the back of the office.

The afternoon before the trip, as Olga packs, Stephanellis comes in her bedroom without knocking. She doesn't get offended because this is his way, his enthusiasms thoughtless and childish. He sits on the bed she has just made, and hurrumphs and stutters about a package he wants her to deliver in Italy for him.

What is in this package, she asks, folding a slip.

Nothing important, he says, nipping at the side of a fingernail.

Then tell me what it is.

It is nothing, just some papers. Official business.

Then why not post them?

They need to be hand delivered.

Then get a courier.

Mrs Stambolis, you are very frustrating.

Why? Because I know when someone is lying to me?

How dare you? What makes you think…

It's in every bone of your body. You slink in here all side of eye, all so very nonchalant, as if you don't care, but when I say no, you erupt. Yes my friend, these papers mean something to you. I will not take them anywhere unless I know what is in them.

He leaves, and is back seconds later ready to argue but looks at her and decides not to.

Can I trust you, he asks.

Don't be such a child.

They are just some documents that help Greece, he says. The Count knows nothing of them. War is coming, the Count could be recalled any time. We need to be ready. These papers will put some fright into the Italians. This is espionage work, he whispers, with a slight smile he can't help betraying.

The idea of this Drago Stephanellis as a spy makes her laugh. She had picked him as a lazy, dull Greek man who could not know the art of risk.

She says no, of course.

He leaves again and comes back pleading. He tries getting angry, but she slaps his face and he leaves once more. When he comes back half an hour later, he is much quieter. He asks, softly, if she will go for a walk. He has something to show her.

Omonios, her favourite part of the city with its big new buildings stone polished, is nothing more than a big intersection but it has light and life. The dark corners are the edge that gives it this life. In Omonios you are never more than five yards from the sick and the sorry, the grasping girls of the daytime night, the men with the knives. A Shanghai of the Mediterranean, Michael used to call it.

Omonios is busy today, with slow Greeks being fast, or so it seems. Drago whispers all the time, talking about dangers from the world, the enemy on the borders and the enemies within; about things she could not know. Greece is about to suffer greatly, he says. Mussolini and Hitler have a compact that will divide up the world. Soon no Greek woman will be free. Greek Jews will die, Greek children will starve. In the end Greek will fight Greek. The people are poor. When they are tired of poverty, they will be angry.

The fishmongers of Pyrmont always mooned about how the Chinese were about to take over Australia. These discussions were usually over a meal in Ming Dao's Chinese restaurant. Ming would smile and everyone assumed he couldn't understand, but he knew. And he took their payments. Talk was talk, frantic, certain, shameless talk, and the next morning these political experts would be back at their stalls with their dead fish, and concerned only with a penny's profit, a profit made by selling to Chinese.

No, Stephanellis says, it is not just all talk. It is people. People living badly. Look woman. See the people living badly.

She looks, and all she sees are the hurriers with their frowns; the sad widows with the girths; the beggars and the businessmen.

Yes the beggars, Stephanellis says. So many beggars.

Beggars are a part of a city, she says.

Not here. Not in Omonios. These beggars are not drunks or opium fiends or the mad ones. These are good people. Just look. Look.

Ahead on the marblesque footpath is a man in a good suit, and as they come closer she can see the man's shirt is blotched but pressed. His face is clean shaven and nicked. Shaving razors that are sharp belong to people who have jobs.

She opens her purse to look for a few coins, but Drago tugs her before she can give anything.

Don't, he says. You'll only draw attention.

She tears out of his grip and puts the money in the beggar man's tatty little purse, more than she was going to give before.

Drago comes to her side. He adds ten more.

The police run at them from nowhere. Drago's nails dig into Olga's forearm, but the policemen are not interested in Olga or Drago. One grabs the beggar's purse, putting it in his own pocket. The other twists the man's arm, and together they push him past them up the street. As he passes, a bare whisper comes from the beggar man, 'I am sorry for wasting your...'

And the messy scene disappears around the corner.

Drago, who has seen this before, and Olga, who hasn't, bear the scene differently. Drago starts to say he was right and they have only made things worse for the man. Olga though, is full of murder for that poor man. He is poor, he and his poor ironed shirt. He probably has a wife at home who thinks him working. No. She would have seen the blotches, so she would know. They would fear together. The wife and this little man who kills his pride to beg.

Drago says the police were waiting for someone to give the man money. There was no point in arresting him until he had something they could steal.

She demands that they see the police chief. Drago begs her not to interfere. It is lost, it is lost. Mind your business. One person can make no difference here, and it will only bring trouble.

So difference can only be made if we are talking of nations. The small man is always lost.

Yes, he says, not getting her point, but thinking he has.

All right, she says, she will pass on the package, no longer caring what it holds and what it is for. Stephanellis had wanted to show her the wrongs in the world, and he showed wrongs much nearer.

She promises to meet him back at the embassy a little later, saying she needs to walk around a little.

Olga

My head was clear in that moment. It was free of doubts and memories. There would be no going home. That man and his ironed shirt, he was as a puppy slapped. I might have murdered there on that pavement and damned the consequences. Men passed me and I wanted to hit them. My fist had shards of my nails. My breast was near to bursting. Where had this come from? I was never an angry person. This came from a deep fight in me that said I would never be the same. Can it be, so quickly?

Omonios, Athens

The police station is easy enough to find. It's the one door in the row everyone is avoiding.

She walks around it. She stares at it. She studies it, figuring, balancing herself with this new country of honest beggars and crooked police. There have been two women in her life. Ellie, the little call girl, fourteen years on earth yet having seen a lifetime's worth of sins, showed her she could have courage; and her Mother Hadjidaki who taught her that courage never comes in a dither.

Olga walks up the steps into the police station.

There are many men, fifteen or twenty, standing against the wall of the waiting room, all with that beggar man's face of shame.

Only two policemen are in the room, both in a clerk's cage. Olga's beggar is in the line, looking at his feet like so many of the others. The dress is like a uniform: neat as can be, coated, slightly soiled and sad. There is no protesting, no demands. This group of accepting men wait without hope.

Olga calls to the policemen behind the desk.

Why have you brought my husband here? Check your paperwork. You have made a terrible mistake.

They jump, as men who are scared of a wife's tone do.

Who is your husband, they both ask, each one's words tripping over the others'.

Olga points to her man.

But he was begging, they say.

How dare you, she hisses, making them cower back just a bit. Are you saying my family are beggars? The Minister for Police is my cousin. I will tell him all about this. And if you do not release my husband now it will be worse for you.

One flicks quickly through his papers, as if the answer to the dilemma lay in them. Finally, he gives a slight movement of his fingers, a 'take him' gesture.

She grabs the well-dressed man, berating him for leaving her in the street.

Your purse, she demands of him. Where is your purse?

She turns back to the two policemen.

Where's his money, she asks, her hand out.

How much money did he have, one asks.

Sixty drachma.

He opens a drawer filled with purses and wallets and drachma. He counts out sixty, and puts them into her palm, saying he is sorry for the inconvenience madam.

Outside she gives the beggar the sixty drachma and tells him to go home.

He kisses her hand and walks down the street with as much dignity as he can manage.

Hotel Greco, Florence

It is the morning of their third day in Florence, and Olga and the girls are at an early breakfast planning their day of museums and markets. The hotel bellboy brings a telegram.

mrs stambolis hotel greco florence

return athens immed stop do not telephone or reply stop see me

immed on return stop see no-one before leaving stop
DS

Keeping her panic hidden, Olga sips coffee as the girls play their game of pinchings and squealings.

So many things could be wrong. A coup here in Italy. A threat against the Count's family. What if someone discovered Stephanellis' little scheme? It was then she realised that by being part of it she was breaking the law in two countries. The threat of Mussolini's jails didn't worry her. It was the girls. They would be alone in the country of their birth, a country they didn't know.

Trying not to be seen doing it, she looks at everyone in that breakfast room, the mothers, the fathers, the waiters, the little maitre de. She sees suspicion in every face. Or was she seeing her own suspicion? Can your own fears show on the faces of others?

She whispers to the girls to get up as quietly as possible. The day's plan has changed.

Irene is happy to leave Florence. She misses her warm bed and father's whispers. The older one, Maria, had been flirting each breakfast with the pretty blonde boy at the next table. Nearly a woman, she accepts the early departure with a woman's stoic silence. And later, as they wait in the foyer for their taxi, she bears quietly the boy's flirtations with someone else.

At Florence station, the man at the counter announces there is a problem with their papers, and points to a bench opposite.

Through the ticket office's dirty window they watch their train leave, then another, and a third. When Olga asks when they will be attended to, she is scowled at by a new man at the desk. She can see her untouched papers still atop a pile to his side.

The girls, knowing nothing of Olga's fears, swing their legs and sing. After only another minute Olga goes to the counter again, asks how long they will be, and is ignored.

A whistle blows for yet another train. At that moment, the official leaves the counter with the pile of papers, including theirs, and goes into the room behind. He leaves their passports behind on his blotter.

Olga takes the chance, grabs the passports and the girls' hands, and runs for the platform, with only Irene grabbing a suitcase. The other cases are left behind. They race down a corridor, through a waiting room and back up on the other side of the wall of glass through which Olga can see the backs of the seats they were sitting on, and the counter. She doesn't dare look to see if the official is back; she just runs, pulling on the girls, aware that they are stumbling and that her arms are jerking them back up each time; listening all the time for the whistle of the train and the whistle of a soldier.

As they reach the platform, the crowds are against them, a crowd so thick that she can't see if the train is still there. She bounces off these people and their coats and their bags, and it is only through the soft flesh gripped in her talons that she knows the girls are still with her. She hears Irene squeal, and assumes her bag has been flung out of her hand in the squeeze.

Through the crowd the dark box shape of the train's end carriage shows up ahead. We can make it, she thinks. Think not of the tight chest or the lack of breath or the cries of the girls. We can make it.

They jump for the train as the guard is taking up the steps. He waves them up, in his hurry not asking to see their tickets. They find a spot at the back of the train beside the toilet, a corner near the breeze of a crack in a door. Without bags, they make a small ball under a man with stained trousers and a stinking cigarette.

A conductor comes by, but Olga deals with him with a lost ticket pantomime and a smile.

Olga

I took the girls with me straight from the station to the embassy. In the taxi they played some game with a button Maria carried with her everywhere. They threw it up and caught it, keeping score in a loud whoop with every catch.

We could have been driving to a home that didn't exist anymore, to a father recalled, to security officers where the doorman used to stand, and I had to watch them play jacks with a button.

I would take them, I decided. I would take them and their little button and not let any Blackshirt twist their collar and push them into a car and make them cry for a father they would never see again.

If there was anything wrong at the embassy I would take their hands, run, and never let go.

We parked across the road from the embassy. I told them to stay in the taxi until I came back. I was not even halfway across the road when they tore past me. They had seen their father's trousers as he stood on the inner stairs. He saw them too and ran down and squeezed and kissed.

My darlings, he cried out. Why are you back so early.

Stephanellis would explain, I said as I went past, never so relieved and, strangely, a little disappointed.

Mrs Pevlakis, the Count's secretary, said Mr Stephanellis was not at work. He had been sick for two days.

One could foresee the cat's piss and rubbish that would wedge into corners of this estate in the years to come. The modernist pretensions of the building were betrayed by sloppy cement work and gaps shown up by sunlight. It is a lazy building, a cardboard betrayal of the people it was built for, people who think they are of the future but whose futures would be rooted in these kinds of tenements. Forty of their names were listed inside the outer doors, names scribbled in all kinds of pens, the owners not caring that the names look like child scrawl. Doors of flawed wavy glass and gaps uneven. A corridor that seemed to suck in the wind. Paint that was already peeling.

This was where Drago Stephanellis lived.

He answered his door in a dressing gown and a body odour. His red eyes were redder than usual and his bald head balder.

He called me a stupid woman, an idiot. How dare I.

I feared at that moment, feared what he had found out about me.

He prattled about a prostitute, saying what if she had talked to someone, or if she went to the police?

I told him I knew no prostitutes.

You stupid woman, the prostitute who passed on the documents I gave you.

I was so relieved, I pushed past him to his kitchen to find something to make a coffee. He sputtered at my insolence and I didn't care.

Why did you do it, he asked in a yell again.

I didn't, I said.

Liar, he yelled, making to strike me.

I grabbed his arm and told him the prostitute was me. I dressed up as a street woman in case it was a trap. That way I could tell the police I had been given the papers by someone on the street. I even had some lira on me to prove I had been paid for delivering them.

His fist dropped, his twisted mouth turned to a sickly smile, and he fainted.

I made sure he wasn't dead, put a cushion under his head, and finished making my coffee while waiting for him to come out of it. He did soon enough, and as I dripped some water into his mouth, he gripped my shoulders. Good woman, he said in glee. Good woman. He kissed my cheeks, his smile so broad his face looked like a China-man's. We make a good team, he said. A great team.

We were stopped at Florence train station, I said.

Random checks. Worry about nothing.

I will tell him tomorrow that he will have to explain to the Count why the girls had lost their cases and about a few other things too because there is no doubt the girls would have told their father about the subterfuge and how we had to run through a train station like criminals.

Those four days with the girls were a joy in this new life of mine. Their squealings and snappings and giggles were so known to me. They complained like Freda; were so easily upset like you, my Nellie. They craved me like your brother Nicky. They came out with moments of genius in the hilarious way of Tina.

Complaining, craving. People need, and I never do anything for anyone. I live the twin shames of what I do and what I don't do. I work hard, but nothing stops my shame, the work just elbows it away until the night when there is nothing to do and I am home alone.

Except that I am not at home. I never have been. Greece is the home of my ancestors, yet I am not with my children. When I am with my children in the land where they were born, my home is half a world away. Is home the smell of places and the cooking of childhood? Or is it where you are weaned?

I was never taken to breast. Maybe that was it. Maybe that broke me at the start.

Piraeus, Greece

She is on a day trip to escape the heat, but the salt and fumes of the ships make the murky air heavier. She is almost annoyed by the sweat and the wet air. People move slower. This queue at the cake shop doesn't move and her eyes examine the grey hair partings of the wives in the line ahead, their armpits making pools that spread around the back of their dresses. The patterns are all the same. Even sweat has no mind of its own. Yet she stands with them still.

There is a bald head four places ahead; shiny and correct. As she wonders if it could be Drago, he reads her thought and turns. It is the first time they have seen each other since the night of the return.

He offers her a place at his side. In Australia such a jumping of places would cause a fight. Here the jumped ones swear a little under their breaths and forget about it.

Drago's eyes are red. He keeps wiping them with his forefinger. He stubbed his toe, he says, and she believes none of it, because there is a redness of eye that belongs to a stubbed toe, and there is a redness of eye that belongs to a hurt heart.

The Count, she asks.

But ever the loyal underling, he says nothing more of it, and asks after her, the first time he had ever done so.

Still recovering from our little excitement, she suggests.

Yes, he giggles. Excitement.

Then, quietly in a loud shop, he asks if she'd help him do some more 'deliveries'.

A Life's Power

(August - September 1939)

Glyfadia, South of Athens

This was wrong from the start, they both knew it. In her waters Olga knew they should have turned around, but the lure. The lure of excitement in a dull life pulled them on.

Train, bus and bus, with Drago always looking over his shoulder. His attempts at furtiveness were so obvious that he was drawing attention to them.

As they approach where they are to meet the contact, Drago suddenly drags Olga backwards into a lane. The same waters have stirred in him.

They circle back around the block and cross to the beach. From behind the stone wall they watch the drop-off point. Their waters are right. Three cars, small, new and clean, are hidden out of sight of the taverna where they were to meet the man.

Italian Secret Police, Drago says. Secret in name only. Everyone knows them. They must have caught our contact and are waiting to see who is meeting him.

They dump the satchel in a drum of water and get away. Skin of the tongue, Drago says, shaking. Skin of the tongue. He is so jarred, Olga doesn't want to correct his cliché.

You are very calm, he spits out, grabbing her hand in examination. God, you look as if you don't care that we nearly got caught.

I care, she says, taking away his hand, and seeing then that he is right. She isn't shaking. Her blood is settled, her head clear.

You are too sure of yourself to get nervous, he almost spits at her, as he marches off to see if it is safe ahead, not waiting for her answer.

If he had stayed, she would've answered yes, of course I get nervous. But it would not be true. She can't remember ever being nervous, not when Michael came for her, not when she was waiting to give birth. Or even when a man pointed a knife at Michael in the shop. As Michael begged for their lives, she calmly threw a ladle of boiling water into the man's face. For weeks after that, she ruled the roost of the little shop.

As they walk, Drago finally tells her what's in the satchels. Forged papers that exaggerate figures about the Greek military power. They are given to Italian spies who take them to Rome, to the Italian military command. Drago hopes that if the Italians think Greece is capable of fighting, Mussolini will not invade. The papers say there are eight thousand Greek soldiers stationed at Lia near the Albanian border, when in truth there is only a militia of 12 to 15 soldiers. The papers say Corinth and Delphi has twelve or more thousand each, with hundreds of half-track vehicles. But Greece has no half-tracks. In these towns the resistance would be with pitchforks and fists.

Drago pumps with pride at his little feast of resistance. She thinks it the most stupid thing she has heard, but says nothing because she doesn't want to hurt him. He is doing something, at least, in a country that waits for fate.

Three weeks later three men from the Italian Secret Service come to the embassy. They walk straight into the Count's office.

His secretary, Mrs Pevlakis, a woman with ears that hear everything, can hear nothing of what is said behind the glass door, but it is a short talk, for the Count comes out after only a minute or so and barks at her to find Drago. It is at that moment that Drago comes out of the toilet. The Count grabs him by the sleeve.

What have you done, he whispers, pulling him into the office.

Olga gets the call at the residence an hour later. Mrs Pevlakis tells her as much as she knows about the Italians of swagger and threat. She tells Olga they are speaking nasty to Drago of spying, forgeries and Il Duce. They are bringing him to the residence to get some papers. That's all she knows, she says, and hangs up.

Olga

I gave thought to going out the Count's solid oak door and running away. To get a boat back to Australia and my fish and chip shop and my smelly soft husband. Back to the kisses of you and your sisters and the eyes of my sweet deaf boy. To a place away from the threat of someone else's war.

But it is not time. It is not safe for me to come back. Could you stand to see me locked away, my darling? One day I will risk it. I will be your mother again one day. I may not know when it is the right time to come back to you, but I will always know when it is not.

I made the hottest tea, strong with too many leaves, and let it burn into my mouth the tastes of Ultimo: a taste too tart, too bitter. My tongue brought back that little table and you and the girls with your drawings and cross-stitch and the smell of lard. It was the finest smell I could remember.

The Count's Residence, Athens

The car is as Olga imagined it: big, black and slow, its headlights as cats eyes stalking, stopping only to pounce; its doors opening fast and piercing. The men in coats were also as she had foreseen. Two very big, one very small. From the window the small man looks the most fearsome of them, with his dapper snappy walk. The others are ungainly and slovenly, safe as gentle uncles.

Drago is out too, roughly pulled, his coat pulled off his shoulder. His glasses are missing and he squints, either to see or to cry.

She rushes down from the bedroom, takes a breath, and opens the front door before they can knock.

What do you want, she demands in Greek. Why are you holding Secretary Stephanellis?

They do not understand Greek. She uses English, and only then, after they look with ignorance, Italian.

He is being held on suspicion of dangerous activity.

Yes, she says glancing at Drago. He's clearly a dangerous man.

They look for a moment at the dishevelled, helpless and blind Drago. She has taken another chess piece from them, even if only a pawn.

The smallest man pulls a pistol from his coat, a shiny polished metal thing that could have been a treasured cigarette case for all the care it had been given. This treasure's presence is its purpose, and on this day it has the effect its owner intends. Olga moves aside, wanting only to be away from its point. Drago is pulled inside by the back of his collar.

They bark out questions. Who is in the house? Not even a cook or maid? When are they expected back?

For no reason other than to get another pawn, Olga tells them she has an appointment in an hour with the Greek-Italian association. The one Il Duce is a patron for. As their official secretary...

Mussolini's name makes them stop their swaggering parade. A flit of fear darkens the face of the leader.

He looks around and picks up the telephone. He tells her to send her apologies.

With the gun pointing at her head, she dials and tells an empty line that she will not be able to go to the meeting. The small man watches her lips, mouthing her words. He looks just a little nervous, and in that moment she understands. He is pretending. He is not beyond her.

After she hangs up, the small man speaks of papers.

Olga says she knows nothing of papers.

Doesn't he have an office?

There is only the library that the Count uses as an office. All the embassy documents are in there.

He orders one of the men to take Olga and Drago upstairs, as he goes through to the library.

They are locked in a first floor storeroom where the linen and mops are kept. Olga holds Drago's hand in the dark, but it is limp. She puts her hand to his face and feels tears, silent tears.

After ten or fifteen minutes, there are steps, the steps of a man and the steps of a woman. A shadow flits in the light under the door, and there's a slam close by. The mistress's room. Footsteps fade down the stairs again.

She hears mumbling. It is Drago praying.

Drago, she wants to shout, don't waste your time, you foolish man. There is no God to save us. We are blood and bone and die by bullets or disease or old age. Why should any God want to save us simply because we sit in a dark room and beg? If God was watching he would never let a baby die. Don't believe in miracles, Drago. There is no miracle after a baby dies.

But Drago's prayers are too strong for both of them. Olga is lulled by his words, swaying to the rhythm of his chants, and starting to feel that nothing bad could happen.

He prays for the Light of His Comfort in these last moments.

The words of His Light and His Comfort. The Light of Salvation. Her eyes strain open and see the light, the only light in that black closet, the light coming in through a one inch gap under the door. Her fingers reach into the light, turning upwards and gripping the bottom of the door. With all her might she pulls up, and in the grace of an answered prayer, the old latch pops and the door opens.

Drago misses the miracle. He is still praying for it.

Crouching to the keyhole of the next room, Olga sees a woman sitting on the bed, a woman with a little fat, too much makeup and a dress that shows too much chubby leg. It is that leg's tight little calf that she knows. This is the calf of the woman who started it all. The woman who promised her so much and cost her everything. Olga has hated few people in her life, but in moments of being alone, she hates her sister Anna.

Yet at this moment she can feel no hate for the frumpy woman with the sad face. The only person in the world who has her shape of face and her nose. They have not spoken for ten years, but weeks ago, for no reason at all, Olga had sent Anna a note to let her know she was working for the ambassador.

Here and now, in this time of life and death, Anna is the worst person to have involved, but God's Light had saved Olga, and Olga will have to save Anna. Italian security will leave no witnesses. It is a time not for bad memories, it is a time for sisterhood.

Olga knocks lightly and whispers for her to come to the keyhole.

Olga, is that you, she wails, too loud.

Shush, softly kyrie. Yes it is me. Why are you here?

Anna cries a story of being pulled into the front door. She says the men in the coats had treated her bad, forcing her up the stairs, locking her in. She says she had only come for Olga, to give her the letter from Australia.

Steps start up the staircase. Loud solid steps. In ten seconds an Italian's eye will see her.

Drago's door is directly at the top of the stairs and if Olga tries to get to it she will be seen. Her little apartment is two doors along on her side of the atrium. It is the only place she can go.

She flops on her belly and crawls the four yards down the landing, alongside the bobbing head of the big Italian lumbering up the stairs. Her door is unlocked as she had left it.

She hides behind her door, jamming herself tight in the gap, not breathing, stilling her heart.

The sounds are as choreography. A hum of surprise from the Italian, a beat, the opening of Drago's door, two beats, urgent and angry words, a beat, Drago's whimpers. A slap, then nothing. For her ears there is no sound after that but the blows on Drago's poor soft body. As she stands, her belly starts a spasming that goes all the way to her throat. Through the door crack she can see it all. Drago crying. The back of the Italian moving up and down. His kicks. His punches as he asks impossible questions. Who? Where? Tell me? Where? Drago's body curls as an infant, rolling left to right, his little shoes, shining as always, arcing through the doorway, to and fro.

Olga is now at her fireplace, not knowing how she got there. She picks up a piece of burnt wood, a long heavy slab.

She sees it all in those last few seconds. The Italian's thinning hair kept in place by an oily cream meticulously applied. He had slopped some on his neck, a little streak of white. She stares at this cared-for head as she steps up behind the Italian and her arms gather a life's power. His head crushes so easily and quietly as if a fragile baby's skull. Then there is quiet again and only Olga, her arm, wood, a mess of man, and nothing else. No terror, no regret. Just as if she had wrung a chicken neck for dinner. Drago stares through eyes puffy, but she doesn't see him.

With the dead man's gun, a big gun, in her hand, she goes to release Anna, Drago's words behind her.

You idiot, they say.

Anna strides to the open door with her bag and coat.

I only come here to deliver a letter, she says. From Australia. From your husband.

Her voice rises. In a moment she would be screaming the scream Olga knows so well.

Olga throws her against the wall and Anna stops, shocked. Never before had Olga touched her, never before had Olga even contradicted her.

Never again would Olga feel the fear of something as harmless as petulance. She lets her go and goes back to the storeroom, knowing Anna will follow. She hears her sister take in a breath on seeing the Italian lying all arms, blood and coat.

Drago is in a bad way, shaky, bloody and leaning. Some of his fingers have been broken, and maybe an arm. As the three go down the stairs, the sound of their creaks are hidden by the smashing and tearing in the library.

The maid has locked the back door, so there is only the front way, across the atrium across the tiles and past the library. In view of the Italians.

As they pass the library door, Olga dares to look in the room, one last time, and sees the most extraordinary thing. In the middle of the room is the Count's unicorn on its base of high Corinthian marble, glass and gold, its front legs raised in defiance, kicking away the moment. The men move around the animal, probably without realising it is there. One bumps into it, and turns instinctively to settle it again before rushing off to rip open something else.

Out on the road, they run. The direction doesn't matter, they just run, watching for a taxi, a bus, or anything that would get them away.

Drago is bruising badly and bleeding. He runs, but only because the others are. He is a man resigned, past fear. His prayers have been said. There is no more for him. He doesn't even ask about the woman who is running with them.

Darlington, Sydney

The skinny, straight-legged boy stands straight and ready. A jeering pumpkin-headed giant runs towards him, but the boy's straight legs stay still. They take the whack of the big body and fly backwards, the giant's jeer becoming a grimace as he feels bones being hit, either the skinny kid's or his own, before crashing nose first into the dusty clumped grass. His face will wear the scar for weeks.

The fallen giant sees the straight legs jump up and stand over him, toe to his forehead. The face that belongs to the legs shows no malice, there's even the edge of a smile in them. The giant stands and plays the ball back, and just has time to grip the jersey sleeve and say good tackle and accept a passing pat in return before the straight legs run off to bring down someone else.

For seventy minutes the boy with the straight legs marks and stops his man, refusing to be dummied or diverted. He'd feel the consequences in the bath later, not now. The headmaster limps up and down the sideline, yelling orders his boys can't hear, telling them to pass the ball, go harder, to back up. Headmaster Smythe is proud to be the coach, it proves that he takes a personal interest, even if bad eyesight means he can't throw them balls in training, and his saggy stomach stops him keeping up with the boys when he orders them to do a lap of the oval.

At the end of the game the boys shake soggy limp hands. It was a hard one. When the Wanderers plays the Institute there is no sympathy, and the deaf boys play harder, giving two hidden punches for every one they get. The Wanderers, like lots of teams, would end up frustrated because their witty taunts went unheard by the deaf heads. The Institute is a team of winners because they look out for each other. It isn't like that in other teams.

At the special ceremony afterwards, the straight boy stands in a bunch with the rest of his team, kidding and tickling and mock punching. He is the youngest but that doesn't mean anything here.

A famous, strongly built man is standing in the middle of the group of teachers, but most of the children don't recognise his distorted features. The only reason they know he is someone important is because he is talking with Headmaster Smythe.

Aloysius Smythe throws a few smiley, head-tilted, knowing words to this companion, who laughs back obligingly, but the man is thinking about what he'd seen today. He likes the style of the straight-legged boy who showed no fear. The boy kicked well too, sending a few over the heads of the opponents to just the right place.

He claps the two sides as they line up for the photo. The Mirror photographer directs him where to stand. Just here Mr Brown, in between the captains. That's it. Maybe put your arms around them. No, around their shoulders. Good.

The man from The Sun arrives late and sees he's been beaten again. He waits till the other photographer finishes, then edges up to the great. Excuse me Mr Brown, could I have a photo of you with one of the boys, you know, just passing the ball, like the great of yesterday to the player of the future.

Dave Brown winces at the well-meant comment. He'd only just retired and he is already yesterday's man at twenty-nine. With his early baldness and all, he had had this sort of thing for years now. Never got used to it, but.

He calls to the Headmaster to throw him a ball, and the bald, fattish man runs to gather one, throwing it wide of the mark. Dave has seen a lot of coaches like this one. He gathers it back and throws it to the straight-legged boy.

Nicky catches the ball and jogs away to a good throwing distance. He tosses a too-hard pass that goes nearly as wide as the headmaster's. Dave laughs and returns it soft and straight. Nicky passes it back a little easier and finds his mark. The Sun photographer shoots from a few angles, and then urges them closer so he can get them both in frame.

While the photographer packs his equipment, Dave Brown passes a few more, and kicks a few short lobs into Nicky's arms. Smythe chats with parents, distracted, always keeping his eye to make sure no-one disgraces themselves in front of the football great, but he can't break away from the mothers wanting dishonest praise of their children's progress.

Soon Dave Brown is gone, and Nicky is walking back to the main building alone.

Nicholas. Nicholas Stambolis, Smythe calls, running to catch up, forgetting that the boy is deaf.

Nicholas, he says with his hands as he catches him on the steps, you were good today.

Nicky's fingers pass an excited message.

He says... I can be... a very good player... and I could play for... Easts one day... if I want.

Smythe asks him if he wants to play for Easts.

I don't know... if I want... to play football... all the time.

You're a level-headed boy Nicholas, Smythe says. You can work in any factory if you want. You'd be the pride of the Institute.

He grabs Nicky around the neck, head-locking him hard with one arm and, giggling, messing up his hair with his other hand.

North of Athens, Greece

They reach a road heading south, Olga guessing that the Italians would assume they would go towards the city. They slow to a walk as she takes Anna's scarf and wraps it on her head. She throws Drago's coat away and tells him to put his arm through hers. Be a husband, she says. Smile. Stroll. Try not to limp.

The light begins to fade. They need toilet, they need food, and Drago's bruises are raising, his breaths are wheezes. They reach a market that is closing, where children call out for last customers as parents sit in the back of the stalls among their rows of jars of preserved fish, eggplant, and olives. The smell of spice and cigarette smoke gives a feeling that there can be no harm here.

They stop for some nuts and lemonade, and in the joy of repast they almost forget what has happened. Anna chatters with the stall man. He is flirting and she likes it. Drago rolls his worry beads absently with his good arm; he's in a trance in this quiet market. The moon calms, the breeze drops. They had not noticed the crowd go and the cheesecloth that is now covering many of the stalls. They must have been lulled for at least half an hour.

The peace is smashed by a roar coming from up the road. It is a car with a big engine; its headlights filling the night.

Olga can't see Anna, so she grabs Drago and they dash away from the car, which is now coming fast up the dirt road past the stalls towards them. Twenty metres. They are the only ones on the road now.

She pulls him down under the table of a closed stall, jamming behind jars of preserved fish, her hand on his mouth, a move of instinct. Everything she does is instinct. The gun is in her hand. She listens.

She can hear nothing else. There are no sellers' voices, no children, no sound at all, but the car's tyres, slow, now crunching loud over the stony road, getting closer. Olga's finger feels her trigger. Anna is there too now, with her arms around Drago, their cheeks together, eyes closed.

Olga watches the road dirt through the table's apron. The crunching stops, a door opens and footsteps come to them.

Hey, those people who were there. The people in the good clothes. Where they go?

The nut seller points to the table they are under.

The steps come to them.

Hey, you want to be driven somewhere, very cheap, good car. American.

They sweep through the countryside, Drago between the two women in the back seat, drifting into stupor, but still aware enough to give directions to the Egyptian driver, not giving an address, just telling him when to turn.

Olga asks where they are going.

To safety, he says, and says nothing more.

Olga

It is funny how you can feel comfort in the smell of old car seats, burnt from too many days in the Athenian sun, and in a man's trouser leg flopping against yours on a sprung seat on a rough road. I reached forward and touched the little fancywork on the back of the driver's seat. It had a design that no-one had probably ever noticed set into the old green smooth material, the pattern now edged with black from years of hands gripping it as they got in or out. It was beautiful and I fingered each groove. I felt exhilarated and I didn't know why.

I turned and Drago's eyes were staring into mine, without blink or care. It was a look of a lover. Or a father. It was a look of an ending to something. His hand came towards me and brushed along my face, but the hand was not for me. It went on to tap the driver on the shoulder for him to stop.

I had never been to a part of Greece like this before, yet we could not have been more than forty kilometres from Athens. This was a dead place. No tree grew, no animal made a noise. The land was black beneath the horizon. I wondered who could live in such a place of no life or hope of life.

The taxi started off with Drago still inside.

You are better without me, he said, as I ran alongside trying to open his door.

Ask for Rena, he called out. Rena. Ask for Rena.

The lumbering rattling car went over the rise and Drago's head fell back on the seat, as if dead.

The car's lights took a long time to disappear and until they did we stood side by side like the sisters we never were, watching the headlight's reflections off the posts and fences, getting smaller and further until they left us in the moon's light.

I realised then that I had come this far only for Drago, not for me, or even Anna. This crazy journey had led us to be standing in the dark wind, Anna and I, two sisters who didn't know each other in a place we didn't know, with no money or food. More than anything, as the wind snapped at the bare bottom of my back, I wanted to eat. I craved the warmth of your father's vegetable soup with some psomme[1] and a little retsina. Here I was being haunted by ordinary things while carrying a gun stolen from the man I had killed.

Anna was watching me with a cocked head, helpless as a child. I would have to mother my sister and forget my wants again.

The only clue I had was the name, Rena. That name I would hold on to, tight to my chest.

Pyrmont, Sydney

Tina runs through the shop's lunchtime crowd, dragging an already dog-eared copy of The Sun, a few of its inner pages falling out along the way. She calls out for everyone to look. Nicky's in the paper. There's a photo of him with a footballer man.

The men from the sugar mill and the docks grab it and pass it around, laughing and teasing, pleased as punch. Even the women who haven't the least interest in football cluck and coo with the pride of the roosting hens they so resemble. Tina snatches the paper back before they've finished looking, and races the remnant into the back room to show Jean or anyone, like it's her own discovery, like she's taken the picture itself.

Her father smiles at the picture of his boy, and his wrongly spelled name. Things like that don't matter; the

---

1 Bread

name is spelt closely enough for everyone to know it's Nicky. Thirteen years old, and he's in the paper.

He hands it back and tells Tina to show it to Jean. She's upstairs. Quick.

Jean laughs and promises to make a special cake for Nicky.

When Tina comes down again, her father is gone.

North of Athens, Greece

They go down the rutted path, holding hands, Anna jumping at every bird sound or when she catches her city shoes in grass roots.

Down the rutted path they go to somewhere Olga hopes will be a key to warmth and food, to somewhere she can close her eyes and not see that mess on the landing.

Down the rutted path they go because there is nowhere else.

The farmer's house is empty, its small windows black as the night. It is a place of poverty and stone. No life to it, no goat or chicken or dog, no broom outside the back door, no washing dangling from anywhere. They are alone and the night is still. The place could well have been empty for a hundred years.

The only other thing on this barren land is what looks like a barn in the valley behind.

Did you see that, Anna whispers. That light. A light in the window of the barn.

Look Anna, I don't even think it's a window.

It's a window her sister cries. It's a window and I saw a light.

Anna is running down to the barn before Olga can stop her.

Be careful sister, she calls too quietly. We don't know these people and they don't know us.

They hear laughter, then the sounds of movement, the thumpy dings of cheap plates. Eating noises.

You see? I told you.

Anna is triumphant, and bangs on the door.

Pyrmont, Sydney

The lone man stands on the bridge watching the clippers and the fat dirty boats going about their business urgently, the singletted muscled men on the decks throwing out orders to each other. There is no laughing, kidding or wasting of time. These men are so different to the Greeks on Castellorizo.

His hair blows just the same way it did all those years ago, back when it was black and longer on the top, back when he was young forever and no-one worried too much if business was bad.

All of a sudden he cries for those days. No-one on the bridge this afternoon notices because no-one looks at other people on this bridge. They have no time to ponder. They are too busy, they need to get to where they are going.

He remembers her at this very spot, when she was easily ferocious, ready to take offence. She was a child then, but never laughing as a girl laughed. Not yet a mother, she never laughed. Was that it? Did he take her laughter away?

It was at this spot that she first took his hand as a woman in love. It had taken a year.

He thinks she should be here for this moment. The boy they had made is in the newspaper and she, if she is alive, doesn't know anything of it. She has never seen how good Nicky is with the football, like she has never seen Nellie blooming. Three years, two years, and these things are done; the children grow into someone else, and the old times, the times they thought would last for always, are suddenly dead.

He cries at this spot that was once theirs, but which is now loud with motor cars and trucks. There is no quiet anymore, no clop of the horses she so loved. Where are those horses now? There is no peace anymore, there is only smoke and noise to mock the slow of yesterday. At this spot where she first took his hand.

North of Athens, Greece

The talking inside stops at the first knock. Olga bangs again, and after a few seconds a woman's voice asks who it is.

Rena, she says. We have been told to ask for Rena.

A woman, short and wide, opens the door. She might be fifty; she might be seventy. Her face shows a hardship that has shrivelled what had been a womanly beauty.

The woman stares at Olga stilly for a long time, ignoring Anna's complaints about being left out in the cold. Olga doesn't know what the woman sees in her face that makes her stop her staring, but she does, breaking into a big smile. She says she is Rena, and would they like to come in for some soup?

The inside of the tiny barn is filled by a table crowded with farmer types. None of them has any greeting. This woman Rena makes up for it with smiles and plates of Spanakorizo, spinach and rice. Anna eats, wolfing. Olga swipes at her in such a way that would look playful to the others.

The men laugh, and Anna doesn't like it. She says they would not giggle if the Italians find them here.

A terror comes into eyes around the table.

Olga has to think quickly. Words wouldn't do, and explanations wouldn't be heard. Never have so many eyes examined her with a loathing.

She takes the gun from her pocket and puts it on the table. A symbol of faith, it was meant as.

But it brings gasps. Taut fingers lift, heads move back, bodies stiffen. They look from the gun to Olga to the gun again. In her tightening chest she knows she has made a terrible mistake.

Anna is the only one not part of the moment. She eyes the gun, and with a full mouth she sniggers, tells the frozen crowd about the mess Olga made of the Italian. You would never think an Italian had so many brains, she says.

Nodding, Olga pushes the gun across the table to one of the men. Yes, she says. He was killing my friend Drago. Drago Stephanellis.

A large, brown-faced man moves his black eyes to hers. He is a striking man with a square jaw and a moustache that drops down each side of the mouth, like a horseman of the old days. He leans across to her and asks, with a softness that belies his tough look, where is Drago.

She tells them it all, the Italians, the escape, the taxi and Drago's words, the killing.

They are judging her with the eyes of fighters and haters. Olga has no doubt that there must be a knife held at the ready in a vest or cloth. Meanwhile Anna continues to slurp, not knowing, and comfortable with the warmth and food.

Olga stands to leave, and a young woman with a twisted face, half a face, with a dead eye dashes at her.

Pyrmont, Sydney

Dad! Where have you been?

Tina is puffing. She's been looking for Michael all over. The grocer's, Mrs Minnie's place, even the pub he never goes into. She sees him coming up from the bridge. She doesn't see his sadness.

Some women from the gu'ment are at the shop. They want to see you. Two biddies.

Now dear. Not that kind of talk please.

But they are biddies. Wait till you see 'em.

There are five women on the bench in the shop, and Tina was right. Only two could be the ones from the government. The others have shifted away from the pair ever so slightly while watching them out of an eye's corner. No one in Pyrmont likes people from the government.

Michael invites them through to the parlour. Whatever they want to say, he doesn't want the other women to hear it. There will be rumours enough already. They pass through the kitchen and he eyes Jean, who grabs Tina and pulls her up the stairs after her.

The women glance around the parlour and its faded curtains, and sit when bid. One is very fat and very floralled: her dress, her shoes and her hat all match in pale lavender blooms; only her purse is different in a good hard-working leather tan.

The other woman is thin as a whip in a close-fitting grey. There is nothing bright about her, even her expression. She carries not a purse, but a satchel, crawed tight under her very thin fingers.

Mr Stambloati, the thin one says straight away, we need to talk to you.

It's Stambolis, Tina yelps. Not Stambloati. Stambolis.

The women ignore Tina and wait, expectant, eyes on Michael.

Yes, of course. Is this important?

Only if you think your children are important, says the thin one, with a touch of venom.

North of Athens, Greece

Olga moves away from the woman, instinctively leaping to cover Anna. The scarred girl still catches Olga, and hugs her.

They are frozen in the strange scene, the three women in a huddle. The others have not moved, not even Rena.

Finally the scarred girl speaks.

You are good. Good. You are good. You are welcome here. If you hurt fascists, you are good.

The girl releases Olga, and Olga lets go of Anna, who by now is starting to panic.

Suppa, kyrie. Relax, Olga hisses.

For once Anna obeys, and starts to eat again, watching everyone with each spoonful.

As Olga looks up, she sees the twisted face fully for the first time. She can't help but touch it. With her fingertips.

The girl asks if she likes her face. A face made when she was stupid enough to think that a Metaxas firing squad would not fire if a girl stood between them and those who were to die. She died that day. Twice. Brought back both times. She says it proud.

Rena breaks away from the still crowd and wraps her arms around the girl's head, squeezing it. Antigone, Antigone she says, soothing the girl with her name and a rocking. Rena talks to Olga through this cradle of arms. She says it is women who are most unkind. They never talk to her. Men, they pay her attention. On trains and buses they touch her. In the street they ask her to come back to their house. She is picked out as a woman who will be desperate for anyone.

Anna rubs her tummy and says this is all made up. The General would not fire on his own people. He is a good man.

The scarred girl Antigone drags her good eye to Anna. Metaxas is another Mussolini, a fascist devil, she says, quietly yet not at all softly. She spits the words and some spittle at Anna.

Well, Anna goes on, reaching across the table for a kefte meatball, if they were going to be shot, then they must have done something to deserve it.

Anna doesn't hear the coo from around the table, and reaches to the kefte, trying to find the biggest one.

A woman knocks the meatball from Anna's mouth. It bounces across the table and lands in someone's hat. The woman readies for a better hit, but the man next to her puts his hand on her arm.

The woman coldly thanks Rena for inviting her, and calls to the man, who follows her to the door.

Olga dashes after the couple and begs an apology for Anna. She was born ignorant, she tells them, and chooses to stay that way.

The man only says it is to be expected. The woman says no, the problem is that Anna is a cunt.

The other guests are leaving as Olga goes back in. Rena and the scarred girl are clearing dishes, putting scraps and bones into a bucket. Anna is sitting back, not in the least embarrassed, as people who never take blame can never be shamed.

Olga's gun has gone.

You will sleep in the barn, Rena orders. The Italians are probably trying to invent a story to explain what went wrong, the amateurs. Your faces are best off the streets.

Olga goes with her to get the bedding, saying nothing, asking nothing. There is nothing to be said.

The barn is cold and becomes colder, and the sisters just have old hay, blankets and each other. Anna nestles next to Olga without touching. They have never touched. Even as lost sisters, brought together after a lifetime, Olga's first kisses found only Anna's hair. Yet Olga has never had a moment when she wanted to grab her sister and hug the barrier away.

Anna jumps up, for once with a face of a child's tease, gazes at Olga bright-eyed, before fiddling in her bag, and producing, as a rabbit act, an envelope. She smiles and holds it out.

It had been opened.

Michael Stambolis
Harris St, Ultimo
3rd May 1939

My Dearest Olga,
I have not heard from you since the night before you left. It has been best for both of us that we have had this time to be apart. I want to say that I understand you had no choice but to leave, and I know I am part at fault for that, but I need to say to you that what I did was the best for everyone, you can see it, can't you? You shouldn't have run. It only made things worse. There are things that must be faced. The longer you are away the harder it will be for you when you come back. Come back now and I will help you. You are the mother of our children, and this will always

mean much to me. Please do not be scared. If you wire me, I will
send you the money for the fare. I will pay anything to help you
when you get back here. We will fight this together.

   With kind regards,
   Michael Stambolis[2]

   She lies back and thinks. He promises to help, but what
happened on that last night cannot be fixed with a few
pounds and a word in someone's ear. If it was not so, she
would be there. He must know this is why she hasn't dared
write.

   Anna watches her sister, wide-eyed, hopeful. Would
she take Anna with her to Australia this time? Michael
would be able to wire two fares. He is still a rich man. Yes?

   Olga sees her old life, the kitchen table, Nicky's smiles.

   I'm your sister Olga. You must. You must.

   It has been three years, three years of rending in her
heart. Three years of kissing the girls asleep as she lies
alone in her bed, three years of touching her pillow where
their eyes would have been.

   You must. I'm your family.

   Yes, Olga says, I will send a wire to Australia.

   Anna jumps and grabs at Olga's hands without touch-
ing them, and says she has to arrange to have Theo and
Theanna and the twins ready. There will be six fares. No.
Seven. She giggles that she has forgotten to count Olga.

---

2 This letter was among Olga's correspondence.

The Dead Ground

(September - November 1939)

Rena's Farmhouse, North of Athens

Anna, Antigone and Olga eat their breakfast of stewed millet in the house while Rena cleans around them. Tables, floors, clothes, vegetables. It's the lot of a Greek woman to always be cleaning something.

A gentle knock comes at the door, and before they can see if their night clothes are hiding their bosoms, the moustache man from last night comes in. He sits at their table and pours himself a chicory, aiming his words at Rena, pretending the rest of them aren't there.

He says Germany has gone into Poland. It is certain to start a war. Perhaps a war of many countries. Greece too.

He drinks the rest of his chicory as Rena dries the plates she had dried only a minute before. No other words are spoken. Olga knows the look that is in the eyes of the other women. They can think of nothing to say.

Olga

Last night I had a nightmare, the first of this new war so many had promised would never happen. I was being hunted through Athens by women in black with guns. Everywhere I went these mothers were there. Up ahead was a corner where beams of light came from a side street. I so wanted to reach that corner and get to the light, for I knew it would be safe there. But I couldn't reach it. My running went nowhere. I couldn't make my muscles move. A hand grabbed my ankle.

I woke in a terror. The terror became relief, became terror again when I remembered the dead Italian. I had killed a man and the sun was shining and the smells of a wood stove were in my eyes and nose. I know he was killing Drago and would have killed me, but truth and reason has no play here. You kill a man, you kill a man. That man will never again smell wood smoke. For all my life, he will never smell wood smoke.

Anna was gone, no doubt to start packing. She had wanted to go to Australia since the first time I met her. To her Australia is the land of gold on the streets, where a beautiful Greek woman could make a fortune with a little work. Anna could never realise that George Street is made of tar, and that there are many far prettier and harder-working women than her in Sydney.

I ate a little, and decided to try for the taxidromeoio[3]. Rena muttered against my hope of sending a telegram. She said everyone in the country is going to be trying to send a telegram today.

Rena was right. The lines at the taxidromeoio were long. By the time I got there they were two blocks down the

---

3 Post office

pavement. I tried another post office, and the line was even longer, so I went back to the first and people were now lined up for a further block. I joined the end of that line, footsore and thirsty in the sun. Some sensible people had their children bring them snacks and water, but I had no-one, so I bore it. I saw people were letting friends in the queue up ahead. It was the way they did it that annoyed me, with a laugh and careless shrug for the rest of us. If they had been furtive and ashamed, I could have forgiven them. I yelled, and pointed them out to the others. But no-one cared, even in this dead line. It is the Greek way to help your friends. If I had met those people at a taverna last night, it would have been me they had let in. I would have accepted the offer.

From 9 o'clock until after lunch I stood in the line, my varicose vein throbbing. Four hours to think of nothing else but you and Nicky and your sisters. A mother in the line with me had brought her daughters, two of them, both probably only six or eight years old. They played and their mother tried to shush them, and they would not be stilled. You were never one that needed shushing. You were always quiet, watching and listening, and somewhere in your eye there was a little bit of judging. I'd see you watching your father and me, looking to see if the way we sniped at each other was serious. You'd have that frown and one of us would both rush to you and say not to worry, we were only playing. The truth is that many times we were not playing, especially in that last year, the worst year of my life, the year that finished with the worst night of my life.

I awoke from my thoughts to see I was only to the door, to see another fifty people ahead of me inside, and only one attendant at the counter. The memory of that night brought me to my senses. How could I think of going back? I would not be going back to you and to our happy shop and its customers and swirls of chicken feathers. I would be taken as soon as I stepped on shore, and I would never see you or my Nicky. My shame would become your shame. I couldn't let that happen.

I left the post office with the tight chest that seems to be with me so much these days.

The lines were just as long at the city bus stations because the buses weren't coming in. A woman at the stop told me the government had just announced they had cut down the services to save gas and the buses for war preparations.

I had nowhere to go. The bus to Rena's would now not be coming until the evening. I stepped back into the recessed doorway of a clothing shop, not knowing where else to go. People pushed past me to go in and out. Eventually, maybe after half an hour, the shop-owner came out and asked me to move. I almost said I couldn't move because the Italians might see me.

It was then that the ridiculousness of it all struck me. I had been looking over my shoulder all day. Even in the line at the Post Office I hid my face with a scarf. This was the country of my birth. The blood rushed to my head, and in that rush I decided I would not hide. I decided then in my stupid impulsive way to go to the eye of the storm, the Italian embassy, for it was the only place where I could find out if the blackshirts were looking for me. The blackshirts could be there, but I feared them not at all. I wanted to stare them in the face and dare them to grab me. I would scratch at their proper moustaches and their leather coats. The thought of having killed one of them exhilarated me. At that moment I wished I had killed them all.

From across the road the embassy looked the same as it always did. An older couple came out of the door in expensive long cloth coats with some fur for show. Their whole dress was for show. It was too hot for coats, and the woman was tripping over her very high-heeled shoes. She snapped snipes at her man in Greek. Her hand was in his elbow, and he let her hand drop when he lit a cigarette. The woman pulled hard on his sleeve and he pushed past her. She clopped clumsily after him up the street.

Italian Embassy, Athens

The waiting room is full. Mrs. Pevlakis is telling a man in a green striped business suit that he will have to wait. He says something back to her, and Mrs. Pevlakis waves him away.

He moves to the wall with the others of all kinds: poor-suited, rich-bearing, a Greek family eating from a tin of beans, Italians wanting to get in good with the Count. Mercenary citizens. The overfed afraid of losing their food.

Mrs Pevlakis sees Olga with a start.

You are dead, she says as a statement.

I am back from the dead.

Yes. A bad time to return to life, she says. This office has been full for two days. They know there's nothing to do. War is war, but they think that by demanding and wanting, they will be welcomed into the new world.

As she speaks, the man in the green suit is there again, this time gripping Mrs. Pevlakis' paperweight Falcon, the one her son brought back from Morocco.

He slams it down, cracking the glass on the desk, breaking the Falcon.

Mrs. Pevlakis grabs his tie and tells him to get out. It surprises Olga that he apologises and leaves through the crowd which had hushed for the paperweight.

The incident leaves with him, and the crowd swirls to the desk. The Count has come out. Olga turns to hide her face, but he sees her.

Inside his office he squeezes her hand. He says nothing about Drago or the dead Italian in his storeroom. Asks nothing.

He snatches a piece of blank paper and starts to write, head tilted over it. His hair is thinner. Thinner than last week.

He tells her she needs a new name, and pointing to her hair, says she will have to change its colour. With her pale skin, some black hair would make her look more Greek.

Olga dares to ask if this is really necessary. She could hide in the city and disappear. Not be seen, maybe carry on working for him.

The Count throws his paper down. Restrained and clipped, he scolds the carpet.

You are no fool, so please don't act as one. We both know what has happened, and so do others. Just accept what I have to give.

Shamed by his generosity, she nods and thanks. Of course. She has killed. The Count is risking himself just to be with her, especially on Italian territory.

As she sits in the waiting room she watches how skilfully Mrs. Pevlakis ignores an Italian woman who is swearing like an Australian. A contrast of women in war. One woman demanding all and the other acquiescing not at all. Two women etching their ground.

After only a few minutes, Mrs Pevlakis says the Count is ready for her again.

He gives Olga a paper and says the British ambassador will engage her as governess without an interview.

There is one other condition of all this, he says, as they hold an end each of the paper. She is never to return to the Italian embassy, and to deny ever working there.

Not even to see the girls?

No, he says, especially not to see the girls.

And with a slip of paper and a touch of a handshake they part.

Olga

The letter of introduction showed me as Olga Mavromati, my family name, dear daughter, one that once had some repute in parts of Greece. I do not know how he knew this was my name. A coincidence probably.

Olga Mavromati, an anonymous Greek woman. I now make my hair black with some concoction of Rena's, and have plucked away my thick eyebrows. It looks nice.

It just isn't me.

Olga (a few days later)

My friends came back for me. Two mornings ago. Rena and Antigone were in the field, and I was dusting the kitchen. It is the only thing Rena will let me do in her house, dusting away the field dust that always comes back so soon.

In that kitchen my friends came and walked right in. They started on me straight away.

What was I doing here in this broken down farm-house? Didn't I know I was wasting my time? What was I doing in Greece anyway? This acting. It's more likely pretensions to acting. You were never THAT good dear.

Your children are better off without you. What can you give them? Really.

Go back to Anna. She's family. Add up all the people who love you. Grab Anna while she's there. Yes she is annoyed about the tickets. Very annoyed. It may be too late. You have lost her too. You lose everyone.

Through the window I saw Rena and Antigone coming up from the field, one short and wide and limping, the other tall and beautiful, more beautiful because of her poor scarred face. My friends had to go. I couldn't have Rena meet them.

But they wouldn't leave. They defied me as they always did. They never leave until they win.

I ran to the stone barn, put a log of wood through the handle and ran to the furthest corner. With my knees to my chest I waited. The crunch of the gravel started soon after, then the pushing of the door. A knock. Rena's voice asking me to come out. For ten minutes she knocked and called, becoming gentler, as if she knew of my friends, but she couldn't know. I didn't know when she left or even when I knew she had left because it was never quiet in that barn. My friends spoke all the time of children and cowardice.

I curled on the floor until the sun dropped, and then through the night. Rena called me for breakfast. I said that I was not hungry and leave me be. I lied that I was writing. Rena argued, then insisted, then beckoned, and finally walked away in a huff. A plate was by the door when I finally opened the barn door as the sun was going down again. I had not noticed the voices had gone.

That is how they are. They come and turn blue skies into dry days. They tell me of the damp in the rain; of the chill in the cool. Their advice is never good. Then they go.

The first time they came to me it was without warning. I was here in Athens, way back, soon after Christopher. I remember it well. I was in Leoforos St. My head was full of clouds, my bag full of things I couldn't remember buying, my feet taking me somewhere I'd forgotten. I saw nothing except the woman with the pram. The baby was just like Christopher. His little chubby arms were reaching for me, and I took them. There was a scream somewhere and a pull on my arm. Run, a voice said. You have a right. Run.

Before I could think, the baby was out of my arms, and being held by the woman, who was glaring and sobbing and kissing his little nose.

You have lost him, the voice said to me. You have lost him again.

The baby watched me through his mother's kisses.

He really didn't look like Christopher at all.

Pyrmont, Sydney

Are you sure a shop is a proper place to bring up three young girls Mr Stambloati?

He nods.

The woman leans back. She is used to fathers fighting or insulting her. This man is unexpected, staring away, and could almost be agreeing. The other woman stays forward, with her elbows on her handbag, eyes trying to pierce his, if she can catch them, for at that moment he is looking at the sacks of potatoes behind her. He looks like he's counting them.

Mr Stambloati?

Yes?

Is a shop a proper place to bring up three young girls?

Michael looks to the women. He learned early in business that people need to have their say. Buyer or seller, it's all the same. They have an offer to make. Turk, Greek, Italian, priest, police or woman. You must hear them out. The women are asking him what he thinks when they don't care what he thinks. He waits. He knows they are not finished yet.

Mr Stambloati, your wife left you with three young girlies and a deaf son. That must be a terrible load.

He nods and they too find themselves nodding like Michael, trance-like. The floral woman even starts silently counting the plates on the wall behind him.

A shout from behind the beaded curtain to the shop breaks the calm.

Get out you frozen old biddies. Go home to your lonely little rooms and leave good families to themselves.

Michael winces.

Err, my daughter. I'm sorry. She feels things strongly.

She is very rude, says the floral woman. A well-bred child would not be so insulting.

I have better breeding than to wear a dress like that, says the voice.

Freda! Mesa. Go cut up the chips and saveloys.

Yes Dad, says the voice, barely chastened.

He turns back to the women and crosses his legs, but makes no more apologies. He just nods more, as if still answering their last question.

Mr Stambloati? You know we can take these girls away.

He nods, and they sit there awkwardly.

Finally he stands.

Ladies, thank you for your visit. If there is no more I can help you with, my governess will see you out. Jean!

You have a governess, one of the woman asks, surprised.

Yes, of course, he says. My girls need a woman's hand.

They pass through the kitchen, by the table, where Jean, Nellie and Tina are pencilling some numbers into schoolbooks.

Jean looks up.

Tina's arithmetic has really improved Mr Stambolis, she says.

The women, flustered, go through the shop and out to the street without saying anything more, glancing at each other. It is the first time they have looked uncertain.

Are they gone, Jean calls out.

Yes Jean.

Good. What I know about arithmetic wouldn't be enough to count to ten, even with my fingers.

The girls leave the books on the table and go to the back lane to play with Nicky and his football.

Rena's Farmhouse, north of Athens

Antigone leads the way to the meeting. Lithe, fast, tonight she is a goddess of land and moon, where a scarred face has no currency.

They criss-cross the valley up to a square stone barn. At the door Rena says a line of words that make no sense, and they are allowed in.

The meeting is formal for this most informal of places. Minutes, gavel and chairman in a barn on a dead hill littered with goat shit and chicken feathers. An English way, Greek style.

Never in Oxford or Westminster could a chairman be so abused. He tries for an hour to switch the objectives of the group from being subversive against the Metaxas government, to supporting Metaxas against the Germans.

The chairman's breakthrough comes when he says they should remember the times Turkey invaded. Greeks, he says, are the most invaded of the world. We must never let it happen again.

It is a good argument for these people. Their hatred of the prime minister is deep, but their hatred for Turks is deeper. The sounds of his victory are a simple quietening but for a hiss and a clicking mouth from the back of the barn.

He can now tell them the British have made contact with the central committee.

They have offered to help us, he says. They will give us weapons and training. They made no demands.

Of course not, one woman calls out. They just want this country to be one of their prizes. They want Greece to be the launching place for their strategy in Arabia and Africa.

Maybe, the chairman says. But who would you rather have here? The Germans, who want Greece to be a jewel in their empire, or the British.

One coloniser for another, the man says.

Yes, says the chairman. It is a choice of the times. The choice is for you to make. I must tell you though, he adds, that the central office has agreed, as long as cells like ours agree too.

They are more muted now. Most of them had never thought twice about the British before tonight, but at this moment of decision they see the British as the enemy of their enemy, the first to stand up to Hitler. These farmers and shepherds respect the British pluck.

For the second time in the meeting the chairman wins an argument in this cell where arguments are hard to win.

Rena stands at a nod from the chairman.

"The British will fight with us against the invaders. They will supply our teams across the north and west. They will send soldiers, we don't know how many yet, to come into the mountains with us and train us in how to use their rifles. The sabotage experts will show us how to blow bridges and block rail lines. And my friends, we need this training. Everyone here will need to be trained..."

At this some of the men start to object, but Rena continues.

"... and we will tell you where to go for this. Just wait for notice, and tell no-one about it. Be prepared to lie to your wives and children. The central command says this will be a war of ears on every wall.

"But if there is an invasion, our first task will be to help British airmen go out of the country. They will be stranded and will need to be moved out at no notice at all if the Germans start to take control..."

The farmers, shepherds, wood-carriers and layabouts listen. Her age, girth and black dress demanding the respect of their silence.

"...because roads and rail lines will be closed almost immediately. We would need to steal bullets for them. We would need to cook for them. Give them clothes, even our own if there are no others."

But their respect for age runs no deeper than the love of their own clothes. The voices start to rise again.

This time the man with the Russian moustache puts his hand up and the noise stops.

He wants to know who is against helping the British.

No-one answers.

He asks again.

The man next to him smiles and says they cannot risk themselves for a few British soldiers. The British are in Greece for their own interests. Sure, let them help us, then let them take care of themselves.

No, Olga says. You are wrong.

He waves her away, appealing to the moustache, who is not the Chairman or the secretary of the group, but clearly the one who matters. The smiling man says Greece will never be free if we keep swapping tyrant for tyrant, occupier for occupier. Use the British like they would use us.

Olga says no again, loudly, on her feet. This is about a debt of honour.

The man says she is talking that way because she is British.

She stands and slowly goes around the table. She grabs his collar, her fingers squeezing the material so tight she can feel one of her few long nails bending back.

I am not British, she whispers at him.

His eyes and her eyes, the loudest things in the room. Her nail breaks.

My children, she says, were born in Australia, but a Greek is a Greek, and this means that anyone who helps us becomes our family. How proud can we be of ourselves when we leave our comrades to get killed, while we scurry around acting important with our meetings and our minutes?

She releases his collar in the silence. There is no laughing, as Michael used to laugh when she gave an opinion on something outside of the kitchen.

Her nail clings ridiculously to his collar, half an inch of her to be brushed off later.

She puts on her coat to leave, but before she can go to the door, the Moustache speaks.

This woman is right, he says. We have voted to let the British help us. They are our brothers from this moment on.

The other man opens his palms and eyes to the Moustache, as easily as he had risen to argue, he smiles that he agrees.

She is barely aware of the Moustache walking around the table talking of killing. Not just invaders, but Greeks if they are traitors and spies. She barely realises he has stopped behind the smiling man and has grabbed his arm and has asked the awful question.

Would you put us in, Nicko?

This Nicko looks honestly surprised. He says if he was a turncoat, he would not be coming to these meetings and disagreeing with everyone.

Unless you were a very smart traitor, Moustache says plainly, his hand still on the man's arm.

Nicko looks down and says maybe he should go.

Moustache grabs him, hugs him, kisses him.

Olga

I have never made friends easily. People resent the truth and I speak honestly. People expect gratefulness and I am not effusive. People want kindness, but what good is lying?

Rena has been different with me since the night in the barn. She talks to me of herself and it is as if she saw something in me that she understood. The nights in her house are no longer quiet and awkward. She talks to me, and last night she told me a story she had never told. It was to do with Moustache, who she had known since he was a baby, a good-looking wildly indulged baby of potato farmers just up the road. Everyone but his parents had thought him mad or possessed, the way he would babble and scream and use words never taught him. He grew into a beautiful child with an eye and ear that caught everything and legs that never seemed to do anything but run. Many were times that he would come across to Rena's little house to chase the chickens with a stick, although she never saw him hit them. This wild child would stare at baby Antigone with the edge of a smile Rena couldn't understand and feared. But Rena's husband would say there was nothing to worry about, he was working the bad out of him, and would he be a good man when the time came. That time came many years later, after his parents and Rena's husband were well dead, after Moustache had spent years in other countries seeking his causes, often fought with a rifle.

He had returned from a war somewhere to find Metaxas had anointed himself dictator and was looking to make symbolic examples of his opponents. Moustache's real war came on his first day back in Greece, and it was to do with his brother, a boy whose nature was as gentle as Moustache's had been wild. The brother had a friend who was a communist. Silly talk about an overthrow got all mixed up. The brother and the communist were caught at a bus stop by a group of soldiers. The soldiers didn't listen to pleas and explanations. In front of children and mothers, the two boys were shot dead.

Rena said that in the Spanish war the Moustache was known for taking bullets without making a sound. But the night his brother was killed he stayed in this house in Rena's bed and cried on her breast. In the morning he dressed and said he was going to Athens to kill the General with his own hands. Rena kept him here, telling him he needed to eat and be ready if he was going to do it. It kept him away from the General until he could think the impulse away. Thoughts of murder turned to the idea of a resistance cell.

Just as she was finishing the story, Rena's door flew open. She leapt across the room to a wood box next to the fireplace, and in only a second, had a rifle in her hands, pointed at the open door. Antigone had also grabbed a pot and was about to fling it at whatever was coming in.

In the doorway was a scraggy dog, long legged and very thin.

Rudolf, Rena cried out. I almost shot you, my baby boy.

She caressed the greying yellow head as Rudolf's tongue tried its best to find a bit of Rena's face to lick. She led the dog gently by the scruff to a place in front of the fire. Antigone sat next to him and played with his ears. It was the first time I had seen her smile.

How quickly these ordinary women were ready to fight.

How quickly they became Greek women once more.

Olga (a week later)

I have not seen Moustache since Rena told me his story, and I'm glad. It is hard to know what to say to someone when you have looked into their soul without them knowing. The story also told much about this. How fearful must he be to kill a child? I, of all people, know killing can be easy. I can bear that I have murdered because it would have been unbearable if I had not. Yet this terrible story of the Moustache's brother is much more than just a death. That is a wrong so bad it aches me in the night.

I have never been reconciled to death. My Christopher, an unjust death, a wrong turning in the world, a slow death for him, a slower death for the rest of us. Stop talking of Christopher, you father would beg. Jimmy Ling's wife, the Buddhist, tried to comfort me with words. Death can be just a wiping of the hands of one life for another. Let Christopher pass onto the next life, she would say. Let him go.

Such belief, and such advice, but never with the secret of how to let him go. It is as if Christopher has crooked his hand in mine, and I can never unclasp it.

Just a Mother

(November 1939 – July 1940)

Olga

Today I started my work at the British embassy and I made my first mistake even before I began. The servants are not to come through the front door of the ambassador's residence I was told brusquely as I tried to step through the threshold. They have to use the back entrance, which is up the side near the rubbish cans. I later found out we were also not allowed to eat our dinner in the house, even in the kitchen. Clothes buttons are always to be done up, even in the very hot summer.

Being the governess, I have the freedom of the house, a paltry kind of freedom, with limits that are clear and loud, like the one that says no visitors are allowed, not even relatives, not even in their own country. I can use their umbrellas though, and was proudly shown some in the hall that look so feeble, they would blow apart in the Athens winds. Next to them are the long wool coats that would stink after the hot rains, yet continue to be the choice of ambassador after ambassador and have been so, I am told, for more than a century.

Yet beyond its gates is a real freedom, for the ambassador's house is in the hills of Pendeli that are so beautiful, a little like Katoomba, where we used to go as a family. Do you remember, daughter? The cool of Katoomba, with a light air that always freshened, and a quiet so quiet that only there you realised how you were perched in noise in Ultimo. Pendeli even has a bedspread of hills in front of it, hills that can never be quite the same as the Katoomba valley, but a memory of it.

The ambassador's secretary, with the unfortunate name of Merder, gave me the city address of a landlord who might rent me a house nearby.

It took me half the morning to find the landlord's office, a very busy place of queues and a kind of desperation. People pushed and accused me of pushing. When I forced my way to the front of the line I slapped the address down and explained about the house. The woman shrugged. I said I was working with the British ambassador. What interest she had in me was lost. Sorry, the house is not for rent, she said, not at all sorry, and tossed the papers back to me. She looked over my shoulder at the next person in the line.

As people pushed from behind I demanded to speak to the landlord. As she put her hand out for the papers of the person behind me, she said the landlord was the sort who would not like to be disturbed by something so trivial. On the wall behind her I saw the flag and the plaque for the first time. This was the French Consulate. There had been no sign on the door.

I drew some drachma from my purse. My dear, I said, you must get awfully upset having to deal with people here. I think you ought to have an ouzo on me.

The woman responded mechanically, taking the money and scribbling with the other hand. The landlord is the ambassador. He is playing golf right now. Here is the address of the club. But don't dare say I told you.

The best golf club in Athens. No more than a field, called a 'course' no doubt by doctors, politicians and lawyers trying to impress.

Only one figure was playing on it, a very tall man with an ambassadorial belly stretched over baggy shorts and white socks that went up over his knees.

I worked out my best French, trying not to let any country twangs into it, then walked up to him just after he took a shot. It seemed to go very high, and right down the middle of the roughly cut grass path. I assumed this was a good shot, and spoke.

Excuse me sir, I said with just enough handbag-clutching humility. I am looking for the Ambassador of France.

He had not seen me coming, and turned oddly, wary.

He said he was the French ambassador, and supposed it must be important. He strode after the ball.

Trying to keep up with him on the clumpy grass, I said I had spoken to someone in his office about his house in Pendeli. I said I wanted to rent it before the white ants… termites… turned it into rubbish.

The ambassador swung one club across the ground in front of him like a scythe. After a time he said my French was very good. He asked what work I did, followed by more walking, his scything and his silence, except to ask did I see where the ball went. I couldn't see it in this fairway where the grass was as long as the rough in any other course. Like a schoolboy, my mission became finding a ball, high heels and all. There sir, I pointed, proud in my now-grey white shoes. With no thanks he strode to it and lined up for a shot. Perhaps another good shot, for he smiled conspiratorially to me. Walking faster, he asked what language did Napoleon the Second learn while he was in exile?

I said it was Napoleon the First who was exiled, and he was learning English. (I don't know where I had learned that. I hoped I had not dreamt it.)

The ambassador said nothing until we reached the ball, which was on the edge between the rough course and the virgin long grass. He stood over it very seriously and without any practice, he hit at it. It seemed to sway to the left, and my house was lost again. Then the god of wind caught it and took it to the patch of green with the flag.

He turned and smiled. He said he needed someone to teach his children. Just a few hours each day. Of course I could live in the house in Pendeli. No, there would be no charge for renting the house so long as I looked after it for him and stopped those famous termites going about their business. Yes, by all means, I could keep working for the British Ambassador too. They were good friends.

He asked faintly if I played golf, and I thought he was going to ask me to join him, but he must have thought better of it. He walked off, calling at me to go tell that idiot secretary at the embassy to give me the key.

Olga (a week later)

I know this silence of servants. It is the same silence the servants gave me when I was a twelve year old at the Greek palace in Athens when Mother Hadjidaki took me there for the springtimes. The new Queen feted her sewing, and for days Mother Hadjidaki would design and stitch, leaving me with the King's children. My, the attention these children gave me, how they would tug on me and each demand me to be theirs, sneaking me around to their rooms and trying to impress me with their toys and their clothes. To them I was exotic. I was their age, but I came from places they were never allowed to see. Market streets of Muslim and Jew. Washer women abusing each other in language they would never understand. Old men you didn't know, who would grab your face in affection and laugh with your mother about trifles. The Royal children tasted these things from me and loved me for them. The seventeen-year-old maid and the grandfather butler they cared not a whit for, brushing me past them with an order for toys to be put away.

Airs and graces, Mother Hadjidaki would say to me, you're getting airs and graces from these children. Yet there was never a criticism in this because I always knew, from the smile that curled on the edge of her lip when she said it, that being a lady was no bad thing.

Twenty-five years later and a chauffeur takes me, in a servant's silence, past that same palace to the ambassador's city flat.

Thomas, the ambassador's son, is a sluggish ten year old. Polite and passionless. I play him music and he fiddles. I read him comedy and he yawns. Open-mouthed.

Thomas' mother, a prissy preening primp of a woman only ever opens her mouth to bemoan her life and bewail Greece. We met for tea this morning at the city flat. She said she was only in the city because she had been invited to afternoon tea by the American ambassador's wife, a crude woman, but one has a responsibility to one's husband to make an effort. The platter was immaculate, with its biscuits arranged into a pyramid with a designer's eye. The tea was poured perfectly to one half inch from the brim. Appearances were kept up, yet she could find no smile and when she spoke, she spoke to my left cheek.

She had thought Athens would be a step-up from Bombay, where her husband worked in the service for five years. But she was so disappointed. In India at least the Indians knew their place. These Greeks, they'll look at you on the street, all of you, from bottom to top and back again. She shivered at the thought, gently plucking a biscuit from the top of the pyramid in such a way that its architecture seemed unaffected. She then brought up her wishes for Thomas' syllabus, or 'curricula' as she repeatedly called it. Greek history was not necessary, speaking of it like it was bitter. English, writing and comprehension were priorities. She said that at this stage her son was attracted to the Bar, perhaps to work in the law of something called torts. I said he was obviously precocious for a ten year old. Yes, she agreed, the point missed.

Half an hour later in a study book-cased with English parliamentary reports and statutes, I asked Thomas. Did he really want to become a barrister? Yes, mother said he did, Mrs. Millemartin.

Mavromati. Was there anything in particular he wanted to study today?

No.

His mother's loathing for my city was in my mouth still.

Did he want to go out? Go to a museum? To the Parthenon?

He looked excited for a moment, then said no, mother said it was a dusty, dirty place.

I grabbed his hand and went to look for the driver.

It was true that Athens was dirty today. There, in swirling rubbish, people in furs blended with people asking for money. The clothes of the girls are grey this year and it suits the mood of the city. Despite what Thomas' mother has said, the men are not looking at the passing women in this Athens of wartime. The dull grey seems to have deadened the soul of this most alive of peoples. Two dogs, grey dogs, were mounting, the only wicked romance of this dull day.

Thomas was sucking it all in. The glass reflected his smile to me.

It is very colourful, he said.

Could the child have been teasing? I hoped he was clever enough.

The driver parked among the stones that were once part of the Acropolis. I held Thomas' hand and we walked up the hill to the Parthenon. We were the only ones there. Greeks never go to their masterpiece. That it is there is enough for them.

Thomas broke away from me and ran to the huge building like a baby, his feet slipping. He stopped after a few paces, prepared for his enthusiasm to be chastised.

I said it was allowed. He could go in it. I wanted him to touch something that was beyond people and beyond the snobbery that would soon be part of him. The acropolis will be here when his mother and her ilk are long dead. I wanted him to feel that.

The morning was glorious. It lifted the boy's spirits and, unable to help himself, he ran through the columns, fell and ran more. When I told him the history of the Parthenon, his little face squinted sideways at me, and I realised he had never looked at me before. Everything he does in the residence is done with a resignation and an averted eye.

There was one moment that was hard. I caught him gouging at one of the frescos with a rock, rubbing, but without the pleasure of a vandal. He scrubbed at the dolphin's faded face with an anger that no ten year old should have. I pretended not to notice. I had a feeling this was a boy who was chastised too much for his years.

I sent the driver to get some lunch for us, and he came back after only twenty minutes. He said they wanted me to bring Thomas back to the flat immediately. Thomas would eat his lunch there.

The ambassador's wife was waiting on the doorstep. She rushed straight to her son, checking his eyes and his palms, her hands frantic in rubbing and patting, combing his hair with her rakish fingers. I went to follow them in, but the driver suggested I not.

British Embassy (the next day)

Olga had expected the ambassador to send for her. Although she had never met him, and had prepared her arguments about yesterday's folly, she knew this would be her last day in his employ. The British were never adventurous. There was procedure. There was custom. There were prejudices that must be respected and passed on. A governess was of a caste that could never challenge the way it had to be.

Readied for the fight, she is stopped inside the ambassador's office by two chairs, backs to her, each with a man in it. She knows neither man nor which one is the ambassador.

They stand and turn at the announcement of her name, and one face she knows. It is the Moustache, a different Moustache, moustache smaller, tidier, hair not wild, clothes clean and well-cut. He is a man of money and purpose and high connections. He introduces himself as Stavros.

The other man is the ambassador. A most remarkable difference from the man she had pictured. A short, paunchy, pasty man with an Oxford accent, an older Thomas, an indoor child grown into an indoor man, and with a Greek lexicon punctuated by hesitation and a confusion of tense which makes his speech not just difficult to follow, but indecipherable.

M-miss. Mavromati. How-how-how were you. I-I was sorry door had time to shut with you s-s-since you built. I hoped th-things are jumping well at Thomas.

Ambassador, your Greek is very good, she says.

Yes, I played shipping at a tutor where England.

Stavros suggests it would be quicker if they speak in English.

The ambassador assents with a cheeriness that can't hide his disappointment.

Thomas. Is he learning well?

She says he needs to see things outside the house. He needs to see Athens. To be excited.

He says he'd heard about the abduction. He smiles approval of her whim, putting his finger to his lip.

He fiddles under his desk and comes up with a file. Her name is on the cover as Olga Mavromati. Her real name, Stambolis, is in brackets underneath.

M-mrs. Mavromati, you know we, the British, are fighting a hard w-war. I think you know w-we have promised the s-safety of Greece, but there is much the

Greeks themselves c-c-can do.. What I want to ask is... would you h-h-help?

He stares with a hopeful smile, wringing his hands. Stavros is in silent stoniness.

Mother Hadjidaki wanted to know, then, there, would she take this man to be her husband, to her life, to her bed forever. Nothing about her heart. This asked in front of Michael, bent over, with arched eyebrow, knowing what the answer had to be.

Olga, a sixteen year old never without word, was without word.

Mrs Mavromati?

Olga says she is nothing special. Just a mother.

He says the British need strong people who could do things like play-act, or speak some other languages. He counts off her languages for her: Greek, German, Italian, French, Egyptian and Spanish.

And that is it. He is on his feet even before she can agree to anything, saying Stavros will explain what is expected of her.

He half-runs, his body bent with intent, to the door, his face smiling. He opens the door a bit, then closes it.

S-silly me. One more th-thing. If you are caught doing any underground t-things, I will have to say I know n-nothing about it. I-I am sorry. And n-never bring any of those things back to the residence. W-we cannot risk a co-co-connection. Do you understand?

He is already through the door. He pulls it shut behind him too hard, boyishly.

Piraeus, near Athens

Dockside cafés are always damp. The walls are streaked from years of cold mornings and steaming coffee and breathing. The customers are businessmen and peasants waiting for the boats to take them to Nauplia or Hydra, and are in this grubby place because there is nowhere else. The waiter does his job with no grace, this making of hot drinks among the smell of ferry fuel, gas burners and sea salt. He'd lost the grace for the job many years ago.

The boat from Crete docks an hour late, three coffees late. As she pays the bill the passengers are starting down the gangway. Choosing her moment to walk across the road fast, she goes past the clumping laughing stewards on the dock who don't see ordinary women. Up past the gangway and the big iron knobs that the ropes get tied to, one door, two, three, and into the one with the cracked glass to the women's toilets to the filthy basins, gritty dirty and stained rusty under the tap. She pretends to wash her hands long enough to make sure no-one is in either of the cubicles. Behind the cistern of the first one the brown envelope is just where they said. She exchanges the papers in it with the one from her purse, and puts the envelope back in the same place.

Back in the café again, she orders another coffee.

Within seconds a man sits next to her.

Is she here on business, he asks dully.

Yes, she answers, I am meeting my employer.

She puts her purse between them, and goes to order a baklava. When she comes back the man is gone, and the paper is not in her purse. She eats the baklava slowly, and leafs through a coffee-stained and stiff newspaper. After a decent time, she goes to catch the train to Athens.

Olga (three days later)

This could be my last note. A bullet through a window, a knife in the hand of a skilful intruder. If it has been deemed that I die, I will not run. I will fight, but I will not run. My kitchen knife is here under my pages, another under my blouse. This would be no whimpering expiry for these executioners. I have done no wrong and I deserve no such condemnation. They have made the mistake and I will not take their justice.

Athens (Earlier that day)

Stavros came to the ambassador's residence in the morning and told Olga he would take her home. She had wanted to go buy some food, but he had a face that would not accept anything but what he wanted.

In the car he gives her no smile and no words as he drives her past the turn-off to her house. He takes her to the dead road to the Pendeli monastery.

He cuts the motor and waits in the stillness, his head bowed, his wrists on the steering wheel, his fists as balls. With his strong arms, they look like clubs.

They did not get it, he says, without lifting his head from the wheel. Tell me why they did not get it. The package. Friday. Piraeus. They did not get it.

He is not shouting, or even speaking. It is a whisper, which was worse.

She tells him the truth of that Friday, although the earthy streets of her childhood had taught her that whether something was truth or fiction mattered not if you have already been condemned.

Staring at the steering wheel he says there has been no sign of the contact.

His is a seething, desperate stare.

Olga feels herself wetting her dress. She struggles to stop her hand going down there. She doesn't want him to know. As the water circles under her knee, she tells him that she never lies, and lashes out for the chrome door handle, bending it the wrong way. She doesn't know what he tries to do or whether he tries to grab her, but she does get out, slamming the door hard. Never running, she goes under the rusty wire fence and out across the little valley between the monastery and her house, her home. She knows he could catch her, or shoot her, or whatever, but she doesn't run and he doesn't come. Neither is he there when she comes out of the field. She knows he can come for her at her home and that is where she wants to be when he comes for her, not in some car in a lane.

A home is a right place for a person to end their life.

Yes, I will start my new life. Yes, Mother Hadjidaki I will marry this old man, I will leave you to go to this place called Australia and have my own restaurant and children who will be brought up well and strong. I will start a new life away from the whores and the hates and the knives of men. And in my new life I will remember my Greekness as I have remembered it in this place of Egyptians. I will live a life anew, a second life, started early with a man starting his late.

With her memories of a life barely started she waits.

Olga

I slept that afternoon, a bad sleep, fitful and broken by odd dreams. I dreamt of lying in an aeroplane, flying too close to the ground, and then so high I was scared of falling into the forests. The cold wrapped around me, lifting me towards the open door. There was nothing to hold onto, and the door became bigger. I was very cold. The plane rose and my stomach fell. I slipped to the edge and fell.

Stavros was blowing warm breath into my hand. The front door of the house was open wide.

The contact has turned up, he was saying. The contact thought he was being followed, so he hid for a few days. He delivered the papers. All was well.

I punched hard at anything of his, and hit his throat. It doubled him and forced a dry retch, making the huge man into a child. No, he tried to say through a broken voice, we needed to be careful. It looked bad for you.

Get out, I told him. Take your suspicions and get out of my home.

But as I watched him, bowed and cowed going out the door, I remembered that man, Drago's beggar, the one who started all this. I remembered too what Rena had told me about Stavros' innocent brother and from Rena I remembered her girl, Antigone, who lost her face trying to save an innocent. From Antigone I remembered you my darling, who could have been Antigone.

Through all these things I knew I would keep on doing their jobs, passing on notes, setting up escape routes and supply centres, making arrangements, doing my bit to turn a paltry resistance into a professional underground for the bad time that is to come. Despite this day, I knew I needed to do it.

Maybe it is a need to have people trust me.

I trust you to be a good wife, your father said, with little trust in his eyes. So many months on a boat with so many other people also trying a new life. We must be careful, he said. A pretty young thing like you. People take advantage, those young men on the crew, they will fall in love with your eyes, he said, making me aware of these men for the first time. Our first night had been a disappointment to he who must have had so many women in so many places. He, a man of thirty-one, with a girl that he didn't know, barely of womanhood, whose face had taken his fancy. There in a swilling cabin, with a tinge of shame for his swelling belly and the smell of engine fumes and disinfectant, we came together, barely learning anything about each other. He would become gentle, and would touch my face, and learn to love me. But not on that night, that night when he didn't trust me.

Olga (three weeks later)

The bus driver took my change and said nothing. We jolted and jarred, me alone in a seat for two, while people of all kinds crowded three into the other seats, chattering and laughing to their own. You don't have any friends, Mother Hadjidaki used to say to me. She wasn't criticising, it was just an observation she forgot about as soon as she said it. She was right though, as simple honest people often are. I never pined for groups of loud pigeon chattering girls who frilled and quipped breathlessly and lightheadedly.

Yet Mother Hadjidaki's words hurt me, and hurt me still.

For an hour on this bus memories of rich Greek Alexandria girls filled my eye. I could see I wasn't the only lonely one. There was Katina, who claimed to be a diplomat's daughter but wasn't, who would rub mud on the back of other girls' blouses as a revenge for a slight and never get caught. There was Emily who nodded agreement with everyone, so fearful she was of losing the esteem they never had for her. There was Mrs Batrouney, teacher of

French, who was also gentle, a grown-up Emily, who was made to cry once when a class wouldn't listen to her, and from then her gentleness was forever a weakness. Someone should have told her never to cry. Get angry, slap them, faint. But never cry.

All off, the driver called, and Katina, Emily and poor Mrs Batrouney became the faces of my fellow passengers shifting past me. Ordinary people with their blotches, their weary treads and their wedding rings. Ordinary people stepping down into an ordinary barren dry country of dead grasses, buildings and ghosts, a place that even the wind had given up. A few flies tried for a while, listlessly, to bother us as we walked, and gave up.

An old widow in black, not smiling as they never smile, pointed us on towards a very big house off the road. There in the dust another old woman, also in black, clacked at us to sit, to wait.

We were allowed in one by one, and my turn came after twenty minutes. Past the toothless widow and three British soldiers in the hallway, to a room on the right. Very plush a room for an old farmhouse, with books and rug and neatly ordered desk. The window was barred. A fat-faced man came in, smiling and offering his hand. He spoke English.

Happy, Mrs Mavromati? he asked.

Happy? A question for a schoolchild at a fair. Here, in this farmhouse it made no sense.

I told him it made no sense. No-one joins a cell for their happiness.

Ah, he said, nodding. Many do. Many see it as an exciting way out of hoeing the ground or adding up accounts. Why did I want to help?

It just happened, I said to this man, this officer. Circumstances.

Ah, he said. How did Hamlet say it? More things in heaven and earth than are dreamt of…

No. Just circumstances.

He flicked through the documents on his lap, and looked down as he spoke.

Mrs. Mavromati, if you help us, we will get you passage to Australia. Within six months, no more than a year, the British Government will pay your passage, and see you home safely.

As I left he said I would need to change my name again. For operations.

From now on I was Artemis.

Artemis. I wonder who thought of that as a codename. The goddess of the hunt and also the goddess of childbirth. The opposites of life and I have known both.

Me with child? No, it couldn't happen so quickly, I told the fat woman, feeling the biliousness that could have been from anything: a tropical sickness, the sway of the boat. The woman nodded with all the knowledge of the world. My deah, you are a married woman, and your husband takes his rights. Of course it happens. There is no sickness like morning sickness. Be pleased deah. It never happened to me. I wish for you and your child to have the best.

But, I pleaded, it's only been three weeks. Perhaps it's seasickness. No, she said, the incessant sea swell having no effect on her solid frame as she applied her lipstick in the toilet mirror. No, you are with child. Sickness and missed monthly. It's certain deah.

Why had I confided with this unknown woman here in a toilet of all places. I knew it was because I had no-one else.

She turned with perfectly painted lips. Take it from me deah. You continental people have no trouble. My heartiest congratulations. And she left. She knew the workings of my womb, this anonymous woman, this fellow third-class traveller who never knew my name, or that I could feel no congratulations, only a prison from within.

Down the hall in the big kitchen at least ten recruits were drinking goat's milk and eating bread and salted anchovies, a sloppy crumbly lunch, with bits that stayed on chins and lips because no water was offered. Only people from a cold, wet place like England would give thirsty food without water.

After a few minutes of this, not enough, we were herded out the back door and down a dusty hill, slipping and backing our way down to a small ravine.

A row of wooden scaffolds were set up in the water with potato sacks hanging from them, making crucifix shapes with hanging victims. The group gasped. Apart from the sacrilege, giant crosses are bad luck. The English should have known that.

A horse-faced man came out in front and picked up a pitchfork from a pile. I had thought he was a Greek, with his heavy black brows and his peasant's dress. But now that he spoke in bad broken Greek, I saw that his pastiness could only be English.

The group had trouble understanding him. He threw the pitchfork to one of us, a terribly thin man of all bones, who caught it without thinking. The man just looked at the thing in his hands. The horse-faced man grabbed the fork back and told us all to watch. He ran across the water to one of the sacks and thrust the fork hard into it. Dusty soil poured out of the four holes. The Greeks stayed still. I think this was because they could not see the point in ruining good bags.

I went to the front and interpreted as he came back. I didn't do this for him, but for the Greeks that he would think were dumb.

He says to pay attention. He says he is your trainer. He says we do not have many weapons, so we will need to practice using everyday things, like this pitchfork. He says this will give you the feeling of what it is like to kill. I think he wants you to take a pitchfork and pretend the sacks are the enemy. I know it's a waste of sacks, but...

The instructor threw the pitchfork sideways at me. Its prongs hit me across my belly, one of its sharp points ripping through my dress, scratching me. I picked it up, and almost threw it back at him. He had turned away towards the scaffolds, but he stayed on the spot. He knew.

I charged past him down the slope and into the ankle deep water. I stabbed at the sack. Again. Slashing, tearing. The dirt flayed out, covering me and muddying the stream.

It helped him get his way. The men went to the weapons pile, picked up scythes, pitchforks, and sharpened sticks, and ran into the stream. Then the women.

My energy spent, I dropped the pitchfork in the dirt, and went back up to the trainer. I watched the group, bodies twisting awkwardly under the scaffolds as they stabbed again and again, enjoying it more. I hoped it was no portent. The trainer's face showed he saw the same thing.

It was well dark when our bus started for home. The trainers had given us dinner packages but I was too tired to eat. I slept to the chatter of men's smiling voices, now confident; comforting me, an alarum to sleep. I jumped awake when the bus went too hard over a bump. It was skimming bushes, seesawing, going very fast, rattling, shaking, seats were lifting and dropping on loose brackets. The man across from me was thrown, dinner and all, into the aisle. For God's sake, someone said, tell him to slow down. But no-one went. They were frightened of being thrown around. Maybe it was that they couldn't be bothered.

It would have to be me again. Prefect girl, interpreter, challenger, questioner. It had been my role all day.

I stepped over the bundle of man and his sprayed dinner, swung my way to the front and called out to the driver to go a little slower.

He didn't answer. The old motor and the very bumpy road made a lot of noise, and I put my hand on his shoulder. Right away he pulled a gun from a pocket in the door, and pointed it at my stomach.

I must have still been half asleep. I remember thinking this was ridiculous, there was no need for him to get cross. It took some seconds for me to realise.

I said we were just workers coming home.

He spat across my dress, and called me a liar. A traitor. He told me to sit.

So I sat on the floor next to him, watching the road. This was not the main road. I couldn't tell where we were. The gun was in his lap, pointing at me still, though his hands were on the steering wheel. If I had grabbed that gun, it would have ended there perhaps. But I didn't.

Another man came and asked the driver why he was driving so stupidly. The driver pulled the bus over hard and stood facing back down the bus, the gun held up in both hands, like a child.

We backed towards the rest of the passengers, not wanting to take our eyes off him, as though we could stop the gun being fired with our very concentration. The driver kept his gun up and fumbled for some clunking rattling machinery that had been hidden behind his seat. He pulled out the first ten inches of a machine gun, jammed in. He jerked it, trying to get it free, and the gun in his other hand fired. The bullet passed by me and hit one of the other passengers, throwing him back into his seat, dead. The shot had hit him in the chest, leaving a big black hole between the two flaps of his shirt. His eyes were still open. Breaths sucked in, a woman started to whimper, a praying voice came from somewhere.

The driver didn't seem to see the death. He was now frantically trying to free the machine gun.

The back of my arm was wet and I knew it was wet with a dead man's blood. What did I feel? There was no time to feel. No time to think of you, my children, or your father, who might laugh. What a mess you have got yourself into, he would say. But his hand was not here to cup my head and love me out of it.

The driver was still pulling at the bag, screaming, telling us to do nothing, not move at all. He let go of the stuck weapon, and charged down the bus with the hand-gun held straight out in front. As he swept it across the group, each passenger looked away this time, protecting themselves by putting it out of their sight. Except me. I looked him in the eye. I could be dead in a minute, a moment, and there would be no reason to it. He would have no thought of the children I had carried while he turned a woman into a nothing, a killed goat, a headless chicken. In a moment a screaming man could end thirty-six years of lessons and faith, this man so close to me I could see his nose hairs, bunches of black growing under a perfect nose, straight and angry, his small black pupils surrounded by as much red as white. There was a madness in those eyes; this, the first time I had looked into madness. Your father says I have such an abyss. It is ugly. It is empty. I wish I had never seen it.

He backed to the driver's seat and ordered us off the bus.

We stood in a clump. He told one of the women in the group to come forward. She was middle-aged, once a beauty, in a dress of little flowers. Camellias, neatly joined at the seam. She had made a real effort to make it look nice.

He shot her in the chest and she fell back bleeding, in a faint.

Two women rushed to her and he kicked at one, breaking a bone by the noise of it. He shot at the other, making a mess of her young elbow. After all this he still showed no fear or understanding. Bang, bang, he called in pretend shots from his gun, breaking the trances and making flinches. He was enjoying this now, and was going to make this last.

Traitors to the General, he said with each pretend shot. Traitors to Greece.

Madness borne of ignorance. Metaxas knew about our group and worked with our chiefs, but the people didn't know this. To the mind of an unhinged patriot like the bloodshot madman before us, we were traitors for being with the British. Unhinged patriots are never smart enough to suspect the truth.

There could be no telling him this. To step out, to make yourself separate would be death. There were seventeen of us, and he had one gun. Four shots or eight shots. I don't know guns, I didn't know how many he had left. It made no difference. No-one was going to move on him. It's about any chance for more life and living on to see your family again and to be able to kiss your children. A man I knew some years ago, a flyer, said life was a precipice. You throw yourself off, and if you lived, you soared. Once you soared, Bert Hinkler said, you just had to remember that soaring, and you will soar forever.

And I did feel like I was soaring as I beckoned to the madman like a friend with a secret. He pointed the gun at me.

Sir, I said. Yes, these people are traitors. But this woman you just killed was a government agent. She was gathering information about these traitors to pass onto the General's office.

He frowned and asked how I knew this.

I was working with her, I said. I suggested we all get back in the bus and go straight to the parliament building. I said that was obviously where he was from.

He stared. No, he said, he was not working for the government, not officially.

A man used the distraction to run around the front of the bus. The gunman fired, almost without effort, and hit the man in the arm or shoulder, but he kept running.

He leaned closer to me, his gun touching my belly.

No, he said, he was here because the other bus driver, believing him a sympathiser, had told him about us and the resistance, so he followed the bus to the village and waited until we were all inside that house. Dead driver. Knife dead. That was good, wasn't it? Good work? The gunman's eyes pleaded approval.

My head floated like when I was in a faint when I was with child, with that feeling that I was not of this world. He could shoot me, and at that moment I was sure I would feel nothing. I had no fear, I had no feeling as I put my hand on his shoulder, and said yes. Good work. As for the woman, he could not have known about her. Luckily there was me. I would pass the details of his bravery to the General.

Had I met him? He was thrilled.

Three times, I said. I suggested again that we get these traitors to the authorities.

Of course, he said.

I offered to try to get the machine gun free. My hands were smaller than his.

I started towards the bus.

No, he hissed.

He gave me the pistol saying he would get the machine gun. With a warning not to let the group move. He ran towards the bus.

Stop, I called before he had gone two steps. I was pointing the gun at him with both hands, as steady as I could.

He didn't understand. The machine gun, he said. What about the traitors, he said.

Someone ran around and hit him from behind, and he fell, his body arched, face first into the dirt. The rest ran up and started kicking. Men, boys and women.

He reached out towards me. Help me, friend. For the General's sake..

A kick in the back of his head, and he said no more, the only sound the panting of the attackers and the crunching of the kicks, the most horrible noise I have known, so much like the crushing of that Italian's skull back in the residence. I did nothing and watched as they took their anger out on the crumpled body, spitting and punching with the sides of closed fists, smashing flat his handsome face. I wanted to help him, to pull them away, to hold his broken body. He had trusted me like a little boy. Like a son.

Spent and satisfied, the group was now looking to me, the woman who had tricked the monster.

I said to bury him, hide all sign. Tear his trousers to use as bandages for the women. Quick.

They did it fast. He was buried in a flattened grave, with a thorny bush stuck on top as a sign of disrespect.

As the rest of them boarded the bus, a man in his early twenties jumped out and urinated on his grave. No-one cheered or congratulated him. After all they had done, this was just too much.

As one of the men worked out how to use the gears on the bus, the dead passenger was laid along the back seat. The floral woman was still alive, and she gave the other women in the group something to do. The woman with the shot elbow was bleeding terribly while a man, I think it was her husband, worked a tourniquet. The third woman with the broken jaw would take no fussing and insisted on helping the others. All this happened down the back of the bus. This left enough places for each of the rest of us to have a double seat, but the pisser sat next to me, asking again and again how he could help. Just sit, I said, not wanting to know this desecrator. He frowned a bit, but stayed, thigh to thigh.

Elias the Pisser, someone called him. They started to laugh, glad to have someone to laugh at.

Back in my home, the floating feeling is no more. I feel a little sick, as if I had gone somewhere I ought not, and now is the price to pay. For I had stepped into an abyss and saved lives and gave leadership. The bad man is dead. Is this the glory that the war memorials celebrate in the Sydney parks? This empty glory, the floating of a dream, like a kite, connected always to the ground. Always looking down to see a handsome face and wispy nose hair that I have destroyed. Bert Hinkler never told me about that.

Athens (later that night)

The bus stops twice. Once to take the dead man to a cell safe house just to the north of the city; the second time at the home surgery of a sympathetic doctor who waves the two women in and orders his sons to carry in the shot woman. Finally the bus stops on a quiet road off Sofias and everyone goes home except Elias, who follows Olga, telling her again and again that she needs his protection. A straggly hungry growly dog runs up fast and Elias the protector runs away.

At another safe house she tells Stavros what happens, and he surprises her by not being surprised. There are many like the gunman, he says. Idiot General lovers. The kind who invent heroes and causes. Most of them are mad. He stops his talk to point at her dress and say she should have washed the blood off by now. If he can see the blood in this dim safe house light, the police, anyone, can see it.

The salt of tears in her mouth are unexpected. She struggles in the shadow to swallow a need to wail at all the hurts of the day and night. But Stavros has turned away.

He is crying himself.

Olga

Don't cry my baby, I begged my Nicky, but in his deafness and his wails he couldn't hear me. Nellie had seen what happened. Four boys, making monkey sounds, imitating him like he was stupid. He was so brave, she said, in how he walked away pretending like he didn't notice. It was only here, in my bedroom, away from the sounds of his sisters, that he could cry as a boy should.

Stavros cried as a man had to, quiet and facing the wall. His brother had been on the bus, a man with a moustache like the one he used to wear. Had I seen him? I couldn't remember. He gave more details, clothes he might have been wearing, his crucifix, a mole on the back of his neck. I couldn't remember.

Yes, I lied. I think I remember him. He made it out.

His brother may be the dead man in the seat and Stavros would be mourning again, but not tonight. His pain would have a reprieve for a time.

I touched his sleeve, and he put his hand on it. My hand went to his head, his face, his eyes. I kissed his mouth. Gently. He heaved a breath of release, and touched my face for just a moment. In a second he opened the door and left me.

Pyrmont, Sydney

The ball skews to the right and snaps the branch off the little olive tree in the corner of the yard. Nicky laughs and runs for the ball.

Tina can never kick straight, unlike Nicky. He makes the girls point to any spot in the concrete yard and he will kick the ball right to it. Every time. Freda thinks it's because he's deaf. With no sounds to distract, he can concentrate on the ball more.

Jean sees the branch break. She goes to the tree and throws the branch over the fence into the neighbour's yard. The olive tree will never bear fruit anyway, not where it is, out of the sun, never noticed in this barren little yard.

Tina balances the ball for her next attempt and talks like she always does, in the middle of doing something else.

Jean, I think I'm forgetting what my mother looks like. I'm awful aren't I?

Tina makes the kick and it goes over the side fence. Jean sees she has a remarkable consistency.

No, you're not awful. You could never be awful. Your mother left when you were nine, and now you're twelve. That's a long time in a girl's life, love.

Besides, Jean says after a while, there must be some photographs around somewhere. Let's see if we can find them eh?

No photographs around here Jean, Tina says. Dad's thrown them all away.

I don't have any, Michael says.

Are you telling me you've thrown out every photograph of Olga? Jean is almost shouting. It's the first time she's raised her voice to Michael.

Calm down. Calm down. I thought you would be happy not to have any of her pictures here.

You can't make them forget their mother.

In the morning Tina wakes to find a picture of her mother on the dressing table. It is an old photograph, and shows Olga dressed in stage costume with a group of performers. Two little girls who look a bit like Nellie and Freda are sitting in front. Mother looks happy, but she can't tell for sure. The pose is strong. She could have been just flirting for the camera.

Tina looks at the photo for quite a while. Yes, that was how her mother looked. She was quite beautiful, she remembers.

Olga

Pregnancy is beautifully measured. Just as I would be out of my mind, each of you came into our lives, and the nightmare would end. Taking you to my breast, overfeeding you because I'd fall asleep. Impossible, the nurses said, impossible. Mothers can't sleep and breast feed. Sleep I did, for weeks after each birth. And Michael was so kind to me, touching me and telling me I was beautiful. How his eyes meant it.

These are the things I know on mornings like today. I can smell, I can see, I can run, I am beautiful. These precious things come in a morning's lottery.

Today I was passing the foreign office building, and feeling the good of the day, I went in. There was no line of people, and the woman at the counter smiled when I asked permission to travel back to Australia. She was very polite, and asked me about Australia and about my family, not for official reasons. She wanted to know.

I signed all the forms with the lady's help. There was no fee either. I walked away feeling good, and knowing this was just a nice day. Of course I would never hear anything from this office and this good woman.

The Brick Wall of Idiots

(July – November 1940)

Olga

The war is closer. Italians getting pushy. Close to the Albanian border. Then withdrawing. Then close again. Being Italians, probably can't make up their minds.

Daughter, if they invade, it will be the mothers who will suffer. Every child I see stabs me with the guilt for the chances I didn't take. A few months ago I had such a chance. A man I knew was going to try to sail his yacht. To hell with the German patrols he said; to hell with the danger of the Horn. He was going because he knew if the Germans took over Greece, they would steal his boat.

No, I said, it was too much of a risk. But in truth I was scared. Not of the trip, and not of the chance I would be locked away as soon as I touched your land, but of what I would find in your hearts. Of the hate that might be waiting for me.

Last week my sailor friend sent me a card from Fremantle. The wonderful, brave man made it. I hadn't even given him a letter to pass onto you.

Olga

Nobody warned me that death and life would be so confused in this world of spies. That one day I could wear the blood of a good man and the next day my cares would be for a sluggish boy and a clothes line. I teach Thomas arithmetic, history and English in the mornings, and in every afternoon's break I walk to an intersection two blocks away. If the house has a pair of stockings hanging on a washing line on the roof, then coded instructions are waiting for me inside. The stockings are my signal. Blouses, skirts, socks, they are for other people. Everyone has their own garment.

No-one needed me today.

On this day, Anna came to the Embassy, snappy and expectant, wanting to know when she was going to Australia, forever causing a fuss. I finally had to tell the door-man not to let her in.

Alas, it takes more than a doorman's no to stop this Anna. Today she broke in past his willowy arm, shouting that she knew there was spying going on here.

I came out of the kitchen, knife forgotten in hand from making a sandwich. She charged at me and impaled her wrist on the knife.

You stab me, your own sister, she said, feigning surprise, knowing it to have been an accident, but trying to push through an advantage.

Don't be so silly, I said. Let's stop that bleeding first. It's dripping everywhere.

See? she accused. You care more for the clean floor than for me. Tell me now. When are we leaving Greece?

I said, simply, that I would not be getting them out of Greece.

Anna stepped up and pushed my face with the palm of her other hand, forcing me into the side of a chair. I tried to grab it to break my fall, but only brought it down on top of me. I jumped at Anna, slapping her across the face hard. She tried to punch me back, but I grabbed her fist and crushed her fingers as hard as I could.

She backed down the hall, cradling her hands. Through the door, she threw her last weapon.

She said I no longer had a family. Nobody loves me.

Anna has more meanness in her than I could ever have. Yes daughter, I can be tough sometimes, too tough, like the time I pushed that busybody woman next door in Pyrmont back into her azaleas. Anna has no toughness. She is mean and weak. I've wished for years that her family was not really mine.

Yet her words made me feel like I'd been punched.

Tinos (a Greek island in the Aegean)

The Elli is a Greek warship that belies the term warship. The sailors dub her The Yacht because that is what she looks like.

Her captain is on shore watching the Assumption ceremony with other officials. It's good luck for the ship and the island for him to be there, so twenty or so of the crew stand with him to impress him with their religiousness. Others, less ambitious, have stayed aboard in their bunks or in the galley eating, or playing cards or backgammon.

The island's pious are banging and singing, hoping for extra redemption by waking those Tinosians still in their beds.

The boom. It's like a big firecracker, and most think at first that it is. Until the crewman next to the captain calls out that the Elli is on fire.

The captain knows the listing. The ship has been hit below the waterline. It is no mine. It's been torpedoed, probably in the crews' quarters.

The teenage boys in altar clothing stare, and the island mothers' eyes are excited. The captain screams at them all to get away from the water. There is a lot of ammunition on the Elli. It could all explode.

No-one listens to the old man. They stay where they are on the promenade and watch the boat die.

General Metaxas' Cabinet Room, Athens

The Greek government is a job lot of men, tall and short, blustery and meek, charming and witless, all scared of the General. Many of those around this table are ministers in name only, doing what they think their prime minister wants. Thinking ahead is a danger here, so they do not think ahead.

The prime minister's chair is out being repaired, so the General looks like one of them today, sitting lower than the others because he is a very short man.

The Minister for Education is protesting. The Italians have killed Greeks. They have sent a submarine all the way to the Cyclades on the day of the Assumption. Greece must attack the Italians. An air raid maybe.

The old General is quietly relieved that one of them has said his piece. He asks the Minister for Defence to respond.

The minister simply tells them Greece would lose a fight with the Italians. The Italians are a poor fighting nation, but they have some weapons and they are ready for war. The Elli was a message from Mussolini to show Greece, and to show Hitler that Italy has a master fighting machine, able to penetrate deep into enemy areas. In a month Greece would be much better prepared to fight such messages. In a year the Greeks would be able to fight off anyone. But not yet. The first of the youth brigades are graduating soon. They will be a new type of Greek soldier.

The Minister for Education murmurs something about national pride, but the General has won the rest of the cabinet by being a man of war who refuses to fight. Metaxas promises to protest to the Italians. This might confuse them, make them get ready for an attack that would not come. Maybe that would hold them, giving time for Greece to build an army. Maybe.

Count Grazzi's home, Athens (that afternoon)

The Italian ambassador receives the order to be at the Greek prime minister's office at five o'clock. It is four-thirty now. The very short notice can only be considered rude, but these are not the times for taking offence. He dresses and waits for the government car to pick him up. When it hasn't come by five he has his driver take him.

The Count is flustered by the time he reaches the steps to the General's office.

He is told to wait. He explains that he is late for a meeting with the General. The woman again tells him he will have to wait. He sits in the uncomfortable wooden chair in the dusty hallway for ten minutes, forced to shift his legs a few times as new filing cabinets and oak tables are carried past him. Finally, the woman calls out to the Count, telling him to go to the lift, the General will see him now. Hurry please.

The General does not offer his hand, or stand, or wish the Count a good evening. Just an abrupt question.

I want to know this from you. Does Italy intend to invade Greece?

There is nothing the Count can say. The General would recognise false promises and, as a friend, the Count doesn't want to lie. Metaxas waits a few moments, then continues.

What is going on Count?

John, I really don't know.

Metaxas waits a moment, appearing to be reading something on his desk, but the Count can see there is no paper on the desk.

I promise you this Count, no invaders will sleep a night in this country… not while I am alive.

As the General finishes, he moves towards the bookcase with the spirit bottles on it. In a softer tone he asks the Count if he would like a drink.

Relieved, the Count goes over and grabs the General's arm.

No matter what Italy does, you must know I respect you as a leader and as a man.

Yes, Count, except I do not have as much luck with the women as your friend Mussolini, eh?

Nobody does.

They drink in a better humour. They are friends after all.

So will you invade us?

My God Ioannes. I really don't know. Who knows what's in Mussolini's head? You would have more understanding of the military mind than I would.

Perhaps my friend, but the problem is that Mussolini is no military mind. And this is making it very hard for me to foresee.

A Greek government car is waiting for the Count as he leaves the building. He signals his own driver to go home, and gets in the Greek car. He watches the wealthier streets of Athens fly past. Shopkeepers sweeping the footpaths, well-dressed couples walking down Amerikis Street arm in arm. There are no beggars. He feels the bad things that are coming, it is in the stomach and it wakes him at three in the morning. He adds up the likelihood of an Italian victory. On the west, Albania is already Italian. To the north, Bulgaria will ally itself with the Italians against the Greeks, an alliance of survival. And of course, Germany is always there too, with great machinery and skill. They were surprised at how easily France gave in, leaving the Wehrmacht with more battalions than they expected.

His family will have to be prepared to leave with no notice. It is a pity, he thinks. He really does love this country.

General Metaxas' home, North Athens
(two months later)

The buzzer rings in the guard's box. It's three a.m. The guard jumps as if he had been dozing, although he hadn't. Count Grazzi is at the gate, alone, asking for an audience. He knows the Count's face from the newspaper, but has never seen him in the flesh; the guard had only ever been on overnight duty, and diplomats never bother a restful night. International relations is a job of daylight hours and cocktail parties.

As he takes in the sight of the Count, the car and silhouette of a driver, the guard realises with some fear that he knows none of the protocols for this. It would have been easier if someone had thrown a bomb over the gate.

The Count says it's important. The General must be woken.

The guard takes the order with relief. A decision has been made. It is out of his hands.

Third door upstairs. The General's room. Knock.

General. Are you awake?

Get out.

I am sorry General, but the Italian Ambassador, Count Grazzi is here, and says he comes on urgent business.

All right, the General replies after a few seconds, as if he too has been given an order he needs to obey. I will see him in the front room downstairs.

The General comes down almost right away, shoeless, putting on his dressing gown on the stairs.

The General sits on his usual couch; the Count takes an adjacent chair.

What is this, Count?

The Count crosses and re-crosses his legs and has nowhere to rest his arms. The chair has no sides. When he speaks it's in French so that his words cannot be mistaken.

I have brought you my government's... request.

The Count hands the General a telegram. Metaxas takes the paper he had been expecting since the sinking of the Elli. But not here, not now. This way there is no dignity for either country. He pats his gown for his glasses, puts them with some deliberation and squints through them at the letter at arm's length.

The telegram accuses Greece of siding with England by allowing the British fleet to use Greek waters; by allowing the British intelligence services into Greece; and by providing fuel stops for English pilots. The telegram demands that the Italian army be allowed to immediately occupy certain unspecified Greek territory for the duration of the war against England. And it wants a guarantee that Greek troops will not impede the movement of the Italian forces.

Ioannis Metaxas puts down the telegram, folds his glasses back into the same pocket, and straightens his dressing gown by pulling down on its side pockets.

Count Grazzi watches the pantomime, and once the glasses are safely settled and the gown pulled down once more, asks the question.

So Prime Minister, will you allow Italy to cross through Greece?

Since the Count had used French, Metaxas decides that he too would use the universal language.

No. No, I will not let your forces cross through Greece.

Count Grazzi has a last duty in that living room that morning. To tell the General the words he had rehearsed and rehearsed, the words prescribed by the Italian foreign office.

In that case, General Metaxas, we are at war.

He could not leave with these words, even though his orders were to say no more. The Count says he is sorry, that he never dreamed…

Well maybe your dreams are too optimistic, the General answers, distracted, already thinking of the work to be done.

I am sorry to do this at this time of night. I suppose you know what this timing means?

The General blinks. Yes, he knows.

The Count shakes the General's hand and, just before he leaves, the General asks exactly how much time they have.

Three hours he is told, maybe a bit less.

As the Count leaves, he thanks the guard. The guard wishes the Count a good morning and creaks the rusty gate closed behind him.

In the car, the Count thinks that the General's gate ought to be oiled. It is not worthy of the man.

General Metaxas' Office, Athens
(forty-five minutes later)

The ministers come quickly. Only moments after they take their places around the table the General enters, giving no pleasantries, shaking no hands. He is followed by his secretary, a petite blonde who, on a normal day, would be eyed by all of them.

The General lights his cigarette, using a silver lighter snatched from in front of the Minister for Education.

Gentlemen. A little while ago I had a visit from the Italian ambassador.

He stops, asks his secretary to take minutes, and resumes relating the events of that morning, including the conversation with the Count, word for word.

When he finishes, the General says he hopes to God that he had been right to reject the ultimatum. His simple 'no' has dragged Greece into the war.

The Transportation Minister stands and makes a slow clap. The other ministers start to stand. They cheer and then stamp. Metaxas tries to settle them down, but they will not be settled.

The General puts out his half cigarette, and lights another, this time putting the Education Minister's lighter in his pocket.

He says that what happened this morning means that Greece has a lot of work to do. The Italians will be over the Albanian border within two hours.

But gentlemen, he says, I promise you the Italians will not be staying in Greece for very long.

The Greek-Albanian border

The Italian army didn't expect the Greeks to move so quickly in the few hours they had. The Greeks are no match for all the Italian machinery lined up on the border, but they have some advantages. The Italian equipment is very old. Mussolini cared most about appearance, and least about quality. The Italians' food is poor, and the cold of the early winter is already affecting them.

When the Italians break into Greece about five-thirty that morning, they march in huge numbers, thinking the war won already.

The Greeks, marching through the hills and valleys to face them, know the Italian soldiers will not like going into the rugged, dry and unknown Greek mountains. These are not the good roads of Italy and are even worse than the bendy holed byways of Albania.

Olga (the same day)

The celebrations of the General's French 'no' is everywhere. Athens needs no newspapers. People tell others the news with the excitement of children.

The children sing crass ditties about Mussolini's lopsided privates and Hitler's homosexuality. Men aren't walking today, they march to their shops and building sites, chests high, looking for trouble, ready to argue. It's in their eyes.

Old men do not bluster though. In the cafes and restaurants these men who have seen war listen to the younger ones talk of victory and justice, and say nothing, yet the curve of their shoulders and the lines on their faces seem to be deeper today.

Nearly a year of training, and now that it's started, I can't remember anything. It is much like having opening night nerves, but with no script.

My God, what have I got myself into?

The Greek Club, Sydney

Michael takes the cards and looks at each one as it is dealt. It's bad luck to do this, but he can't wait. He needs to know. First a two, then a five, then the others. The hand is a bad one. He bets on it. He loses, the seventh in a row, but the winner, the man across the table, takes his money like it's a burden. This annoys Michael more.

What's the matter with you Constantine? Deal again. It's your deal. Come on.

Constantine flicks them out.

Settle, Stambouli. We are all upset, okay? My village is close to the border. I still have cousins there. Maybe you should think about going home to your children.

Michael throws out a card and waits, staring at the dirty tablecloth. Constantine deals him another, and this gives Michael an Ace, a King, a Queen, and a ten, all spades, and a five of hearts. So close to a great hand and so definitely nothing.

Someone says the Italians are not so bad. Most Australians think they are the same as Greeks.

There is now only Michael and Constantine left in the game. Soteris, who had folded first and is scratching his ample tummy says he had a cousin who fought in the Great War. He says the Germans are barbarians. They don't know when enough is enough. Yes, the Italians are much better enemies.

The fishman from the next table shouts for him not to be such an idiot. The Italians want the islands, that's what they want.

Constantine reorders his hand and yells back that anyone who would rather have the Germans on Greek soil is an idiot.

Michael raises by a pound and tells Constantine to finish his hand before going off to punch people. Constantine throws the cards down in a fold and leaves the table to go chin to chin with the fishman. Michael scrapes the money towards himself, the first bounty of the war.

Fat Soteris says that at last General Metaxas proved himself when he said 'no' to the Italians. It is a great day for Greece. Soteris remembers, and says he is sure Olga is safe. She's in Athens anyway isn't she?

Michael stops playing. He has no stomach left. He sweeps the winnings into his baggy pockets and quietly, head down, passes the counter where Constantine and the fishman are drinking together.

At the table the others are already talking about Michael, because he is usually the last to leave the table, and never before has he left any with money in his pockets.

Michael walks, not towards the shop, but up George Street to the city. These men in the club, they have no idea. They think he is worried for Olga, that he is picturing her cowed and open to Italian soldiers. They know nothing. He believes now that his wife is dead and he drove her to it.

His friend in Greece couldn't find her. Someone as loud as Olga would be seen everywhere.

No, it is his girls that he worries for. They need a mother. They pretend to be happy with him, but the question always hangs, their life can't be settled.

Tomorrow he will send a telegram to Olga's sister Anna and ask if she knows anything of Olga. If she has heard nothing, then he will go to the government people and put this all to rest. He will tell them that his wife is missing in western Europe, and they will understand. Sure, they will ask him questions. He will answer everything and they will give him a piece of paper to say he is a widower. Then he will make a decent woman of Jean.

Olga

We are winning, the streets say. The streets, full of flags and anthems and folk dancing. Full of young men feeling their power, pinching at girls and women, as if it was all allowed now that the world is topsy. I heard of one boy who grabbed the bottom of an ample woman in a crowd, asking, without even seeing her face, for a place in her bed. He should have waited for her face. She was his mother. But she only laughed at him, such is the joy of the day.

An invasion is an enema for the lethargic soul. This afternoon's meeting was full of new faces, people not brave enough for when we were just an underground.

Again the meeting was spoiled by the professor droning on about this war being an opportunity to build a communist Greece. The faces in the room winced each time he said this war would see the end of the fascist King.

Communism and fascism. Your father always said they were the same. Communism, he would say was the worse of the two, because it takes your dignity away. Without dignity you have nothing. This he told me once as he was chasing a chicken around the back yard.

The professor had a plan, he said, patting his front pockets until he found a scribbled sheet, and flattened it out on the table. Then he searched for his spectacles, as the new women stood impatient, shifting their heavy children from hip to hip, their men glancing at each other.

Should we not save such plans for later in the campaign, I suggested. We have only just started fighting.

But this man of liberty and fraternity was indifferent to a woman who didn't know her place. He, a professor of mathematics, who thought his title made him Sophocles.

I left without voting on his resolution.

Afternoon rain had greyed and emptied the road outside. The water on my head made me feel like a little girl. More responsible women were rushing to pull in their washing, cursing the rain, while their children scrambled between and around them to get into it.

Older children in one of the church schools were staring through their windows, probably wishing they were me. They couldn't have imagined that I wished to be them.

Athens, Greece

Anna smiles at the telegram that has come to her all the way from Australia, from the man who should have been her husband. She would've been so much a better Australian wife than her sister.

She feels the lightness of the paper. So light for something that can change all their lives.

She plays with it, weighing it on her palm. It never occurs to her to just answer it honestly, there are too many things to be considered. If she tells Michael that Olga is dead, she will be strong on Olga, a final spit in the eye for the sister who refused to help her. The thought makes her smile. This kind of revenge has been a way of life in this house. Everything they have gained has been through someone else's loss. This has not been a house of smiles, but they have always had food on the table.

Her palm moves up and down with the telegram floating. It flutters off, and she grabs it and thinks again, because if she wires back to tell Michael that Olga is alive and working in Athens, he is likely to renew his offer to bring them all back to Australia. He is a businessman, he would find a way to make it happen. Her head swirls at this chance she had thought dead. That is what she will do.

Her mother bangs her way in the house with bags, grumbling, and Anna starts to resent the life she has, as she has resented it almost every evening of every day of her life. The sound of the old woman brings that familiar tightness to her chest.

Anna, the old woman cries out. The house is filthy, you dirty dog. Clean it. What have you been doing? Out whoring, I bet.

These are the taunts that have been thrown in this house since Anna was a child and, unknown to Anna, these are secondhand taunts, the same ones that the old woman's mother threw at her when she too was young. This house has always been alive with the hates of women.

Stop it, Anna yells at the old woman, who as usual pays not the slightest heed.

Stop it, Anna calls again. Stop it and let me be.

Whore, the old woman mutters, pushing past her onto the kitchen. In all the years of Anna's life, her mother has always had the last word.

The forgotten telegram is still on Anna's palm. She sees it and remembers. She remembers the telegram, but not the joy of the chance to get to Australia. She only sees a chance to spite the women in her life . She takes her tatty coat, the one she stole from Olga, it must have been twelve years ago, and heads to the post office in the next building, to telegram Michael that his wife is dead.

Pyrmont, Sydney

Jean's heavy shopping bags bang into the doors on each side as she heaves them through the shop. Michael trots around from the cookers and tries to take them from her.

Jean says it's all right, not giving them up. No-one ever takes her bags from her, she isn't that kind of woman.

Through to the back room, she lifts the bags onto the preparation table. Looking to see no-one else is around, she goes back into the shop to tell Michael the news.

The baby's good Michael. The doctor says the baby's good.

Michael agrees of course the baby will be good. He will be a little god.

She takes his hand to put it to her belly, but he resists because this isn't the kind of thing they do. Jean takes no offence and smiles a bare smile at his fears. She knows that everyone knows.

Tina and Nicky should be told, she says. They should be told soon. It's bad enough that Nellie will have to be told on the telephone.

Michael feels old for a moment. He has created another life, another Nellie or Freda. He is glad of the baby, glad to be putting the old life behind him, glad of this sweet woman to share his hours. What was it the priest said? The priest who used to be a builder? Something about marriage being a cementing of two lives, cementing like two bricks. To Michael this baby and the marriage will be also a new way. The church, the Greeks, the children, everyone would understand him marrying an English, especially now they know Olga is dead.

The girls cried and railed when the news came from Anna, but not as much as he had expected. It has been four years since their mother left, and in those four years the girls have become young women, and these are the years that matter the most to a child. As the bible said, these are the years when you put away the things of a child. They have done that, and they have become new people.

Nicky though, will not cry like his sisters. He says his mother is alive. He doesn't say it as though he is willing himself to believe. He says it with a conviction that is definite and unchanging. He says it just like Olga would, almost offhand, brooking no contradiction.

Nicky gives Michael some pause. He knows that to marry Jean will break his son's heart, but there is nothing for it. To not be married is a bad way to have a baby.

Olga

Today we hear we are winning less. The Italians push through, killing thousands of Greeks and sacking villages. They are only days from Athens. These things we hear from our parlour maids and the gossip wives of the gardener and the plumber.

Today I also had the first loss of the war.

I loved the French ambassador's twins too easily. Marie's shyness has become so very much like yours, my darling girl. Antoinette's sharpness is like your sister

Freda's. Time with these girls is time with you, my own. Yet as a cocaine fiend can't know their danger, this time I didn't allow the danger of making the children of others my own. I had lost the Count's girls too easily.

Please come with us, they begged and wailed. Please Madame, they cried. Please.

Please. The word they use when there is no other left. A word that no mother wants to refuse.

I wonder if Tina begged of your father. Please dad, make mummy come back.

Or maybe she said, good riddance to that gypsy.

French Ambassador's residence, Athens

The ambassador's office is a mess. Open boxes everywhere. The ambassador is behind his desk, reading and throwing out papers almost in one movement. His golf clubs are buttoned up, lying across boxes in the middle of the room. Worry on his leathery face.

He looks up, sees her, then goes back to his piles. He says her services are not needed anymore. She had another job did she not? Working for the British ambassador?

The children. What of the children?

The children will be fine, thank you. It is best to leave this morning. Best not to prolong such things.

His face shows he doesn't know about the bonds of women, of how close the twins and Olga have become.

Is there anything else, Olga?

Asked without an eye to her. She thinks the French are supposed to understand women.

The house you rent me, she manages to say. Will I need to move out immediately?

He tells her to forget that house, it is a wreck. His weekend house in the same street is much better. If she wants it, then she is welcome to it. The Italians will take it anyway when they reach Athens. Number four, he says, apologising that he doesn't have time to find a key.

And in a moment she has all she'd wanted.

She says she doesn't know how to thank him.

The ambassador stops his sorting and looks at her through his very thick reading glasses. He has no time for games of embarrassment, and says, rather impatiently, that she has done good work with the girls. They cannot take the house with them. He tells her to take what she wants from here too. Linen. Crockery. Go outside, get a taxi. No, wait. He pulls out some papers from some desk drawer and tosses the folders onto his desk one by one till he finds a brown envelope. He writes on it and stamps it with a seal. He tells her to take it to the records office in Athens in the morning. They will list her as the official owner. For what it's worth now. The worth of the world changes with the whim of a posturing Italian idiot.

He starts sorting again and says nothing more. She stays across from the desk for a minute, not knowing how to leave. Somehow she does sidle out after a while, bumping into a maid dashing out triumphantly with a box of envelopes. Of all things to take, a box of envelopes.

Hailing a taxi is easy, for there are many. Their drivers, sensing desperation, are circling the diplomatic area, heads craning like capped and bristled scavenger birds.

She must have made a dozen trips, loading linen, lamps, books, silverware and crockery, anything, into the cab. On her last trip she saw the twins at the top of the stairs, watching their teacher take their heirlooms.

Olga

I held them tightly until they squeezed back. I was only holding these things for their mother. I will love these things for them. Distance doesn't lessen love. I brushed their hair and kissed their foreheads, eyes and lips and together we wailed as women.

Looking back up at them, they looked even more like you and Freda, to whom I never gave such a good-bye.

You will like this house, your father said. It is not what you're used to. Proud he was as he showed me the vats that could fry two hundred pounds of cut potatoes in an hour; his concrete tubs in the yard where chickens are dispatched and dressed at the perfect height to stop splashes on trousers; and his new ice box. The biggest in the city, said proudly. Proud too he was of the stairs and their worn and newly-painted bannister. Steep steps that curved not for convenience, but to suit the ease of a designer's pencil. Small rooms. For our children. I, barely pregnant, still bearing the morning inconveniences, and I am informed that more are being planned. My children will grow in these dark sided rooms that smell of old paint and lard.

But how he cradled me that night. His fingers did none of the groping Ellie had warned of. They touched my forehead, they cupped the back of my head, they discovered the lines of my fingers even I did not know. I had never known of such a loving, and sometime during that first night in our house the smells of the kitchen, that I had hated, became sweet.

How to describe my house. It sees the Acropolis. It sees over the houses of Pendeli with a majesty. It is above. It commands. It bears a stale sweet smell of ordered linen, childrens' picture books and grey silverware. It is three stories. A basement, a living floor, a small bedroom and balcony. A phonograph, packed with records. I wound the spring, expecting it to break with my indelicate hand. But La Traviata came from the cone. That story of tragedy and loneliness. And with memory and music, I feel less alone.

Beside the house a tarpaulin covered the motor car, a beautiful shiny Citroén, all polished and proud. A saloon they would call it back in Australia, curvy and tall for its size. It reminds me of Tina. Little Katina. I will call it Little Katina.

A beautiful house. Its grey streaks of the weather on the outside walls are beautiful. Its musty sweet smell is beautiful. It is my house. A place that one day I will share with you, my children. No Italian, no-one, will take this house from me.

My last act I had to do before dark. To plant my olive seed. I have carried that seed with me, waiting for a piece of land to call my own. I celebrated tonight with a scraping of dirt and a thimble of water and love. They say it's very difficult to propagate an olive tree from a seed. Please that they are wrong. Please that it grows healthy and fruitful, bringing a little of Ultimo to this land that should never be foreign to my girls.

Pyrmont, Sydney

Michaelo, you old Oriental. How are you?

Ted always calls him that, and Michael has never got the joke. The sunburned man's satisfied smile stays on his face as he pulls up a bag. Here you go Michaelo. In here me boy. Three tins of the loverliest butter you ever seen.

Michael had been hoping for butter. He gives back a smile, but not a big one, The stuff is stolen.

It cost a bit more than usual. There was someone new on the docks, says Ted.

I can go another few shillings, but no more.

Ted carelessly drops the bag on the counter and pulls out the tins, in the view of people walking by. That's part of the price of buying from him. Everybody knows what he does, and he is happy for them to know. He isn't a dishonest man.

He takes the coins and whistles out of the shop, promising some fabrics for tomorrow. For the girls. Maybe he'd have an evening bag, even.

A wink and a whistle and Michael has someone else's tins. Well, he needs them. If the police show up for their cut, they'd probably end up with one of the tins.

In some ways this place is just like Greece.

Olga

I only have Stavros' account of what happened, and it is a story as rich as the ancient tales of this land. He told of the Greeks fighting the Italians with one foot forward, the other planted backwards, so they could not be pushed back from where they came. They were solid with a defiance that killed so many of them because they would not allow themselves a sensible retreat. To the Italian soldiers the Greeks were a brick wall of idiots who pushed and kept pushing when the bullets ran out.

Nine days ago, on the 4th of November, this brick wall pushed the Italians out of Greece. The invaders then became invaded, and were pushed back further and further into Albania.

Stavros said that Greek soldiers of all kinds, in uniform or rags, strolled arm-in-arm through the newly conquered

Albanian towns who welcomed them as liberators. In Athens, Metaxas was cheered as a saviour wherever he was seen. For the first time, General Metaxas was Greek first, and a tyrant second.

Even Stavros seemed to be proud as he said it.

Not Loving Enough

(January -June 1941)

In a café, Athens

The radio announces that prime minister Ioannes Metaxas is dead. It says he died in his sleep. Over and over it says it. Died in his sleep. She wonders if he would be disappointed. Don't soldiers prefer to die in battle?

Yet as he turns to nothing, the beggars he made lived on.

The thought comes to her that time is passing, people are dying, children are growing. Minutes matter. Her girls.

There is a pencil in the crack between the seats next to her. She starts writing.

Dear Michael,

I need to get out of here. There'd be no need for you to worry. What if we try it out until the war ends, then maybe we could come back here. I have a house now, in Pendeli. It will be perfect for them. We could open a little taverna and the girls can serve and learn how to cook. The air is wonderful in Pendeli. Nellie would be…

The British ambassador's secretary is suddenly next to her. He is worried about her, he says. Her chin has been down, he says. Is there anything the embassy can do?

She scrunches the napkin letter.

A few tables away, two girls, they might have been ten or eleven, are bickering about something. Their father is drinking coffee, ignoring their hissing.

The secretary sees it too and laughs. Just like him and his sister, he says. Even now, with her married to a viscount and living on a large estate with dozens of servants. When he sees her, they fight like children.

Family.

Well, Olga says, flattening out the napkin again, family is full of loving and hating, but when people get to the end of their lives, it's their brothers and sisters that they ask for.

The two girls are now drinking their chocolate quietly. The father hadn't said or done anything. He just knew the storm would pass.

Not just when they die, the secretary says, but when they're lonely.

Olga folds the napkin and leaves it on the plate.

Olga (the next day)

Well, I asked him. Are you happy or not?

About Metaxas?

Of course Metaxas.

Stavros just shrugged and said Metaxas doesn't matter. He never mattered. Now it's Koryzis. At least he has a heart. Perhaps…

Perhaps?

Perhaps one day there will be a new politics for Greece, where people share everything. Each according to his ability, to each according to his needs.

More communist talk. I never thought anybody was listening to the professor. Of all people, Stavros. He had hardened lately, his heart had sunk in his eyes, their wetness now a glaze. He was careless of people who were his friends.

I said it was stupid talk, all these whispered roarings of quotes from a man who had invented a system of yokes. This Marx had not lived to see a single one of these yokes made. His brilliant system was only brilliant ideas invented on a toilet seat and easily scribed on a notebook. The people had to make his idea work, and if they didn't wish to…

He left the room, saying political talk was not for us. I knew he really meant that political talk was not for women.

Olga (five weeks later)

Sixty thousand British troops are in Greece. Sixty thousand to help us fight the German invasion everyone says is now sure to happen. Sixty thousand British everywhere, swaggering and flirting, cockneys and Australians with their swags and shiny belts and their comforting familiarity. The streets are green and khaki and alive.

My part is to find them homes.

Many are the houses that are open for all. The poorest take the most. One women insisted on fifteen soldiers.

Fifteen, I asked. You barely have room for your cats.

One could never have too many men in one's house, she said with a wink, this woman of at least seventy-five. Wishing for no thanks, she would rather be considered a romantic than an altruist.

Yet my sister Anna says her house is full.

She in a four room house. Please, just take five…

Anna almost dropped the mounted sea shell she was dusting. Five! No. No. Find someone else to take them.

Of course. Anna does no favours. For her life is a deal and a bribe.

I told her not to expect any favours from me about going to Australia.

Yes, all right, she resigned. But only three of them, and only for a fortnight.

Five, I said. Five, and for as long as we need. It might be two weeks, it might be for the rest of the year.

As I left, I called out that her lot was arriving in the morning before daybreak. It would be good to have some breakfast for them. They would be hungry.

I closed the door on her screams. I felt good. Five had been taken care of, and Anna had been beaten.

Olga (two months later)

Time has run out. The British ambassador's secretary told us all, the maids and the butlers and the cleaners, and we knew he was serious, for he hadn't shaved and he wasn't bothering to whisper. The growth made him look like a different person. An ordinary person.

Time has run out, he said simply. They are coming. Swastikas would soon fly over Syntagma.

The little ambassador called me to his office a little later, welcoming me with both hands and thanking me for the work I had done with Thomas. The ambassador's stutter had gone, his stance was not childish. This was the diplomat in him I had never seen before.

He didn't dally. He asked me to do extra work, for the King.

The King? King George of Greece?

No, he said. Greek King George is going into exile. George of Britain. But the work would be for the good of Greece. The two Georges are related after all.

He quickly told me what he wanted. I would be a British agent, unofficially of course. There would be no records of it. Records in an occupied country mean risk. Only he, the Americans and a couple of people in London would know I even exist. The fewer, the safer. My cover would be as a housekeeper for the American ambassador. I would be contacted to be told of my duties.

I asked why he wanted me and not Stavros.

You have the right politics, he said with a sharpness that told me it was a subject to be left alone. I looked over his shoulder at his trophies. The thought of this awkward little man winning a sport tournament was ridiculous. A rugby shield too. The ambassador saw me looking at them, smiled and said his one regret was that there was no place for his Oxford wrestling ribbons. I laughed. We both laughed.

His secretary walked me to the ambassador's car, and told the driver to take me to Psihiko. The secretary gripped my arms and told me to look after myself. I grabbed and hugged him tight and long, giving him a chance to put his arms around me too. He didn't. When we broke, his eyes were wet. It would have to do.

A thin uniformed man was waiting in the doorway of the United States embassy. He came forward as the car stopped and opened my door.

Mrs. Mavromati. Hello. William Demerest. Ambassador's secretary. Welcome to the family.

Where the Italian and British embassies are dull and dusty yellow, this American embassy office is shiny and ornate. No dust is allowed here. The woman behind the desk is perfectly made-up, young and collected, the opposite to the harried Mrs. Pevlakis. But the twenty or so people on the padded bench seats were nothing like the neat and dapper Americans I knew in the Alexandria days. These people were too fat, too loud and too careless in their clothing. People of the good times. People who have never been invaded and never thought they could be.

Demerest took me into a small room. He sat close to me, almost nose to nose, and told me what I had to do. There was no question or request. Allied soldiers, mostly British, would be stranded in fields and villages as the Germans come down from the north. I was to help them escape from Greece. The underground would hide them, and I would be leader of one of the teams that gets them out.

He reached over to a pile of maps lying in the corner. He unrolled the largest one and pointed to an area marked Zone 1.

Athens was a zone now.

My cover would be as his housekeeper. But I would do no housekeeping, he promised.

Would I not be suspected? Working for the Americans?

He smiled in that wide American way and said the U.S. of A. was still officially neutral. The safest cover I could have.

I didn't ask for a promise of escape to Australia when it was all over. I had been promised help so many times. The U.S. may not be in Greece by then. Demerest may be back in Utah or Colorado bringing up his own children. I would only be asking for another lie.

He wanted to know what was on my mind. I said there was nothing on my mind.

Northern Greece

The German advance is fought hard. In the north, General Tsolakoglu's troops slog and batter themselves against the artillery and the ridiculous numbers of troops in the advancing Wehrmacht. On the Albanian front in the west, the Italian forces are pushing through again, threatening to trap the Greeks and British from that side. The Allied troops are being squeezed into a retreat, leaving the timeless settlements open to the Germans and Bulgarians. The young men of these villages are in the hills fighting, leaving the old, the women and the children, who can only resist by burning their fields or acting dumb. The very old ones can do no more than sit in the sun and wait, as they do in normal times.

In these easy villages the invading soldiers walk the dust streets seeing the impassive Greeks who offer them nothing but a hatred that had neither sneer nor word. The young welders or students of Hamburg and Dusseldorf can only wish for a smile and an invitation to have some of that wonderful smelling soup and coffee.

Some of the villagers have welcomed the invaders. These villagers long for the supplies the Germans have for bartering, like tinned food in exchange for fruit, or woollen scarves for sex. It is a war of deals and agreements. There are no reprisal shootings, rapings and looting. This is still a gentleman's invasion.

In the hills above these villages, the British soldiers are learning. They see how the Greeks step in the paths of the goats and leave no foot print. Quiet, the British urge to their laughing companions at night, quiet, we can be heard for kilometres across these mountains. No, the Greeks say, you cannot. And the British believe them and learn to laugh too.

These little groups fight their battles hard and roughly. Bombs are made of nails and rocks. Ambushes are fought with picks and nineteenth-century rifles. Stabs are thrust by knives that have only ever been used to cut onions. The invaders are attacked so they can never win, ambushed all around, with the radio operator the first to be killed. Their bodies will never be found. The Greeks got the idea from the British and perfected it.

Yet they are losing.

Olga

This Sunday just past I went to Athens with Anna to see the start of it. Others were there, making a crowd at a parade. But it was a crowd only of women, because it is only women who will dare. We all needed to see if it was true that we were no longer the mistresses of our own country. Across the road from me a little woman was clutching her daughter to the front of her apron so tightly that the girl was struggling to get her arms free. An old woman waved a Greek flag. Most though, just stared.

Half-tank monsters led the parade, topped with German officers waving and smiling at the people who did not wave back.

Except the sluts.

The smell on that street was of gardenia and sweat and something else, the smell soldiers bring. Wool in the sunshine, machine oil like Mother Hadjidaki's Singer machine, only much more, much stronger, the oil of war machines. It is now a ruined smell, one that until now

166

always brought me Mother Hadjidaki's earnest brow and tongue between lips as she threads the needle.

That was enough for me. Just as we had to come to see the new, we now had to know the old was still there. Arm-in-arm, Anna and I strolled the shop windows, trying to be sisters on an ordinary day. We went past a Plaka bakery that opened in stormy weather or Christmas day, and it was still open on this day of invasion. We pointed at the cakes we would like to eat, and teased about how fat they would make us.

We let ourselves be lured into a restaurant in Monastiraki by a waiter who was probably hopeful for a few last Drachma before the change. The service was wonderful and I knew why. Now that the country was no longer ours, they wanted to show pride, the kind that isn't so important in normal times.

We ate our plates of rice and tomato and wished for wine. Sensible wine merchants had hoarded their last stocks for bartering with the Germans, and there had been none in tavernas for days.

The waiter must have heard our wishes. He came back with two small glasses half-filled with retsina, saying it was from his own bottle. We knew from the first taste it had been watered, but it didn't matter, and we were grateful.

The wine made Anna remember. A man had come up to her when I was in the toilet and asked her to give me something. He was very scruffy, she had to add.

The crumpled piece of paper had the familiar signs on it. The movement could always find me, even on a day of madness and crowds.

Back in the cubicle, I translated the simple code.

It said a British soldier had to be picked up, somewhere north in a few hours.

Another risky thing thought up by another clever man in the underground who had decided to play it too close, a rescue on the invasion day. And handing over notes to a relative too.

But of course I would do it.

The time for the rescue was for ten o'clock that night. I had seven hours to organise everything and get to the mid-country. Not enough time. Never enough time.

I ran back to the table and pressed drachs into Anna's hand. I told her I had to go, and that she should go home too. I had some embassy business to get to.

She grabbed my purse. No, she said. Not this time. I was always leaving her without a word. What was that note? Who was that man?

I tried to pull her down, shushing.

Anna shouted that I didn't care about her, or Aunt Theanna, or the cousins. She said it was my fault that she was trapped.

I said calmly that if I didn't go, I would lose my job. Her family might be relying on me for money very soon.

She let go.

Three-thirty. The mail box was, ironically, at a post of-fice. An envelope was taped underneath its porch.

How are you dear Olga? Your cousin will be visiting this week. He will be staying in your mother-in-law's home. He knows the address, cousin Steffi gave it to him. Sadly, he has a cold, so do not catch it from him. He dearly wants to see your mother, and has perishable presents for you all. He has a new job, working for a grocer.

The code was the same one that had been used when I joined the underground. Three times I had suggested changing it.

Your cousin..

A Cousin is a person to be rescued.

Your mother-in-law's home.

One of the four pickup points.

He knows the address.

He will be outside the back door, waiting.

Cousin Steffi

A German name in the letter meant there were Germans near the pickup point.

he has a cold…

The pickup is important. People of great importance have influenza. Very Important People are dead.

He dearly wants to see your mother…

He has important information to pass on to Britain.

perishable presents…

This information must be passed on quickly.

a grocer.

Escape from Athens is through a cargo ferry from Piraeus.

The 'mother-in-law' pickup point was two hour's drive away. I couldn't use my car. Even in the well-organised resistance, there was no spare gasoline.

I would have to take the country bus. If it was still running.

I tore the paper and put bits in rubbish bins as I walked.

Four-fifty. I had just left a confirmation message in a mailbox and was at the safe house, telling them to expect the arrival the next morning. A rescue kit was being prepared for me: some money, a few basic papers, coded emergency directions hardly readable on a handkerchief.

Five-fifty. Everything ready. The sun fading.

Usually the city would come alive in the hours following twilight. The shopkeepers would be fresh after their naps, and children would be playing ball games and being loud, but this Sunday was quiet. The Germans had dropped leaflets saying this would be a peaceful occupation; that they were friends protecting Greece from the war; that citizens should carry on as before. But the people would not believe the tanks and patrols were protectors. They stayed home.

Six-ten. I walked into Syntagma Square. The bus stop was at the top end of it. The square had looked quiet, and that's why I went through it, between the saplings and the dry garden beds. I was walking too quickly, so I stopped and breathed. A cigarette. I looked for cigarettes in the bag. They weren't for me normally, but for contacts or bribes. I lit up, nervous. This was Syntagma. My home. Just walk normally. I could see the bus stop, a hundred yards only.

Madam, do you have a cigarette, a voice asked.

I flung around. Seven Germans were sitting in a dark café. No helmets, feet up on chairs. The voice had been in good Greek.

Here, you can have the packet, I said, fumbling for it stupidly. The men became restive.

Well, bring it over to us then, said the man with the good Greek.

I took two steps and reached to hand it to the closest man, but the leader, sitting further inside, called out.

No. To me. Bring it to me.

Where was my wonderful confidence? What had happened? I wanted to run, but some stupid part of me refused to show them the indignity.

Certainly, I said to him, if you need to smoke so badly, I will give them to you.

I threw the packet at him. He made no attempt to catch it, and it bounced off his breast.

Come here woman.

Some of the men were behind me now. I had made a mistake. My play of pride had only evoked his.

Pick them up.

As I bent, I felt my dress being lifted.

I wouldn't do that, I said strongly, but it sounded weak in my throat. I work for the Greek government. Anything you do will be found out.

We are greatly scared of the Greek government, he said, his smiling mouth almost kissing mine.

And in the darkened café the soldiers had their play. Never showing their faces, and never knowing my name or the names of the babies I had fed. For a quarter of an hour they used me. Just a woman, just a Greek. It was so quiet, a ritual, the only sound a snigger once from one of those waiting. After each had had his turn, he went away, perhaps shamed and sorry. Not for me, but for themselves, for their mothers and sisters. They knew I was not a whore. I was just a woman.

My mind stayed with the bus. The contact was waiting, alone, in danger. This kept away all the hurts... my neck spasming under the hands of each man, my stocking knees torn on the rough ground, my stomach sore from the edge of the chair I was being forced over.

Then I heard the uneven roar of the bus. I had to get the bus.

Please. My bus. I must catch my bus.

The leader, having had his share, looked sickened of the play. He was out in the square, smoking another of my cigarettes. The man on me eased off.

I got up, stupidly putting the seat back in its place. I pulled my dress down and picked up my handbag. No-one stopped me walking out of the darkened café and running, not away from the men, but towards the bus. I couldn't miss the bus.

I was the only passenger. The driver looked at my clothes and flirted a smile. It will take hours to get there, he said. A little kiss would make the journey seem shorter. It was nothing, a simple Greek flirt, playfulness, no harm meant. He could not have known why I snapped, telling him to do his damned job. His smile died, and he jammed his long lever into gear, almost jerking me into his lap.

The back seat. The only light bulb still working was above my head. Blood was on my stockings. Had to clean my knees. Handkerchief. I had the one with the instructions on it, but that was too important to dirty with my blood. So I cleaned myself with a dirty day old newspaper, scrubbing hard to wipe away the night.

Hey. Hey. Here you are. We're there.

I see red skin with thick hairs in large wet pores. The driver's nose almost to my face. I screamed at him to get away from me or I'd kill him.

He waited until I was off before he yelled out. Well you fuck dog. Get out of my bus. Slut.

I tried to be erect. My joints stiff, my knees fighting every bend, his words behind me and with me, my thoughts on the passing seconds. I was twenty minutes late.

The house was locked up and empty as it was supposed to be. The contact was not there. Just this house. All I had gone through to reach this place, all that for a dead house, and there is nothing as lonely as a dead house. Where are its children? Is there no remnant of the years of lovemaking that happened in its warmth? Does all this die when the people leave?

North of Athens (a few minutes later)

Bill has been watching the woman standing up close to the door, like someone sheltering from the rain, except that she is facing the flaking paint and there is no rain. She is heaving.

He stays on the ground and wills her to do something, just so he can know, but she only heaves.

For a long time he waits, until a single word breaks into the quiet.

Please…

The woman has turned around and is calling to the dusty grounds.

Please…

Bill backs further into his ditch. He had wished for her to do something, and now she does, he doesn't know what to do. After a while there is a banging, as a hammer on wood. Bill takes the risk and runs to her, trying to make his boot steps light, but the gravel and rocks make him loud. The woman turns quickly, making him realise, ten yards from her, that if this is a trap, it is a clever one. He is in the open, without an escape.

Olga

Under the threshold of this house I wanted for the warmth of Rena's soup; the love of Michael's arm across my belly in his sleep; Ellie's kisses on my lips; the sound of Mother Hadjidaki's sewing machine. I wanted for the good things of my old life.

But there was no warmth. There was nothing for me, only the cold of Germans, the bus driver, and now this phantom man who was not here waiting and grateful.

No-one should feel that kind of aloneness. It is not right. It is cruel.

I wished to be caught.

I wished Germans could grab me and shoot me there, with the voice of Anna despising me as my last thought. To end all this. I banged my head against the door frame. Harder. Four times. More. Let my head split. Let me fall dead.

I didn't fall dead. It just made me dizzy.

A man was standing in front of me, his voice Australian, though I couldn't hear his words.

A truck's light flashed up the road, two miles or so.

For God's sake, he said, tell me the words.

Words.

Words.

I had none.

Come on missus, something, he asked, he begged, as the lights got closer. Tell me something. The other contacts told me you would be a number...

Three. That was what he wanted. That number.

He smiled a vast set of teeth.

North of Athens (minutes later)

They run. They run trusting that the ground they can't see in the dark won't have a ditch that will send them sprawling like fools. Their eyes are just for the corner of the road where they can hide together behind a tree.

When the driver slows to turn, they jump from the tree, hooking their arms over the wooden slat across the back of the half-covered tray. The man lifts himself in, then pulls Olga up after him. Inside with the hard boxes and steel poles, Olga feels the stickiness that can only be blood. He has slashed his arm on the slat as he lifted her into the truck. His blood is everywhere, on his jacket, on the floor, on her dress.

He tries to bind the wound with an oily piece of cheese cloth he's found somewhere. From the other side of the tray she watches his fumbling, and the grease and the dripping blood. Without deciding to, she leaps over to him, snatches the rag, tears it in two, ties it properly. Then she shuffles back to her corner.

The flow is stemmed but they are covered in his blood. They will have to leave the truck before it hits a roadblock where the Germans' dogs would be sure to smell it.

Some miles on, at a bend in the road, they jump.

They land upright and run into the ditch, and as they lay on their backs in the dirt, panting hard, he lights and offers her a cigarette, the last one in the packet.

She says it's a risk, the dogs might smell it. But she takes it anyway, and they have turns drawing long deep drags, and feel warmed by the smoke blowing back at them.

And in that warmth and dust, and without invitation, she tells this man she doesn't know what happened that day.

When she has no more to say, he says not a word of it, knowing it is the listening that is important. She prefers it this way. They lay in the quiet, staring out at the hills against the sky and the old sign that points to a junction, an old sign of flaked paint and words no longer readable. Their trances seem intermingled in her story, in the night, in the quiet.

Without quite realising, he starts to tell her his story, about how he joined the air force to defy his much older brother who had taunted him as a coward for not doing his bit for the war effort. Out of resentment, out of spite, he was flying missions within months, glad every moment he was in the sky, high above the small clouds of grey and the noises of death. He wrote his brother stories of his new life, of the people he met. Of Bernie Carpenter who flew Spitfires and used to play for Arsenal. Of the women he never met and of the loving he never had. Of the forty-two reconnaissance sorties he flew in his Gladiator that had purred like a kitten every time. The very same plane brought undone three days ago by Greek mechanics at Yannina who serviced her wrongly. She started playing up somewhere near the eastern coast. When the engine went out he glided, hoping to make Larisa and knowing he never could. After he parachuted, and as he hung in the air he saw her for the last time flying on, quiet and flat, graceful, to her inevitable death. He stayed in the air forever, it seemed, until he landed on a dozing sheep, and caused a ruckus. The local resistance seemed to come from the very ground itself to hide him and feed him, and arrange his escape down country.

Olga takes a last puff of his cigarette and grinds the buttend into the dirt with her thumb. No more is said of their confessions. They have at least fifteen kilometres to go into the city. Eight, nine miles, through an occupied land with soldiers who by now will have set up their first roadblocks.

He tells her his name is Bill. Born in Newport in Wales, but grew up in Australia. With the 5th British, on loan from the RAAF in Melbourne in Australia.

She considers asking him if he had been to Sydney, or maybe even Ultimo. But that would be stupid.

They tramp on through muddy plots and thistle bushes, keeping out of view of the roads, Olga's thin coat buttoned neck to knee all the time. She wants to keep the blood and her dress closed away. She fears the moment when she will have to undo the buttons.

Lights appear. They thought the glow had been the shine off the stars until they were revealed over a little crest. The lights are spread out across the road up ahead.

Although this road block had to be at least a mile away, the lights outline a truck like the one they had been in. There is a lot of movement around it.

Olga and Bill run further from the road, away from the sound of dogs barking and lights that seemed to be reflecting towards them. Further they go, into the low, black, foul smelling mud, to make it harder for the dogs and the soldiers.

After half an hour they are past the line of lights. The mud is thinner here, the beginning of a stream, and its water breaks the claggy mud from their skin. But still deeper into the stream they go, drinking the water too, not caring whether the blood or foul muck is scooped up with it.

On and on, having not eaten or stopped for hours, for they know that light might bring surveillance planes, and with the dull dying grasslands there would be nowhere to hide.

She promises that the outskirts of Athens could only be a few miles ahead, but they see no lights of homes. For all they know they could have been going in a circle. Her little kit has no compass.

There is a hill on the right. It's a hill that could let them get a bearing, but they would have to cross the road to get to it.

But the hill is across the main road. The British trainer had warned her of the Germans' rat cunning. They would, he said, plant soldiers in roadside ditches for days on end, just to watch for people who avoided roadblocks. These soldiers would bear none of the niceties of peacetime. If they saw someone trying to sneak across, they would shoot them.

Olga does it first, not trying to hide, meandering as a lost woman might. Everything in her wants to run across, but she fights her instincts, stops in the middle of the road, looks up and down, and goes to the other side just as slowly. Ten minutes later Bill follows.

They cram behind a rock, both wishing that Bill's packet has one last cigarette. Like a miracle, it does. This time they smoke in a huddle, Olga shivering from her soaking dress, Bill rubbing her arms, she letting him.

They climb, low to the ground, often on hands and knees, following a goat trail, a well worn path that thousands of hooves have made smooth and free of stones. It leads them right to the top of the hill. The night is dying so quickly now that by the time they are able to see over the top there is just enough light to make out the city coming awake in the distance, with red and white glints reflecting off far away windows and stone walls of north Athens.

Before the city is the steep downward slope of their hill, and at the bottom of it, a small road. From there a few more fields and farmhouses, dirt tracks, then the city.

They scramble down to the ten-foot cliff overhanging the road and prepare to jump.

Voices. German voices directly beneath them, hidden in the overhang.

They fall to the ground, not afraid this time, strangely, but annoyed at how these Germans always seem to be everywhere.

Without discussion, without needing one, they know what to do. Bill crawls off to the right to see if he can get a look at them from a bit further around, and Olga stays to try to make out what the Germans are saying. She edges close enough to hear their young voices talking of feats of mountain-climbing and girls. They speak with the limited vocabulary and tongue of simple folk.

Bill is back soon enough to say there are two cars parked under the cliff. The two Germans are of no rank, doing nothing but smoking and talking and not even watching up and down the road. They look useless, but Bill's assessment is that it would be best to wait for a distraction and then decide what to do.

Olga has already decided what they need to do.

The distraction comes within minutes. It's a car rattling up the city road. One of the boy-soldiers waves it down, and it squeals to a stop ten yards past the little roadblock. A portly boy soldier saunters out to the road and up to the driver, shouting with an edge of derision in his voice. The driver's voice, that of an old man, has an edge of fear in his, as he tries to explain and apologise.

Bill and Olga drop down the cliff, the noise of the jump covered by the rough idling of the old man's car. The other much thinner German has not found the nervous Greek worthy of his attention and stays with one hand on the bonnet of his car, watching the view of the city.

Bill pulls out a short thick bladed knife from his belt, treads softly up behind the German, one hand thrusting his father's butchers knife up to the hilt, his other hand covering the boy's mouth. He helps the body to slide to the ground next the car while never taking his eye from the other soldier. When Bill rolls him over, he and Olga both gasp at the face. This uniformed German is an unformed boy of no more than fifteen years, his last expression one of mild surprise, as if caught in a sneaky schoolboy prank.

Olga opens the car door and pushes the body into the back seat. Small drops of blood on the road are kicked over.

Bill has taken the boy's gun. Olga now has the knife.

It is her turn.

The rough rattle of the Greek's car revs up again and through the imperfect glass of the dead German's car window they watch the distorted image of the other uniform walking back towards them, his rifle slouched over his shoulder, his body lollipy.

His voice young and friendly.

'Heinz? Wo bist du?'

This child takes a moment longer to die, long enough to call for his mother and for his eyes to ask Olga why. Olga's eyes stay on his uniform, badly pressed, and the smallest of oil stains inside the collar, made by sloppy eating.

It is this stain that makes Olga scream. She grabs the child's fat mouth, pushing her fingers into his downy jaws. Bill makes to pull her away but she will not be moved, and kisses the dead lips as a rattle comes from the boy's throat. She sucks in his last breath on earth.

And that is all she needs. She stands, grabs the body by the hands and pulls it towards the boot.

Olga in the larger car leads the way down the road, and Bill follows in the small one with the bodies in the boot. Their funereal procession rolls, hill on one side; fields and houses on the other, until she passes a deep hole in the hillside, a big notch made by centuries of summer rains. She signals to Bill, who drives his car right into it but at a wrong angle. It jams, with the car's tail sticking out.

Just then a car comes over the horizon in front, maybe a mile away. Bill reverses, and drives in straighter. The metal scrapes, but he forces the car through until it is well off the road.

He has to break the windshield to get out, and after throwing some branches on the roof and boot he walks, head down, to Olga's car just as the other car passes them. They are relieved to hear it run roughly. A Greek car.

They drive three or four miles, through towns and villages, thinking of nothing but the youth of the soldiers and keeping their thoughts to themselves. Soon they join the local traffic of early morning trucks and donkeys carrying loads. It is not until they pass the ritzy Pantheon night-club that Olga knows her bearings have been right. They are not far north of Omonios, about a half-hour's walk to the safe house.

She chooses to dump the car in the old foundry. It was a place where, years ago, there had been an accident, and workers were killed. The owner then died of a heart attack. Taking the omen that Greeks were all too willing to take, the workers walked out, leaving the building and its heavy equipment to decay. The first floor collapsed long ago, leaving an inverted tin sheet cone in the middle.

Olga edges the car into this ghost building and around to the other side of this cone. Bill is neither Greek nor superstitious but he shivers in that dark place for this all to be over soon. If Olga feels this, she shows no sign.

They open the car's doors and let down the tires, they put an iron sheet through one of the windows and pull the wiring out of the motor. Finally a thin, ageing spray of dirt is thrown over the car. No-one looks in the old foundry to see what is going on. The memory of death and the fear of superstition is so strong that the car might not be found for years. The city couldn't even find enough workers to pull the old building down. It will be left to do the job itself.

In this part of Athens, things are still the same as before the occupation. Clothes hung across the narrow, dirty streets. Fat women sit in upstairs windows watching for men to walk past, smiling at their approach, abusing when they are ignored. An old woman throws a bucket of brown water across the path in front of Olga and Bill, splashing their shoes.

Ay, maee, Olga yells.

Bill lightly jerks her arm and tells her to settle down or they would be noticed.

As the old woman disappears behind a paint-flaked door, Olga whispers that this is Greece. They have already been noticed. It would be suspicious not to complain.

Several pairs of Germans are walking towards them, but their attention is in shop windows. A peasant couple holds no interest for them.

A quick strained cat's voice fires at Olga. The voice belongs to a waspish woman who is calling from her stool at the front of a sandal shop.

Olga Stambolis. What are you doing here. Who is that man? He is not your husband.

The Germans look.

What is that blood on your leg Olga Stambolis? What have you been doing?

Bill's arm tightens on Olga's. All four Germans are staring now.

There is so much blood. Right up your leg. And your dress too. Let me see.

And the fat bandy-legged woman makes for Olga, her talons ready to pull away the coat.

Olga tells her something about a car accident, and that this man was helping her because she was feeling ill.

The fat woman believes none of it, and in the way of Greeks she says so out aloud.

Olga makes like she is bilious, puts her hands over her mouth, jams a finger in as far as it can go, and forces a vomit of phlegm on the woman's feet.

Ayee. Not here, the woman screams, moving her feet too late to avoid the muck. Go, go, she commands. Get home. Oi my shoes. Go home.

The Germans laugh.

Olga and Bill walk all the way to a Plaka back street, to a cellar hatch which is almost completely hidden in a weedy crumbly part of the footpath. The cellar is not tall enough for them to stand in. This is deliberate. It discourages searches.

At the furthest end there is another hatch hidden in the plaster, its edges impossible to find in the darkness unless you know where they are. Through it is a tube passage, six foot long and half that across. They crawl through it to a larger room, which has been stocked with food. There is a box in the corner covering the hole that makes do as a toilet.

Bill surprises Olga as she turns to go, kissing her gently.

She kisses his lips as softly as he had, and as she leaves he tries to tell her his full name. She stops him. It is a dangerous thing to share names.

Bill Luckett is my name, he calls out after her, and to hell with them if they find out.

Olga

I felt the vibration of them. I heard their boots on the gravel. I smelled their machine oil and their sweat until I saw them, men in a line, a single line, coming on and on past the housewives who were dressed in their colourful skirts and Sunday shoes. On and on the soldiers walked, under the lines of washing, over the dogs of the street, past the faces all the same, except for Bill Luckett, who was standing with the housewives across from me. I called out, 'not long now Bill, just a bit Bill. Soon Bill'. And he reached toward me through the men. Fingertip close. His hand touched my arm. Gently, then roughly, until it shook me.

Was this my house, he asked.

Yes Bill. My house.

But the face was not Bill's. This face was wide jawed and tanned, and his collar was the collar of the violator, of the marchers I had just seen.

I woke enough to know I was on the sofa where I had been writing, my pen still in my hand, my feet and calves bare.

The officer knelt down to me, for I had not had the presence to even sit up.

Your dress. Carnations.

Yes, I said.

The flower of the American Mother's Day.

And, I remembered, your middle name, my Nellie.

You have had a busy night, he said.

I could not remember a single thing. It was probably the only moment in my life I would not think of the rape, of my murders, of Bill Luckett.

It must have been a bad accident, he said, as I tried to sit up.

What accident?

The blood on your dress. Perhaps my medical orderly can help you.

No need, I said. I am fine.

This German officer smiled. Is this your house, he asked.

Yes, I told him. All mine.

He asked to see the deeds, pleasantly, as a family lawyer might.

As I tried to move I smelled for the first time the blood that covered me, and my sweat, and their sweat and the heat and the dust. His soldiers' boots were as dusty as their belts were shiny.

And on the floor where it had spilled from me there it was.

My diary.

It was open. Even facing them. Any one of the soldiers could read it and its names and dates and places. With its story about dead boy soldiers.

I swung my legs off the sofa lounge, my fingers tingling to reach.

His eyes following mine to it.

Him picking it up.

Flicking through it in a literary roulette, stopping at a page and reading a little. Looking to me over the top of the diary.

Yours?

Yes. It is a book of stories for my daughter.

I see.

He read more and nodded.

He complimented my writing, saying that he wished his students could write with such imagination.

The diary was given to me.

The deeds please.

My head swirled as I went up the stairs, heady either from the escape or the compliment.

The captain did not bother to look at the French ambassador's papers before handing them back at me.

I like this house, he said. You are very lucky to have such a view. He smiled.

The soldiers stood back to let him out, then followed him into a glorious sunset.

I followed them and saw that my street was filled with Germans. German trucks. German soldiers with their frantic movements. An officer in the cap walking through the scene. Soldiers carrying boxes into the Petrakis house across the road. Strips of cloud casting patterns over the Acropolis in the far distance. It was beautiful, even on this day.

I stripped off in the kitchen. Thick blood was through my underwear, the blood of me, of Bill, of boys.

I stuffed the dress and pants and brassiere into the wood stove, but they wouldn't burn because I had over-stuffed it. In a panic I sprayed lamp oil in, and it made no difference. The matches burned themselves out, the clothes staying like an ember. If the Germans returned, how suspicious would this seem to them, because few people in Athens were destroying perfectly good clothes. Please burn, I begged it. Let the match stay lit, let it catch.

There was a knock at the door.

Anna shied when I grabbed her fingers and kissed them. She was limp and not understanding. Come now, sister, she said, pulling her hand away and going to the kitchen. The fire was burning in a loud whoosh. She used the embers of my clothes and the blood of boys to heat a soup. As she spooned it into my mouth, we said nothing at all.

I woke in my bed later, alone. She never said why she had braved the German soldiers to come here.

Dear daughter, Mother Hadjidaki was not my real mother. I was a foundling, given up by the woman who bore me. I had always known that, but this was all I had been allowed to know. Anna and I only came to know about each other by accident, through a person in Crete who had known us both.

It was 1929. You were six or seven when Anna's wonderful letter to Australia came. Could I come back to Greece and meet my real mother and cousins? They wanted to bring me into the family at last.

Your father let me go to visit them. You, Nicky, Tina and baby Christopher. I was not surprised that Freda wanted to stay behind with your father. She always loved him more. I would see her jealousy in the side of her eye when your father touched my back in passing or rubbed my hand. It was a jealousy I could never understand, but that's probably not fair. Children are children. They take sides and play favourites. Nicky and Tina were always fluttering around me; you adored your father, but none of you ever had the angry jealousy Freda had. Your father couldn't see it, so I let it alone, and when she fussed about not wanting to come to Greece with me, we let her stay behind with your father.

Three months on the boat, and this new family gave me the grandest of welcomes in their threadbare home of whitewash and rotted timber.

Then came the questions, asked with a thrill and impatience. How many properties do you own? Is it true you run a large restaurant? The old woman, my mother, wanted presents. I remember your face when the little koala you had made was tossed on the sofa, so greedy were they for money, for a set of tickets to Australia, for deeds, for titles. I will always remember how their happy faces soured when there were none of these things for them. The old woman snapped at Anna. Anna barked in turn at me. There was no room for us in their house. Go find a hotel.

Why didn't I walk out on them there and then? I would have, I would have, but for the smallest of things. The old woman had a mole on her foot, an ugly black mole. I saw this mole and knew where my life had come from. I have such a mole, the same kind in the same place. I know it seems trite, but the little things are the clues to life, and at that moment I knew this old woman was my own. Mother Hadjidaki I loved, but her body was not mine and mine had not come from hers. This moment, can you understand, it was a moment of learning I was not alone, that I came from something, that I came from the centuries, and might come for centuries to be.

As bad and mean as these people were, they were me.

I took you all, baby in arms, Tina barely walking, you were only a little girl yourself, and my howling Nicky, and we muddled along a footpath to find somewhere to stay that would not take all our money. In the end I took the first place I could find, a pension that charged too much for a room with one bed and a sofa. That night we crammed together, you asking questions about my family until you fell asleep to Nicky's howls and the landlady banging on the wall. The wails and the bangs stopped eventually, but I stayed awake, disappointed by the day, but with a part of my heart so very full.

We would spend each day with my new mother and sisters, never really wanted, buying our way in with cakes and offerings. So sad you were, my darling girl, for they would never treat us as family, hardly even as visitors.

Olga (the next day)

The Germans lean on their half-tracks in the road outside. Others walk around smoking and throwing their cigarette ends into the dirt. They do it as if they own this place: Pendeli, Athens, Greece. This is invasion. I have lived it before. During the war, women in Alexandria were raped, and Mother Hadjidaki would tut and say the British ought to stop this. My school friends cared less, saying that the girls asked for it by spending too much time with the soldiers. I would walk home and see the oriental soldiers holding hands; or an American rolling up the sleeve of a private who had been hurting from the Egyptian heat. There was something in the way this private let his sleeve be rolled. He sat as a child, blinking and looking around as his comrade did this in a time of war. How could such men become scoundrels?

Olga (three days later)

It was early evening yesterday in the city and the Germans seemed to be everywhere. Some Italian soldiers were there too, but they kept away from the huns, their allies.

They know.

Soldiers from both armies smiled at me as I passed their clumps.

At a dead-end lane there were sounds of protests, pleasurable ones. A pile, a German uniform mixed around a long white leg that looked very young. The soldier saw me and was not at all embarrassed by the pants bunched at his calves, and the gun belt around his naked waist. I kept walking. She was laughing, but maybe she had no choice. What woman wants to do this thing in a dirty lane with a man of no shame, no class. Her laughing started again.

My note said my orders would be at Shop Six, a taverna that becomes a bar speakeasy at night for anyone interested. It's well crowded almost all the time, and no-one pays any attention, they mind their own business even though they see everything.

It was across town from where I was. Past Syntagma. Past that place.

Face things, girl. Never run away.

I walked through Syntagma.

The café in the park was closed. I touched a chair that could have been the one those men had bent me over. I hugged it and couldn't cry. It was only a chair. What did I expect? Ghosts? Thank you Ellie.

In Amalias Street there was a big group of invaders, Italians. I crossed to keep away, but one of them ran out and crossed in front of me. He was a young man, twenty-two maybe, smiling broadly with open arms. He wanted to show he was friendly, but it made me think of capture.

Hello missus, he said in appalling Greek. Would I like an escort through the streets?

I said no, but he fell in beside me anyway. Ah, what husband would let a beautiful woman walk alone at night…

An empty compliment is still a compliment. I couldn't help smiling. He laughed and jumped in front, jogging backwards to keep his face to me.

There is no husband, is there?

Yes there is, I said. And five children. Four alive and one baby dead. I have a husband.

He stopped and let me walk on. He said, gently, that he was sorry about my bambino, then he ran back to his friends.

This day the speakeasy only had men in it, some playing cards at corner tables, some reflecting over coffee cups of ouzo or whisky. The sad ones like whisky.

I asked the waiter for a special coffee, one like the old waiter used to make when he had the coffee shop called Shop Six. The waiter wiped the table and left, returning in a minute with a thin black coffee, American style, the kind I hate, but he was not to know. As he put it down his left hand swept its base, spilling it onto the table. I moved my legs out of the way of the stream of brown moving down the table. He wiped it just in time. He promised another coffee, and left the cloth, saying it was in case he missed some.

I took the top layer off the cloth.

Two more cousins coming in tomorrow. They will be at Cousin Maria's house, you remember, with the red curtains. Your cousin William is doing well. He thanks you for helping him with his exams.

Bill made it. I laughed out aloud and banged my fist on the table, not caring who saw it.

God I felt good. Not even the memory of my Christopher could ruin this night. In this feeling I went to the message corner on the next block.

I should have known good feelings can be fatal.

A flash of light.

From the window.

It took me a few seconds to understand. The message corner. It had been changed a week ago after a security breach. I had gone to an old place. I had gone to the wrong corner.

The Germans had my photo.

I walked away slowly, wanting to run, to tear like a child and hide. There was nowhere to go. Certainly not home. I couldn't risk a halfway house or a friend.

I spent the night in the national garden, alone in the weeds and rocks. Thank God it was warm last night. No sleep on the longest night of my life. With grass itching my arms and the smell of gardenia and wood smoke, I looked up at the always moon and thought on it all… the flash, the German in my house, the quickness with which my body was taken, the lightness with which we grip this life. Around these thoughts went, to no answer; to no more understanding; just around.

So this was what it was like to know you were going to die. Where was this terror and desperation I was supposed to feel? I had no terror.

What I did feel was furious. Again men were deciding what was to become of me. A man takes me from my mother when I am a child, makes me bear his children, and thinks that is all there is to me. For twenty years I have been half a woman, needed only for the milk of my breast or the feel of my thigh. Here I am more, and the joke is that I will die. Yes Michael, you have won.

I rose from my grave as the sun cleared the moon away.

Demerest was at the desk at the U.S. embassy. He looked up and asked nothing of my trials, and showed no surprise or relief.

Not more complaints about pay is it? Isn't it always? This was said loud, him glancing at his waiting compatriots, half winking a mockery of me.

I leaned over the desk and whispered that I might have been discovered.

Look Missus... I can't pay you any more... There's a war on... All right. I'll see what I can do.

He pointed me to a room, and after about five minutes he came in and I told him.

There was a moment of weighing, weighing the danger, weighing the value of me, no doubt. When he spoke, it was the voice of a diplomat, of a fixer man.

He said I must keep working for the ambassador. If I went underground now, they'd know for sure I had something to hide. That would be bad for the ambassador.

Surely they couldn't touch him, I said.

Any excuse, sweetheart, he said.

German trucks were still outside my house, and this calmed me. As the British taught me, when things are different, that's when you have to worry. Inside, the house was the same as I left it. The body powder on the drawers and doors was still there.

Surprises of a war. I think I am to live.

Olga (The next morning)

I woke in terror last night. It was not the terror of death, but the terror of realising there was no way out. This was someone else's war, miles from my life. But I had been pulled into it. It tore me as I realised that this was now my war. Yesterday I could have died, and if I had, I would have passed out of this world without a word to you, saying not one of the things a mother is bound to say. Five years have passed now, and I have always believed it better that you don't hear from me, that you think me dead. I have always believed that by being on the same compass we would feel each other, but last night I felt like I was dead to you. It cannot go on.

In the night I found an old card that had been left in a drawer by the French ambassador. I cut it into a postcard. It didn't leave much room to write, which is good. I am never much good with sentimental things. It always comes out all wrong. All I wanted to say is that I love you, but we have never said that, and you would not be expecting it. So I wrote 'Hello Nellie' on a silly little card with a puppy dragging a Christmas stocking. A card from the wrong time of the year. A baby's card.

The time for babies has passed from my life, but all through the night my head was full of the sound of you as a baby. It haunts me even now, louder in the quiet dawn.

From the moment my hand left the postal box in the square, I wished I had written all your names on it. Now it is too late. By now some postman will have taken it. If the Germans will let this little nothing of a card get through.

I can only hope that your father knows that by writing to you Nellie, I am writing to all of you.

Pyrmont, Sydney

Michael holds the card by the corner, as if afraid of it.

He leans against the window of the shop, faint. All he has read of it so far is that it has come from Olga. This little card, from nowhere, from the grave, destroys everything he

194

knows. Last night he had a new life with a new wife and baby. His daughters have settled into a new truth with a new mother. This little card turns Jean into a woman who is wrongly married. Their little Jimmy is now a bastard. It brings back to him a ghost that has left him alone ever since the marriage, the ghost nagging him that Christopher was his own fault. If only he had gone to Greece with Olga that time, Christopher would have lived.

He gathers himself and tries to walk through the shop as normally as possible, past Jean, whose arms are covered in batter flour, and doesn't answer her. In the bedroom he sits with the card on the bed next to him. Feeling woozy again, he puts on his glasses and looks at it properly. It is addressed only to Nellie in that familiar strong writing in thick ink. He smiles at how she always presses too hard on the pens. He flips it over to see the Christmas dog. Olga always did love dogs. He remembers her bringing home a stray for the girls, a nasty, snarly thing that seemed to resent being helped, and ate two chickens before he managed to let it escape by accidentally leaving open the back gate.

These are the things he loved about her. Her flaring passions, the way she could love, even the way she could hate, the life that was always in her until near the end. How many times would he have to bear the unbearable memory of her last words to him:

No, not my children.

There is no message on the card, apart from a Christmas wish. Perhaps there was too much to say, too much to explain, so she thought it better to say nothing at all. She had written a return address, but the bottom of the card had been wet, so the street and number is an unreadable smudge.

Thank God.

He takes a breath, goes to the wardrobe, and drops the card in the dusty gap behind it.

It is the kindest thing to do. For the children, for them all.

Olga

Nellie hasn't written back to me. If she had received my card, she would write. She would insist. She would steal the money for the stamps. She would stand in the line at that musty old post office with the old ladies, and not leave until she gave it to the postmaster directly and saw it go into his bag. She would count the days until I got it, then imagine the kinds of joys I might have at hearing from her. Then she would wait the same number of days for my answer. It would be the start of a correspondence that would let her share my time here, and let me see her growing into womanhood. She would tell me of her woman's troubles when they begin, and how her school-mistress has planned for her to become a teacher, and how she was drawn to seeing the world, and would it be all right if she came to live with me here in Greece for a while first?

Yes, I will say, the world is a great place, and the continent is where a young lady can learn to master the subtleties of life. Then we will go to the theatre together as sisters, and talk on long walks, and she will come to understand why I had to leave her back when. And we will be one.

But her letter hasn't come yet.

Mother Hadjidaki's Daughter

(June – July 1941)

Olga

There was a nice thing yesterday. The man from the Athens Dramatic Society sent me a letter, a summons to see him.

In his ruffled office of yellow papers the man with a constant cigarette and yellow fingers told me he was putting on a new play. Only the best people. He had seen me in something, but couldn't remember what it was. I was very good at whatever the play was, he said with a wave of that perched cigarette. He thumbed through a pile of yellow papers like a man counting bank notes, and found some sheets. An English play. It was based on a book by Daphne Du Maurier. He said the Germans, for some odd reason, liked English plays done in English. I could speak English, couldn't I? That's what he'd been told. This was my part, he said, finding the character sheet. I had to play a severe woman who was very angry. My part would be a Mrs. Danvers. Severe. Strong and severe.

I should have refused. Me with my own cell, with no Stavros to give me a night off, no-one to ask permission for indulgences. I was the person who did that now for others. I said yes, I very much wanted to do it.

The rehearsal was a surprise. The actors were good, there were no clipboards, no complaints and no upstaging. It gave me strength to do the night work, even though some nights I got no sleep at all. My little cat ate even less.

Olga (a week later)

After I came home tonight I had a hot bath, as hot as I could bear, as hot as the Japanese man showed me that time in Brisbane. So hot you could not stand it. Do you remember, daughter, how we shared hot baths when you were young? I had that sort of bath, and here in a mean sort of way, I was with you. You played with my fingers and pulled my rings and loved the way the soapy water would make them shiny. Yet you would never try to take them off, as though you knew the magic in the rings is in the wearing of them. A marriage is much more than a band of gold, but I have never taken it off. This year it will have been twenty years that I have been wearing this wedding band. Then there's the other one, the gold one with the circles of little diamonds and four pearls raised in the middle. It was the last thing your father bought me before I left Sydney. A great gift indeed because your father didn't have the money to spend.

A slow shiver came on me. Something was wrong somewhere. Somewhere in these rings.

I jumped out of the bath so fast I almost fainted. I moved as if I was guided. I put on madame ambassador's gardening pants, sandals and shirt, took my diary, got a knife and tore off a piece of plastic that had been covering the floor of the pantry.

Behind the house there was only a few square yards of uneven sloping ground, but it was too close to the house. I went over the back fence and up the road, looking for somewhere that would not be built-on or tilled, somewhere no-one could ever look.

At the end of the road the cliff-top overlooks the steep road up from Athens. Below the edge was a little ledge. I tucked the diary and the plastic into my pants, and lowered myself, belly to the cliff face, down the three feet to the ledge, hoping it was solid, hoping the night light wasn't playing tricks, and the ledge wasn't a mirage.

My feet found the ledge, kicking stones and dirt down into the dark.

It must be barely two feet deep, this ledge, just deep enough to get a balance. I held onto a tree root with one hand and chipped at the rock face with the other. I wasn't getting very far, when I saw a big root covering a rock wedged in a crevice. I pulled at the rock and used the knife to pick at the dirt around it, until the root let the rock move enough so I could get it out. I pulled your father's rings off, wrapped them in a piece of the plastic, and jammed them as far as I could inside where the rock had been.

This is the last thing I write in this diary, here on the ledge, with just a part of the moon to help me. When I am finished I will put this in the plastic too, and into the hole. Only I will know it is there. Maybe I will come back and take it out again tomorrow. Maybe not.

Tonight I tell you, daughter, how it was.

It is ironic that to find ourselves we often first go to those who came before us, thinking that in the deeds and seed of our mothers and our grandmothers there will be some explanation for how we are and what we do, as if what they were will explain who we are. From the time I was sixteen, from the day Mother Hadjidaki told me she had adopted me, I yearned to know of my birth mother. No-one could be a better mother than Mother Hadjidaki, but she was not my flesh. I started seeing my eyes in those of other women, my hips. The mole like mine on the top of a market woman's foot once convinced me that she had birthed me. I asked her, causing a flurry with her husband. I ran off, leaving them to fight over the child she denied having. So intent had I been on her mole that I hadn't noticed she was a half-caste negress.

Mother Hadjidaki wanted me to leave well enough alone. The story was a sad one, she would say, and would say no more. Her friends, the old baker's wife and the knife maker's widow, would tell me stories in expansive tones over cups of tea when Mother Hadjidaki wasn't in the room, about how my real mother was a girl who worked in the royal house in Athens, and who became pregnant by a very high ranking Scots officer.

The story said that my mother, this girl, was too young to look after me, and so even before I was suckled, to clear up the embarrassment of it all, I was given to Miss Hadjidaki, the royal seamstress, Miss Hadjidaki who had never married, her bullish figure a barrier to any chances of a love of her own. She took me as the child she could never bear herself, and suckled me in her own way. Tins of soldier's milk instead of the breast, herself as a father and mother, pampering me with her skill of the needle, making me the finest of clothes, better than those she made for royal children, and made no doubt from material which was meant for them. She would parade me with her along the streets of Alexandria and Athens, proud as a mother, me dressed as a princess, while she kept herself plain, not wanting to shadow my light.

I remember the tight dresses and the little hats that made my head hot in the heat. I remember how Mother Hadjidaki's face would drop if I complained about them, and these were the only times I saw her disappointed. Customers in Alexandria and the Princess Royal in Athens could treat her with a snobbery and disdain, and she would bear it with a smile and a bow. She would say that their words and their thoughts were their business, and only we can upset ourselves. So when she dropped her head for my complaint I resolved never to complain again.

From the time I was ten she sent me to all kinds of lessons: drama, languages, and made plans for me to go to the university. Marriage was not life, she would say. Learn something first. I could marry later. I was the only girl in my school who had no glory box.

But life intervenes. Mother Hadjidaki did give me the choice. Your father, decent man that he is, promised me nothing he couldn't give but my ears heard those promises how they wanted to hear them. To my ears he was offering me love in a home where I would be Queen. A home, a nest in a quiet place away from all these beggars, thieves and stinking heat days. I would be the Princess of Sydney, mixing in the best Greek circles in a clean new city of the sun. I would be able to act when I wished and have children if and when I wished.

Mother Hadjidaki heard your father's promises too and I couldn't tell whether she heard them the same way as me. She offered me no clue except by the wringing of her hands in her lap. Her eyes would not meet mine and I could not tell if her hands were anxious for me to stay or go. It was left to me in that minute of decision to think of the streets of Alexandria, which had hurt me and loved me. My Ellie had gone and my ghosts were staying. I made my decision, the first of my life, balancing the old against the new, the fear of what I didn't know against the comfort of the expected. With those thoughts and doubts I resolved to leave my home. The twentieth of November 1921. I was seventeen, although I put my age up to eighteen for the priest. Your father was fifteen years and a world's experience older. The wedding was a small affair, Mother Hadjidaki on my side, and a Cretan friend as a witness on his. A grim wedding among the gold of the Evangelismos Church, a wedding that no doubt the priest and the witness thought was a forced one. The papers were signed with a mechanical resignation, no hands were shaken, and we were out on the street with the witness, who had to dash off to see someone. That was the moment Mother Hadjidaki walked away. I had passed on and there was no more to say. With barely a goodbye, her plump calves were across the road and out of my life, and I was without mother, without family. No matter, your father said, you will soon make your own.

Within hours we were on the ship, and on the deck I passed by the places of my childhood. The fortress that stood sentinel here every morning of my life, the mosque that was bleating out its beautiful music I knew I would miss, just as I used to miss it when Mother took me to Athens. We slid past places of bad memory too: the sea wall of that ear twister, and the pink house at the end of the esplanade that belonged to that British importer who took me and made me watch him and ruined me as a little girl. I was only nine years of age and spoke not another word until Ellie. Twelve months of being a mute that neither Mother Hadjidaki nor doctor could remedy. Watching this house from the boat I remembered my shame for it was I who had spoken to the man first. I had said hello and asked about his dog, and for that transgression I always believed I had invited seduction. Even as I watched that house from the boat all those years later I felt that same shame, as I do now in my mind's eye. I have never told anyone of that house.

There was no-one to greet us in Sydney, and while Michael ran off looking for a horse and dray, I waited alone at this spot on the other side of the world, the furthest, I realised, that I could be from my home. I watched mothers pulling children roughly. I watched husbands talking to friends and ignoring their wives. I watched policemen strolling with pride and just a little menace.

I worked until my confinement, if it could be called a confinement, two days in a bed above and within the smell of the hot lard. You were brought out by a midwife of a neighbour and at the sight of your round black head all my fears vanished. Don't hold her so tight, your father would say, half-afraid, proud: you'll suffocate her. For nine months I had you in me, and for another nine I kept you to me, wrapped to my chest as I worked, even after I was pregnant again. The cycle went on after Freda, with Nicky, Tina and dear Christopher keeping me suckling. In this way I made my family, my circle, my ring, and I was content most of the time. I bore no ill-feeling towards your father for his bad promises, for he believed them to be true. I couldn't bear to blame him, I couldn't bear to hurt him. He wouldn't understand.

Then in 1929 came the letter from Anna, and my need for my real mother came back to me. I hadn't thought back in the eight years we had been married. And contentment can turn as easily as a few words in ink on a page. Michael saw it in me. It was he who urged me to go back to Greece to see her.

It was only a week after Christopher, Tina, Nicky, you and I arrived in Athens that Christopher became very sick. He would cough in fits till his little eyes cried and his fists clenched. I remember the fists. Every night I sleep to this sign of him bearing the fits. His fists clenched. For two days he worsened in colour and his little arms would be more like rubber, but his fists stayed clenched. I couldn't do anything for my beautiful boy, just dab with damp sponges and brush his hair. Do you remember me telling you Christopher was getting better? You would smile and say 'good, then he can play soon,' and you would go arrange his toys and his clothes. This would break my heart.

The doctors said it was not a disease; something had been done to him. After it was over, these doctors lost their fragile sympathy for me when I asked them to carry out a post-mortem on him. This was a sacrilege to them, a mother wanting her baby cut open. But I needed to know what took my baby away. Of course he was buried with his secret. He was fifteen months old.

It nearly killed your father. He blamed me and hated me. He came with Freda and took you back, leaving me in Greece. Only Tina I kept with me, for she was barely two years old, barely off my breast. I had never seen your father in such an anger, dark and seething, as he loaded you all into a cart, not even inviting me to see you off at Piraeus. You cried, my darling, for me to come, but there were too many things stopping me. Your father's fury, my shame and grief for my Christopher, and my fear that if I jumped on that cart, your father would take Tina too. So I let you go, tearing myself as you sobbed, Freda barely casting a backwards look. She was with her father and that was all that mattered. Nicky had been without hearing for just over a year, yet he knew everything, and stared, just stared. Tina could not know what was happening but she cried too with the terribleness of the day. After your cart had gone I stole a bicycle and put Tina in the bag around my neck and followed you to Piraeus.

I watched you all go to the ship. I saw you with your little cases, the ones I bought you at Plaka. You weren't crying anymore. From a corner in a port of many corners I saw the cases loaded onto the tray and your father waiting with you in the sun. All I could think was how foolish he was. It was stinking hot and he did nothing to take you to the shade. Yes, you had stopped crying. I even saw a laugh. You and Freda started to chase each other, seven and eight years old, playing as children. Tina was starting to struggle, so I left you to your game. I let you go because I saw you could be so easily happy without me. I let you go because I couldn't stop Christopher from dying. I let you go because your father hated me, and that was one hatred I couldn't bear.

For six years Tina and I stayed in Greece, managing in any kind of job and house. But times were good in Greece in those days. I cleaned for people to start with, then I worked at the university for a professor, typing his notes, taking Tina with me until she was old enough to go to the school. The days were full and the nights were barren, until the professor, who worked in the drama department, asked me if I would help on one of his stage productions. For him I cut sets by day, and when the play was running at night, I sat Tina on a stool while I set the props. She was such a good girl, your sister, as fascinated as I was with the student actors. I watched how they could turn the words with an inflection and hold an audience with a pause. I had always acted, but this was something more. I so wanted to do this, to capture people, to have the faces in the audience stare at me. The professor's method came from the work of Stanislavsky, a Russian man who said acting must come from within. If an actor was to be angry on stage, then he must be angry. It was no more than what Ellie told me. Find a character girl, and find it from yourself. Men will always know if you're just pretending. After seeing this acting on that stage, my old ways of being could never be anymore.

Life went so fast for us in this way until, after six years, your father sent his brusque note for Tina to return to Australia. My first reaction was to ignore the letter, but I couldn't for long, for when I looked at her, I saw him. She looked nothing like him, she was so dark, but she sputtered her words, just like he did, and in the way she shrugged and laughed. After some weeks I showed her the letter. She couldn't read it. It was in English and I had never taught her English. She had been my little Greek monkey, and seeing her not knowing what it meant, I could not bear it. She had sisters and a brother she had also left behind, sisters and a brother she had never really known, and a country of her birth she had not walked on. For many more weeks I didn't answer his letter, excusing myself by thinking it would be too dangerous for her to travel the seas alone. This cowardly excuse could be no more when my friend Helen Kalatzis told me she was taking her family to Australia. So after six years I watched that same pier as my little girl, looking so much like you, my Nellie, in her coat, standing with her case in amongst the Kalatzis trunks. This time though I could make a kiss good-bye and touch her hand until it was time to let her go up the gangway.

Yes I thought about coming back too, but I thought of the hatred of a man, and the death of a baby, and I knew that every time I saw your father I would remember my

Christopher, for he looked just like his father. And Christopher was here in Greece. His grave needed tending. I could not leave him alone in a strange land.

For eighteen months I lived here alone, pining for you all. The professor saw my distraction and put me into the plays, first as an extra, then giving me speaking roles. In the new year, it must have been 1936, I was giving testimonials to his new students about the fear of acting and how to overcome it. Now I had no Tina, I was free to do anything I wanted. I had a wage, yet I wanted to do nothing. After the performances, as the students would go to the clubs and bars, I would go to my room, spending my nights in the dark thinking of you, imagining what your life had become.

The professor was the one who convinced me to go back to Australia. He helped me with the fare, and helped me pack. A kind man who I was told loved me, but never told me such himself, and never could. His dockside promise was that he would always be here, along with the job, if it didn't work out. But by the time I came back to Greece again he was dead and General Metaxas had closed the drama department. All I had bowered for myself in Athens was no longer, but my grief was only for my generous lonely professor.

And so after seven years I was in Ultimo again. Do you remember how Freda didn't know who I was, how she thought I was a customer, and how I ordered fish and chips and sat on the bench in the shop waiting for someone to recognise me. You didn't know me either. It was Nicky, who hadn't seen me since he was four. He ran to me and held me so hard that the battered saveloy he was holding pressed into my coat. Tina recognised me too, but only stared, for girls are never so forgiving as boys. As for your father, he was not angry or reproachful, but we had our burden, and we carried it separately in the same bed. He is a good man, but people turn corners.

I had come across the world to be with the people I adored, and slowly you, Tina and Freda came to me to tell me of your school adventures. I came to know that it wasn't just that you didn't know how to talk to me. You didn't know how to talk to any woman. You had grown up in a house without a mother.

Nine months I stayed in that bed at night, turned away from the man who had fathered my babies. I don't remember ever sleeping. My mind would go to all things. To the day Ellie was taken. To the barrenness of Mother Hadjidaki. To Christopher's fists. To Nicky's illness. As the nights went on I became sure I had caused all these things. It was to this bed that my friends came to stay with me for the first time. They would seduce me and rejoice in my wickedness. They would talk of blame, they would talk of not loving enough and not being loved enough. They would talk of getting older and of not having much more time and of wasting it. They talked of ruined lives and of how I must make things right, how things needed to be started afresh and never could be. My friends came every night, regaling and rebuking, all while my husband slept next to me, facing away, snoring, his smell that I used to bathe in, so close that it stifled me. Morning after morning I would get up with him and cook the breakfast and clean the shop. Until the time I realised I didn't care to live, and yes, that night in the car, yes I fear I was going to kill us all. Your father stopped me, and in doing so I am left never knowing if I am the sort of person who could kill her young. And when one has such a question in her mind, the answer is always the worst.

Together your father and I bore what nearly came to pass. For weeks we each bore it alone, each with our thought of it as we lay side by side in that bed, not a single word passing between us until that last terrible night. I know I must tell you of it, and of what happened that night. I just can't tell you yet. Please be patient, my daughter.

Darwin, Australia.

Steve Kafcaloudes lights a cigarette outside the café, letting himself be seen through the glass. After a minute he glances in to see Nellie making a milkshake or something for a customer. He gets through half his smoke then takes it inside.

He comes around the counter and gives Nellie a tough hug, as much for the customers as for her.

How is my Fee-oonce-say? You ready for tonight?

Yes Steve. I'll be ready, she says, pulling away without realising she is.

He leaves with waves to everyone, this man of the well-known builder family who is now engaged to the Parrelis girl.

After work Nellie straightens her hair in the corroded mirror in her room, wishing Jean to be here to tell her she looks good. She takes her good handbag, her little cardigan just in case it gets cool in this awful heat, and gently closes the door behind her. The Kafcaloudes house is only a ten-minute walk, and it takes her twenty.

It is a night of loud laughing and hot cheap Greek food. All the children of Soteris Kafcaloudes compete. For their father's attention it might seem, but the boys and girls of this rough builder's family are acting this way trying to impress Nellie, and she doesn't see it.

Nellie, truth be told, is glad when it's time to leave. It's Steve's mother. Future mothers-in-law always ask everything. Nellie had been scared all night that she would ask why Olga had left, but this woman asked no such thing. In fact she said nothing in particular to her, or nothing that she could remember later on the walk home. Nellie's memory of that night would always be of the old woman watching her from across the room with a face that told her nothing. There was no malice in it for the girl who was taking her most beautiful boy, but neither was there a mother's love or welcome.

As Nellie sat on the bed in her room with the loud laughs and squeals still in her ears, the thought happened to her that in these times of a new life, maybe people didn't care about lost mothers and old marriages gone bad.

Nellie seemed to be thinking of her mother more and more lately. It wasn't that she doubted she was dead; there was the official paper from the government that said it was so. It was that her mother just jumped into her brain at odd hours, like when she was in the bath, or working in the café. Sometimes the thought would be thrust on her, when a woman might come in to the café who had her mother's wide jaw or beautiful black hair. Nellie would stare at this woman and see things she had long forgotten, like the way her mother would kiss her all up and down the side of her face, or cradle her chin and squeeze just hard enough. All these memories would hold Nellie up; take her out of this café and out of Darwin. She would come back suddenly, maybe to a call by an impatient Mick Parrelis to stop daydreaming.

Then there were Nicky's letters. They would come from Sydney every week regular as the clock. In every one he'd write about how he knew their mother was alive. Tina wanted to believe, he wrote, but Freda would have nothing of it, and every week Tina's head was being turned more and more. Nellie wrote back but never said anything about their mother, perhaps hoping Nicky would grow out of it, perhaps never wanting to contradict his hope.

As she falls asleep, Nellie says her mother's name, as she has every night for five years, making her the last thought of the day, a thought that helps her to sleep.

The Story Between Baths

(July - December 1941)

Olga

For half a year this story and these rings have been in the wall of rock. Holding them again, I can breathe. I have taken no breath in six months.

I think it best to start my story on the morning after I put this diary in the rock.

I awoke that morning to noises in the house, little noises, like rats. I opened my eyes to Germans around my bed, a ring of uniforms. Two held pistols that they were not bothering to point anywhere in particular. That same officer who came into the house those weeks before was standing at my foot, smiling.

My sheet, a blanket and soldiers' honour were the only things between me and these men.

I tried to be firm, insisting they leave, but how firm can one be lying in bed amidst guns, surrounded by men?

The officer talked over me, announcing we were to go into the city, if it wasn't too much trouble. Said with a smile that looked deep into my eyes.

There is a finality in a man's voice that is not often practised on women. It is a finality which is gentle. It is a finality that says a man will not be moved. It is a finality that cannot be negotiated, as a father might be when denying a child a charm he would love to give her, but does not have the money for. It is a regretful finality, a definite finality. This was the finality in this officer's voice.

Would this take long, I asked. My play was due to start at eight o'clock that night. I needed to do a costume fitting first.

Yes, he knew about the play, and about my acting. A stage production of the movie Rebecca was it not? Opening night? He said he was hoping to go. If we hurried, we might sort all this out and I may still get on stage.

In this way promises and assurances were made, and I believed them. This commander had the charming smile of a charming man. All would be well, I thought, not thinking of the fact that the request had been an order, made by intruders around my bed, with guns. Still, I had to believe.

He left two soldiers with me and went down the stairs. They watched me change because they could. I slipped a dress on under my night gown. How to play it? High heels would make me look more formidable, but too rich. Germans pay attention to those with power, but they also seemed to enjoy hurting them. I chose flat soles. No jewellery. A cane bag. Hair pulled back and held in place by a cheap comb.

I had been to the office building on Leoforos before, when I put in a passport application. It was the sort of building just right for passport rejections. It was a sad building, an edifice for Metaxas and worse. How we need Metaxas.

They pulled me up the stone steps quite roughly. There really was no need to do that. The escort wanted to make a display I think. Greeks on the street turned their heads down and away, knowing it all. Inside the doors, the guards let go and I was surrounded by five other soldiers who walked me to the elevator. As we went up, the captain seemed to amuse himself by watching the gaps at the top of the elevator door flicking past. He must have been only thirty or so, his jawline strong, his tanned skin closely shaved, his hair perfect. His jacket could have been new. I wondered what he did for a living outside war. Upper class. Too much self-pride to be a soldier. Too hard for an actor. Too neat and clever for a politician. A lawyer.

The captain pushed the metal grille over and made room for me to pass.

The second floor was grubby, yellow walled, the wooden floors greyed with age and neglect. It was the window at the end of the corridor, cracked and opaque with dirt that scared me. In some way it said that people suffered here.

Your father's voice came to me, scolding. You fool. Above your station. Too good for a fish shop. I take you to the safest country in the world into a business where you will never want, and you throw it away. Stupid woman. Beyond saving. Your choice. Go to hell.

A guard pushed me hard in the back for no reason.

Ellie and Mother Hadjidaki's voices scolded too. Head up girl. You can better these people. That time when I was five years old, when that man tried to steal me, dragging me into his little canvas shop. Stay there, he screamed at me. I stayed, quiet, until he came back with rope and tied my hands together. Mother Hadjidaki always said if that police officer hadn't been made suspicious by the man's rushing gait and his sweat, I could have been sent to the desert. Did I have a chance to escape, she asked. No, I answered, and learnt that the only ropes that bind are ropes of twine, not ropes of threat.

As the soldier pushed me again I saw what all this was. An attempt to rope the soul.

Again the captain held a door and let me pass. As soon as I was through, it was closed. A slam actually.

The room was small, maybe two yards by three, a new and quickly built room within a room, with thin ply walls that stopped short of the ceiling. They were badly put together, with gaps at the bottoms and corners, made by people who were not trying very hard. Greeks either patriotic or lazy. Two stiff-backed chairs and a small table took up all the space. On the table was an ashtray crammed with cigarette butts and ash which filled the room with a stale dead smell. People were talking in the next room in calm, everyday business voices.

My head had its own voices.

Find a character girl and find it in you.

Still my thoughts stayed on the danger, on what this really meant. I shuffled through the people who might have put me here. The flash? It wouldn't be enough surely. I could have been any Greek woman among millions. But if they had a photo. Could someone have been following me? Or someone from the village, going to the invaders with a story about the parade of English knocking on my door. The English, even dressed as Greeks, could not look like anything but English. Oh God, to have washed. My thighs were sticky. In this heat I worried I would smell soon. I had to think of a story, to tell as much truth as possible. Say anything so I would not be tortured. I knew my torture would kill many good people.

Find a character girl.

My door was flung open, banging into the side of my chair.

Guten tag. Wie gehts? A man came around the chair quickly and leaned on the arms, trapping me beneath his sour breath and piercing blue eyes.

He came close. Wie Gehts. Did I not hear him?

His breath was worse than sour. His Greek was smooth. So smooth I almost apologised. No sir, I mean, yes sir. My name is Olga Mavromati.

He backed up to his full height.

Didn't I speak German, he asked me in Greek, as if surprised.

No sir, I said. Maybe a few words I hear on the streets, or read on your posters. But that is all. I will learn more, sir, I promise.

I dared not break away from his eyes. He said his name was Herr Stern, and asked if I worked for the Americans.

Yes sir, I said. I am the housekeeper for the embassy secretary, William Demerest. He is the only contact I have with the embassy.

He put his hands back on the chair's arms and asked me why I called him a 'contact'. He asked if I had any other 'contacts'…

A bad mistake. No, I could not let myself think it was. I would have to be careful with every word. This man was an experienced interrogator. An actor with a sharp eye.

I pulled a voice of a maid servant being wrongly chastised.

It is an American term, sir. They are always talking about making a contact to buy shopping from, or a U.S. citizen is called a contact. I suppose I have picked up another of their stupid habits.

What were you doing last night? 'Schnell, schnell'.

I almost stammered some quick reply, then saw the trap.

I do not understand. I do not know a Mr. Shell.

He sat and leaned back, looking away for the first time. He asked if I went out the night before. He asked it looking like he didn't care whether I had or not.

I tried to look flustered, confused.

No, I went nowhere, except maybe when I needed some herbs. I went down the road to get some from a market garden that a friend has. She does not mind me taking some things. I help her with her washing sometimes. So really, it is not stealing. Is that what this is about? I am sorry, but really I am allowed to do it. Did she lay a complaint against me?

He left the room, and I heard him whispering to another man just on the other side of the petition in fast German. I know the language well, but they were going so fast, it was difficult to keep up.

Either she's very smart or a fool, this voice said.

She's a fool, look at her, said the other man.

A third voice was louder, telling my man he'd better be sure, because there were a few things that pointed to me. He said to throw me something.

My man sounded exasperated, and asked what, how, why bother?

Trap her, the other voice said. Use that professorial head. Get her to say something only a resistance member would know.

I have it, said my man, my professor. When she was at the docks a few weeks ago with those two men. If she denies being there, we have her.

It was agreed. My professor came back, looking ferocious again. He pulled his chair close, so his knees were touching mine. He put his hands on my thighs, not hard. Just enough.

I have a question for you.

Yes sir, then can I go? I need to get to the theatre.

On the night of May eighteen this year. It was a Sunday... just a few weeks ago. Where were you?

I stammered deliberately, as an innocent woman might.

I do not know... how many weeks... what is the date now... oh, two weeks... I don't know. Last week I was at the market in Athens... two weeks... Sunday... I think... Yes. I went to Piraeus in the evening. I had to meet some people for the ambassador. Just to give them some papers. Their boat had been held up, so they could not come to Athens. I was stuck in a smelly café for hours. I was really scared, not of the Germans, I do not mean the Germans, I mean... I was just... scared.

The professor waved that he was not offended.

I said I told the ambassador I would not do it again. I could have been late, and broke the curfew. Is that what this is about. I am so sorry. I will not break curfew again. Please...

Forget the curfew, he said. Go on.

Thank God for that, I almost cried out. I am sorry I should not use the Lord's name in vain. I understand you Germans are very Christian.

I made a Greek cross across my body.

What was in that package you give these men?

I am not allowed to know... some papers. It was soft. The people, they pulled the papers out. I saw the back of them. Official stamps on them, Greek and U.S. Oh yes, they signed one of them and gave it back to me. I gave it back to Mr. Demerest. Should I be telling you this? I might lose my job. Please, please do not tell anyone I told you all this. I will never get another…

He was already standing, and at the door. There were muffled voices from the corridor. When the door opened again, my professor was in the doorway, looking more than ever like the lawyer, not looking at me, chewing something. He motioned with his thumb for me to get out of the room.

I walked to the stairs, my head spinning. I gripped the handrail and started down, my knees not able to take the weight, and only doing so because I forced them.

Then hands came under my arms. I turned to thank my rescuers and to say that this really was not necessary, when I was pulled back up. I stumbled along with two uniformed men towards the elevator. We got in, me not looking at them, them not looking at me. The elevator started down, but instead of stopping at the ground floor, it continued to the basement, crashing to a stop in blackness. One soldier pulled the grate to the side and flicked a very loud switch. There was a corridor identical to the one two storeys up, but instead of walls on each side of the corridor, there were rows of paint-peeling columns. It was like a sewer in a way, the floor littered with papers, boxes and crushed piles of old carpet. Stains on the floor. Deep, long drips. No windows.

They shoved me in this mess, gently. And I was alone.

I stared at the button for the elevator. You think you learn a lesson. You think that you never make a mistake more than once. For a long time, perhaps hours, I stood before that button. The old Egyptian with the rope. I was not tied.

As with diving in a freezing lake I was determined to do it, and my arm would not come up, my leg would not move. Ellie and Mother Hadjidaki would not be proud of me being no better than a bewitched moth before light. Ellie, smiling as she is shoved into a car, never to be seen again. Mother Hadjidaki, not allowing herself a tear for my forever departure. Brave women, honourable women.

My arm unlocked and with an ease that surprised, I put my finger on the button and was about to push when the siren of the elevator jolted me making me fall over. The cage rattled down to me, and when the grille was pulled aside, my professor came out.

Through the light of the lift his silhouette said some fine Greek policemen would be sent down to take me to another place. Goodbye.

He went back into the lift, but stopped before he pressed the button.

He said in German that he knew I didn't want to go to a rat hole. So now was the time. Was there anything I wanted to tell him? I would be rewarded very well. I could live out this war in luxury.

I looked at him as if I could not understand, and he sniggered as if he expected no more from me, and pressed his button.

I saw then another figure was standing in the back of the elevator, covered by the shadows of the guards. Even through the bars, the dark and the guards, I made out the figure of womanly hips and a large bust I thought I knew.

The elevator started up again with the professor and the figure of a woman still inside, leaving the basement as cold and black as before.

The elevator came straight back down again for me. I was marched into it by two young men in uniform. One used his elbow to push me where he wanted me to go, the other put his palm under my elbow.

We went to the ground floor and out the back of the building, through a small grey lane to an old open-back vegetable truck already filled with women. The guards put a box behind it, and I stepped up in amongst them. The guards did not bolt the back properly, they just shoved a loose rod into a half screwed clip. They did not bother coming with us; they didn't even give us the honour of a guard.

Again I could have escaped. I could have jumped off this truck and run into the crowd and they would never have found me. Could I excuse myself that the truck was going too fast? No, because it wasn't. I just didn't jump. I stayed on the truck with all these women who also didn't jump. There's a silly hope prisoners have, that if they do what they're told, things will work out. We hope, despite all that has been done to us, that the invaders are in essence good people. If we act sensibly and maturely, so will they. We were yet to know that in times of war such mores mean nothing.

A squat woman, dressed in something like home-made army fatigues, came to the middle and said there wasn't much time. Had anyone told them anything about the Piraeus line? Quickly.

A young fat dark girl jerked her hand forward, saying no, she said nothing to them.

The fatigued woman studied the teenager. She asked the girl if she had worked on that line recently.

I threw myself on the floor between them, clutching my groin, screaming that they had made me bleed.

The other women, including the teenager, gathered around me. I grabbed her long plaits, pulled her down to my face, and whispered that she must say no more. The woman in fatigues was a German spy.

I let the girl go, and screamed out to God to kill me now.

The rough truck jolted, bringing a collective 'oh' from the sea of concern above me. Women, probably with sons, husbands, and perhaps daughters fighting in the resistance, were glad of someone to look after. But it would have been wrong for me to continue my deception.

I said I was better. God had taken the worst of the pain. I took my place as one of them again. The teenager said no more. The women in fatigues asked no more.

As the truck moved through the city, street people looked at us. An occasional man, seeing that women had been arrested, had to be pulled back by companions from doing some brave stupidity. Others crossed themselves, or dared not look. Some spat at us.

The truck stopped in front of Averoff prison.

A row of guards came to the back of the truck. Out here please. A shocking politeness.

The woman in fatigues was not with the group. I wished I had killed her in the way the British showed me. Suffocate so that it looked like a heart attack. Now that silly teenage girl will die in her place, along with anybody in her group that she talks about under torture. She's a child. She will talk. The third lost chance added to my shame.

I held the girl next to me as the group was led through the huge edifice. There were a few Greek police officers sitting behind the counter, their faces deliberately blank.

A Greek woman was used for the stripping of us, and she did her job with no sympathy, wrenching off rings, hurting joints, trying to impress the German supervisor, who neither saw her diligence nor cared. Stockings, watch, everything of value was taken. These bits of a life were thrown rattling in a chrome dish like it was rubbish. A guard then pushed me barefoot towards some stairs.

At the bottom of two flights was a corridor, brightly lit and of cold concrete.

The guard banged on a door, a hatch opened and the door rolled to one side, opening on near darkness. A clang, and the door was behind me. New guards took my armpits and pulled me down yet another walkway.

The smell was like old carnations and the sweet damp of unwashed people. I tried not to hold my breath. Take it in, I said to myself, accept it. Easier said.

At some point a light was flicked on and I could see. On the left were small barred units, cells, separated by concrete walls a foot thick. On the right was a rough stone wall. A groan from somewhere, a groan of despair not injury. A woman stood at the bars of a cell, her face red and hands white. There were women on beds, others lying on floors, one to a cell. All squinting, shading eyes, trying to see.

I was stopped at the end of the row. The guard fumbled with his keys, cursing as the door failed to respond to each one. My hope, the hope of the condemned, lifted with each wrong key. The guard might say to forget it. What was one woman worth? Let her go if she would promise not to get into any more trouble. Just be a governess, a housekeeper. Yes, I would have promised anything at that moment, and kept that promise.

Of course the door gave way, giving out a cloud of rusty decay. But the guard didn't force me in. He stood to one side and I walked into my cage.

There was quiet in the corridor then, no groaning, no calls for freedom.

This was the welcoming silence to a sister. I later understood that all the women knew what I was thinking, because all newcomers think the same things. It takes weeks to know the hopelessness. They knew that. They had been through it.

The cell was small, no more than two yards square. The bed, a wooden slab with nothing on it. Two buckets, both half-filled with water, one perhaps for toilet, the other for drinking, but it was a guess which was which. A very small table of old wood, that even in the dark I could tell had gone to grey.

Another guard came up without noise and pushed a blanket through the opening, a corner dropping and soaking into a bucket. Here prisoner, he said. And was gone. Prisoner. I was not a prisoner. I had to get to the theatre. Demerest was going to the performance. He was expecting me to play Mrs Danvers.

As the bars were closed on my face, I am shamed to say my thoughts were not for you my darling girl. My thoughts were only for one living creature.

My cat. She needs to be fed. I said it to no-one, as the light was turned out on me. Entirely dark it wasn't, for after my eyes got used to the shock of the black I started to see again. A single dim light was still on, a single globe down the corridor.

My tight fists pressed my nails into my palms until they bent back, one, two. I opened my hands and felt my ruined bent short nails. Another thing damaged.

Help me, please. There has been a mistake, I called to obviously no-one.

But it was to someone. From through the walls and up the long corridor a hopeless, lacklustre chorus sang a hymn. It was for me.

I sat on the stiff blanket. It smelled of cat's piss.

Pyrmont, Sydney

Nicky's hands are working so fast that Tina can't read them. She calls out to Freda. She's faster with the signs.

Alive? How do you know?

He doesn't know. Mother is alive, that's all.

Freda says everyone knows she has to be dead. Daddy has married Jean. Of course she's dead.

Don't say she's dead, Tina screams.

Nicky signals no, he'd know if she was dead.

They all let out a breath, even Jean, who has every reason to want Olga never to return.

That night Jean lies in the big bed listening to Michael and baby Jimmy breathe. They look the same, the little round month-old face and the big round haggard face. She wants to tell Michael about Nicky's vision. Michael believes in them. But he'd worry about everything, and when he worries he gets so old.

Jimmy sputters a cough. Michael's arm is across him. Jean lifts it and kisses the hand and lays it on the pillow. She feeds the baby there in the bed, in the darkness. Jimmy finishes and goes to sleep as if he'd never woken.

The touch of her baby and her own motherness decides her. She will tell Michael about Nicky's vision. He has to know.

Olga

I woke shocked at realising where I was. I wished the sleep would bring me a different morning. But this was the only morning I could have.

A woman called and pounded from the other side of the stone wall. She knew of a newcomer's need for noise. All the prisoners took turns to keep up a chain of noises: shuffles, whistles, rhythms, songs, all gentle, motherly, sisterly, kindly; stopping only when the guards came down the corridors.

In Averoff we didn't know time because there was no morning or night, no clock, no windows. Food here was just food, not breakfasts nor dinners. The days were for lying and wasting. I lay with the wall pressing and scratching the side of my arm. Without realising, I had started picking softly at the render. I stopped it. They would be here to release me soon, and a damaged wall might upset them.

I saw a small white box inside my bars. It had not been there when I went to sleep.

It had little things. Some dolmades wrapped in thin paper. A bar of soap. A little cloth. Two paper packets of tablets. One had water purifiers, the other a single red capsule. A note.

I went to the bars to try to read it. It was in tough code from someone saying they were a friend. I was not alone in there, it said. They would get me out. Germans in my house. If there was anything incriminating, be ready to give an answer for it. Trust no guards, Greek or German, and be careful choosing friends among the other prisoners. Keep the box hidden. All the wrappings can be eaten. The red tablet a last resort. Keep it close by. If they take you down another level, be ready to use it. Once you bite, you are gone.

Then a line, written for the stupids:

'Do not store it in your mouth.'

The note ended with the worst of all…

'There will be no more communication with you.'

I pushed the dolmades under the blanket, against the cell wall, but the smell was already coming through. There was nowhere else to hide them, so I ate the seven. No, five. I passed two around the bars to the woman in the next cell.

I broke a water tablet and dropped a bit into the full bucket and waited for the fizz to end before scooping up the water with my fingers. The rest of the tablets I crammed into the support under the bed. The cardboard from the box I flattened for extra warmth under the blanket. Sleep came again quickly.

Darwin, Australia

The wedding is loud in the Kafcaloudes way. There are a lot of people: family, business associates, aboriginal friends, the workers. They all came because everyone wants to be there to be part of the hitching of the Kafcaloudes boy to Nellie from the café, Mick Parrelis' niece. Michael came up for the wedding and treats his new in-laws like unfamiliar family. Love is for people you love. He respects them as good workers, if just a little too tough. He still feels a little like Nellie has short-changed herself

Steve is admired by all, and Nell is like a bride should be, a little overwhelmed, a little hidden. For Steve, it is the happiest of days, he has collected his wife and everyone is looking at him.

The Greek Orthodox Archbishop surprised everyone when he turned up from Sydney to do the wedding himself. All suspicion for this happy turn falls to Mick Parrelis, who had nothing to do with it, but does nothing to stop people thinking it was his idea. The families have their

Greek wedding, the Church of England organ blending somehow with the quarter-tone singing of the priest.

Afterwards, Michael is waiting by the cakes at the trestle table to see his new son-in-law. Like a caesar, Stephen strides through his crowd of admirers to grant time to the old man who is standing so restlessly by himself.

Michael hopes Steve will say something to relieve him. It doesn't come. Michael begins to speak, unsure, when the Archbishop comes between them. He doesn't shake hands with Michael, he'd already done that in the church. It is Steve he has words for.

I have known Nellie since she was a little girl, he says. If you do not treat her right, I promise you, on these robes, that you will answer to me. Do you understand?

Yes, of course: a little taken aback, and a little frightened. I will treat her like she's a princess...

The Archbishop doesn't stay for the assurances. He has said his piece. He's said it for Michael too. Michael puts his arm around Steve and they go to have a beer together.

The new Mr. and Mrs. Kafcaloudes moved into the top floor of a house just outside the centre of Darwin, one built by Steve's father, quite a man in these parts.

After a suitable couple of days, Jean brought the family to visit. They found a home that said nothing of Nell. There were the wedding presents, the good tablecloth, the awful pitcher someone had given them.

Nellie played the hostess to her former family, trying to be happy for their sakes, making the tea, putting their sponge cake on one of the new plates and laying a shiny knife next to it. Even the starving Tina held down her hands in a way she never did with her sisters. After they left, Nellie put the rest of the cake in the meat safe. She had no hunger, just a regret that she couldn't talk to those closest to her. She had to remember she was married now. There were things between a husband and wife. She washed the cups, taking off the lipstick and tannin.

Olga

If there is one true torture, it is to give a human being nothing to do. There were never beatings. There were never sex things from the guards. Never interrogations. They just left us, and that was by far the worst of all.

We had one good thing in that prison. The trough, a long concrete sink in the half dark, within the smell of the cells. We were let out to wash in its cold water, without any soap. But we loved it. I loved it. We could rub against each other or touch a hand, just to feel another human being. The more decent of the Greek guards left us to wash in privacy. This was when there could be talk about what was happening on the surface. The war, relatives, the government, who would be released next. There were never visitors, so how this information came, I never knew, but new prisoners confirmed that the most important of it was reliable.

The Greek prison guards were much kinder to us than it was safe for them to be. An occasional piece of fruit, or women's pads would be pushed through the bars. One afternoon at the trough, after I had said I missed writing in my diary, one of the women, a tough grandmother whose name I would not come to know, whispered something to a guard. He left, and came back with a child's exercise notebook, and pencils. The grandmother took the books from him without thanks and gave them to me.

For all my dreams of having paper and pencil, I couldn't write anything. I had become used to thinking my thoughts, writing in my head. I had learnt to be satisfied with a thought, edited in mind, with a conclusion reached in silence. I couldn't write anything. This child's book became an intruder in my cell, a demand that my thoughts be written out, to be marked forever on paper so they could never be forgotten.

I did pick up my pencil after some weeks, after another of the many nightmares. The director of a play was ignoring me; other actors not caring for my dilemma. In the audience you were all there. You, Freda, Nicky and Tina, who was scowling. My Nicky was clapping me for the lines that he couldn't hear. The only one clapping me in that audience of children.

I wrote.

My Nellie.

In this cell I ponder who I am.

The Greeks think I am British. The British think I'm Australian. Australians never accepted me, even the Australian Greeks. They called me 'theaterina' behind my back, and thought I never knew. Theaterina means actress, but the way they meant it was a sorry use of the word. Whore. Prostitute they meant. By calling me this they were telling me I was not one of them. I was more Greek in Alexandria, where Greeks were refugees or fugitives. We banded together. We were proud. Australian women are much too proud. They mock your difference. Not to your face. Never to your face. Here in this Hamlet's dungeon I have the love of more women than I ever had in Australia. But what does that make me? Australian? British? Greek? A woman who doesn't know what she is?

This last one, I think.

It was late October, as best as I could figure. Nearly six months after I was first put in the hole. On this day the trough talk said the Germans had found one of the lines. They had traced it back to the headquarters. They got ten people, all men. Shot them. No trial of course. I couldn't tell who among the little splashing flock had spoken because of the dark.

Someone else said the Germans were now doing everything in public. They didn't do it like the Russians, in some room in a farm. These Germans make it a show. Another said people were starving on top. The winter cold had killed most of the farms, and the Germans took the rest.

Cold. When I had come down here it was stinking hot. Now it was cold on top. Two seasons lost.

Mothers and children starved on the top, yet we prisoners, we the outcasts, we criminals were given our food every day in this topsy turvy new society of the Third Reich.

We didn't usually dare mention the resistance. On this day at the trough though, someone said the resistance was being more organised, making it a proper resistance, called something show-off, the Front of Liberation or something.

EAM, another said. Just remember EAM. That's what everyone calls it.

Communists, said another.

At least that's better than the dictatorship, said a fourth.

We were making noise now, and the guards came in. It would be days before another trough.

As we broke up someone whispered to me that I would be released. Sometime in the next week.

I went back to my cell trying not to be excited. My dim grey little home of the past six months was a little more lively than when I arrived. I had hung up the bright clothes and cloths that came in the Red Cross packages. The Germans had opened them, taken the food, and left in the Red Cross list of the box's contents, so we could read about the delicacies we had come so close to receiving, tins of beans, nuts and chocolate that not even the Geneva Convention could deliver to us.

I fidgeted with my things in the dimness, straightening, dusting with my palm, preparing them for a new companion. For I would leave everything. The two oversize shirts, and the women's magazines that it was too dark to read. I stacked them neatly against the wall, and lined the buckets up to the bars. I realigned these rusty things until they were perfect, and held to my ablutions all night. I wanted this cell to be perfect for the moment when the guard came down and ruefully gave me back my life.

He didn't come.

Day after day I would feel the closeness of my new freedom. By sleeping time I would fear the lie. There was no sleep on these nights, not until an hour or so before the time I was due to get up for the accounting, when we would have to stand and be checked through the bars by the guards. This of course was for no purpose, since there could be no escape. At least it gave us a routine, a marker for each day.

Days, maybe weeks later I was woken in the middle of the night, and all drowsy, I was taken to the concrete stairs. I had the sense to grab my red pill. To go down: to die. Red pill. To go up, to live.

We went upwards, the German guard even smiled that I was being let out.

I had left the cell a mess. I asked to go back and clean it up, and the guard stared at the stupid woman who wanted to go back to hell.

There were no possessions for me in the possession room, and I did not care enough to argue about the missing brooch, the christening cross or the handbag.

In thirty seconds I was facing the big door which had flashes of daylight coming through the spaces at the bottom and sides. It was daytime, and downstairs they were thinking it was night. A Greek guard moved me to one side, slammed back the huge bolt and pulled against the might of the iron to open it to a blinding light. I almost called for it to be turned down, this first daylight I had seen for six months. Then I was alone, the door behind me slamming on the prison, the cell, the trough, the kindnesses. I had to shade my eyes. The street in front of the prison was empty.

I walked, flinging the red pill away.

I had ten minutes of joy. My country was occupied, I had been betrayed, I had no money, I had lost six months of my life, but for ten minutes in the sun and the air, learning to walk again, I felt such a joy. I saw every gate, every crack in the pavements of Alexandrias and Ippokratous, every tree with its bare branches high on Lykavittos hill, and I smiled at every dour face and took no offence at their scowls. Even the cramps in my leg couldn't cramp my spirit in those ten minutes.

Ten minutes. Ten minutes brought me to where guards stood useless on every corner over beggars on pavements, and families making homes of cardboard and tatty suitcases. I floated through the people, my tight legs stepping over tawdry possessions. Nothing was clean, everyone had given up. I saw, after my ten minutes, an ancient city dying.

Can I begin to describe what was there? I only have words, and they are not enough to tell you of this horror.

An old woman was lying up against a wall unconscious, her long dress rucked up, showing the loose skin on the front of her thighs. Nobody was helping her, not even a woman had tried to protect her modesty, so I went to her, and saw what Greece has become. Her emaciated face had the alabaster translucency of death, maybe some days' death. This woman is dead, I called out to anyone. But the beggars and the mothers looked at me like I was the strange one. I was the only one who had not seen this before, the only one to whom death was sacred. There was nothing to do. I pulled her dress down and left.

I had heard about frightened horses showing the whites of their eyes, but here I saw it in women. Mothers. One dashed across the road in front of me, her hands cupped, looking like a child who has found a hurt bird. I saw enough of it to see it was a bird, but it was dead, a stiff thing that was now a meal.

It is a strange thing to see children not playing. They were beyond teasing and fighting and games of domination. They were languishing, roll-eyed, craw-hands out to anyone who passed them, even other starvelings. I had nothing to give them. No coin, certainly no food. I cradled one, no more than six or seven, who struggled weakly against me. I was blocking his begging.

It was like this all the way to Athens. Their weakness gave me the strength to walk. At one little patch of green, some kind soul had crumbled bread for the pigeons, this bounty unseen by the starving. I gathered it and gave it to the nearest child who was too weak to eat it, a child beyond saving.

The Athens shops too were ghosts. Again and again empty. Uniform windows like frames of a black film. G. Cassimadis, Chemist, stencilled with pride across the top of an empty double shop. I wondered where G. Cassimadis was on this day. Was he one of the dead or dying? Was that his wife with the bird?

It was in the reflection of G. Cassimadis' window that I saw the white haired woman standing next to me. I turned, but the white haired woman was gone. In the next fruitless shop the woman was back. This time I caught my own image turning to see the white haired woman. There was no other woman. This was me. I pulled at a curly lock, but couldn't see.

I stopped the boy who was running past, and asked him to tell me the colour of my hair. He just looked strangely at me and ran off.

White, he called when he was safe distance. White, old woman.

I wandered on, every window showing my hair's whiteness, me an old woman at 36. No, I was 37. I had forgotten. My birthday had passed down in the cell.

Pendeli. My home was the only place I could go, the only place I knew anymore. There was nothing for it but to start the long walk home. The further I went, the shorter the walk seemed. My feet were not able to keep up with me, and the loose shoes I was wearing were not mine, just two the guards had taken from a pile.

My feet were bleeding when I went into my gate that night, my hand almost reaching for the drink I left in the icebox nearly six months before.

There was someone in the doorway. A German guard with a child's voice.

Who do you wish to see...

I went on past him through the door, and across the room with the sofa, the officers on it paid me no mind. The kitchen's stove was lit. A Greek woman was bent over a pot of boiling water.

She pushed me out of the way and barked. What are you doing in my kitchen. I have food to prepare.

This was my kitchen, I said, and to prove it I picked up her cup of coffee and drank.

Artemis, she said with a small smile to the corner of her mouth that was gone just as fast. She pulled me away from the door, always looking through to the lounge.

They released me, I said.

Her eyes searched mine, suspicious. A rightful suspicion. Only spies and turncoats were released.

Come back tonight, she said eventually. Two houses down that way. Eight o'clock. She would get me to friends.

She stopped me going back out the front door. It was my house, I argued as she forced me out the back. She replied that it didn't do to try the devil twice.

Rena held my hair in each hand and cried for my ageing. Change had been wrought on her too. Her healthy plumpness was gone and her eyes were widow black.

The stew she made was plucked from the remnants of a garden that had been plucked too much. Seeded horta and parsley and blackened tomato she magically made tasty.

It was here I learned what had happened to my Greece. It had started a month after they caught me. The underground started a push, ambushing Germans, blowing up bridges, attacking convoys. This brought retributions. The Germans shot menfolk in the little villages. Ten Greeks for every German. Sometimes to make up the numbers, even the old were killed. They killed also by taking food as revenge, leaving nothing for Greeks. It made Greek betray Greek. Sister betray sister.

The thought that I spent six months under the ground because someone feared missing a meal was more than I wanted to know. If you start to think about the Judas at your shoulder, then there could be no room left for life.

I had just been sloppy, I said and cried suddenly. Rena and Antigone touched my hair, arm, shoulder, breast and back, and cried too, rocking me on the flimsy little chair, this clump of womanhood.

You see, daughter, I never cried in jail.

Each morning after that I would kiss them goodbye and go to see Pendeli. I would walk past the house and the trucks, and sit on the little hillock at the end of the road and look out on Athens. Then I would walk back again past my home, rubbing my hand along the old stone wall. Just feeling it made it mine again. Rena would scold about my stupidity in going there, but the dear heart always gave me the bus fare.

Until the day there were no army trucks and no guard at Pendeli.

The front door was open a little. I pushed it, and there was nothing. No people, no furniture, no paintings, only faint squares on the wallpaper. They had taken my womanhood in Syntagma, my youth in Averoff, now the soul of my home.

In the kitchen I picked up one of the rags off the floor and started to wipe down the dirty, smelly sink. It stunk of something like piss, but I couldn't let myself think on it. Of course there was no food, and not even newspaper for toilet. My bedroom still had a bed, and there were sheets, in scrunched piles on the floor. I picked up one. It smelt of men and sex. My wardrobe was there too, open and empty. It had no dresses, no coat that your father had given me those years ago, and no shoes, just a broken heel blocking the robe door. It was red, a maroon red. I tried to remember the shoe.

I laid on the floor in the living room where the sofa used to be and looked up at the rosette on the ceiling. Yes, there was the same rosette and the same pretty cornices.

Hello said a voice, young, frightened.

A child in the doorway, a black-eyed girl. With a basket.

My mother told me to give you this. We live across the road. She said to tell you welcome back.

The sound of her floppy feet slapped back down the garden path.

A gift of fruit, a sliver of cheese, and bread. I fingered through it, and was overcome by the kindness. Life-giving kindness.

I feasted alone in a homecoming, savouring the safety of the food. The food closed the 'dead ground' the British instructor told me about. If you look across a valley to a hill, and can't see the ground between you, the dead ground, then the distant hill will seem closer. This food was like that. It made me remember the last time I ate here, and while I ate I forgot the prison. I decided to bathe like the last night I was here, the night before they took me. I just wanted to keep that ground closed.

There was barely wood for the water boiler, just some old palings, twigs scattered in the garden. Enough.

The water stung as I lowered myself. My belly was so white and loose, my knees so round, my arms though were tight, still the royal skin, as your father would call it. Pale and without blemish. The night was quiet like the eye of a storm. Not even wind could make a noise tonight. There was just water and me. My head was under the water and the heat seemed to be gone. I could hold my breath for a long time, and tonight I held it until my head swirled. It would be such a peaceful passing. I would sleep and the water would fill me and I could leave all this. A fine end to a day. I could leave the Germans and my betrayer, my husband who cannot touch me, my sister who hates me. I would be just another of the dead. Would they not find me for three days like the old woman of alabaster, and when they did, would they not mourn? Would you mourn? Would you remember me?

I jumped out of the bath just as I did that night six months ago, dressed myself fast in the only clothes I had, the peasant's shirt and pants Rena had given me, and ran from the house. I felt nothing running up the road. My head was drunk yet I couldn't stop. Lowering myself down the cliff ledge, I had a panic that even this would be different, that there would be nothing for me.

I pulled at the rock and it slowly moved around enough so I could get my fingers into the hole. I had a charge of terror as my finger couldn't feel anything inside. Then I touched plastic.

The rings came on my fingers, a little looser than before.

My diary was as dry as if I had put it in yesterday. It had survived Averoff too.

I prayed there on the ledge for the first time in twenty years. I prayed for forgiveness and for love, I prayed thanks for all in my world, for my children and my house, for Rena and Antigone, for second chances, and for the stars in front of me, as they were six months ago.

It is dawn now, and the ground is closed. My story between baths has been told.

Pyrmont, Sydney

Jean puts little Jimmy into his cradle and slips into bed beside Michael. She does what she has never done. She wakes him. He jumps with a start, wanting to know where the fire is. No fire dear, she says, regretting already, I just thought you'd like to know that Nicky is sleeping sound. No jumping around, no noises. For the first time in half a year.

Something is right in the world, Michael says, as he drops to sleep again.

Mother Hadjidaki's Dance

(December 1941)

Olga

My Citroén Seven is gone. The bastards would have no use for her. She is so small and helpless, and they don't know about the oil problem. She will go dry and die.

But my cat came back this morning, still plump and unworried. And my olive seed has sprouted in its little patch. Their mark is all around it, heavy boot prints. One man, one tread and it would have been killed, yet the tiny sprig avoided them all and lived, just like my little olive bush in a few inches of earth behind the Ultimo shop. Michael said it had no chance, and it lived. This proves there is magic in this world of hate, enough to make you laugh.

I laid down with my sprout of broad leaves and looked at the sky. I was here again with my tree that waited for me.

Olga (two weeks later)

Stavros was my driver today, a corpse of Stavros, wearing clothes that hung loose, hair that was wild for its new thinness, and a body stink where the sweet warrior's smell used to be. Even his heavy moustache seemed to pull his face down.

He drove like an old man, slouched over the steering wheel, peering into the passing side streets. He stopped in the diplomatic zone and as we walked, his grip on my forearm was desperate tight.

We passed some Greek sentries outside one of the government buildings. Pressed uniforms, healthy, well fed. Lackeys for the Germans, conspirators in their home city.

Stavros tilted his head to the sentries, who gratefully smiled back.

I asked him loudly what he was smiling at them for. They helped our enemies, they were our enemies.

The words of the British ambassador pushed this out of me, that thing about Stavros having the wrong kind of politics. A small part of me suspected him, but didn't know what to suspect him of.

Stavros stammered they weren't all bad. They didn't shoot Greeks, and they carried out German orders slow enough to let the Greeks get away. He said he would rather it was a Greek on that corner than a German.

I looked back. They had already slouched back against the wall, their uniforms comfortable. Yes, they were Greeks. The times have changed so that I don't know who I should hate.

A bird-bony woman pulled on my skirt from the ground. She was nursing a baby. Even in the fading light I could see the baby's colour was wrong, grey and yellow. Its puffy legs stuck out from a tight wrapped blanket.

I knelt beside the woman and put my hand to the side of her face. The eyes were a little opaque, something I had never seen in a woman so young. Her weak claw hand gripped mine, capturing me.

I asked to look at her baby, I might be able to help. She pulled the bundle away quite viciously, almost setting me off balance. She held her package tightly and rocked and sang a discordant lullaby.

A man's voice said the child died three days ago.

It was an old man sitting against a wall, holding a smouldering miserable buttend of a cigarette. He said she had not eaten since, or slept. She begs for help and does not know what to do when people give her money, so the others take it from her, he said pointing to women, who I saw were looking at me with hope. The man said he tried to stop the thieves, but he could not be here all the time. The little mother cared nothing for herself, just her baby, and was terrified someone would take it. He said he would get the baby from her when she goes to sleep. Or dies.

Stavros was bending beside me now, telling me to come. We could not be late.

The man with the cigarette butt asked quite gently, as we started away, if I happened to have anything to eat, or a few coins for food for her. She was his daughter you see.

I watched them all again from the fifth floor of the hotel building. The young woman with her dead baby; her father; and further on and everywhere, the dying. Hundreds or thousands. In every street. In the squares and the parks. Lying alive and lifeless. And Germans walking through the debris. Italian soldiers were the only ones stopping and talking to the Athenians.

The Council members came in the room at short intervals. Blinds were pulled, and candles lit. It was a meeting different from those before I went to jail. The people were nervous and officious, suspicious and uncertain.

At the head of the board table was a striking woman. She was no beauty, but she had carriage. She eyed everyone in the room except the man next to her, the chairman, a man they all called Proteus. She had the menace of a bodyguard, never returning greetings, never allowing herself into small talk. Just those black eyes going around the room.

When she looked at me, I stared back, pretending to feel no anxiousness, determined not to break away from her accusing eyes.

She was the one who moved her eyes first. I thought I saw a tiny wink on the serious face before it looked to the next man along. It had been no competition for her, just duty.

Her name was Nikotsara. They had talked about her in prison. She was supposed to have run a thousand missions, saved a thousand Greeks and killed a thousand Germans. Just on her advice a person would be killed, or so they said in the jail.

This Proteus rapped his knuckles on the table, and attention was his. He was as impressive as the woman, with his wide face, dimpled and unshaved, cheeks lined with angry strong scars that somehow did not look at all ugly, and tattoos on broad forearms. He must have been more than fifty, and looked more powerful than any man I had ever seen. He was a maverick uncle, some family's seafaring dark horse, the kind who will laugh when his nieces and nephews are mischievous, and slap them hard when they are bad.

This strong pair talked of sloppy work in the lines. People at the table gave excuses, which were returned with scoldings and glances of warning.

When Proteus finally stood, the rest of the table stood too, but he motioned to Stavros and me to sit again.

Nikotsara stayed by his side while everyone else left.

Proteus offered his hand and a smile. I saw in this transformation why he had been given this codename. He truly was like his namesake god, a being of many appearances.

He called me Mrs. Mavromati, and then apologised immediately for doing it. (I recognised his old technique. Show that you know a person's intimate details to put them at ease with you.) Nikotsara smiled a smile of teeth and shining eyes. She was a different person to the one who had scared everyone for the last two hours. She took my hand from across the table and held it in a dry tight grip, just as a man would do it. Proteus put his hand on my other one, so I was held, kindly, but held. For a moment it seemed they cared, but nothing was asked of my time in jail, no sympathy, no consolation. Just business. As it should be.

They said they needed someone to use the black market, to make new contacts, to buy from anyone and to sell to anyone, so long as there was a profit to buy bullets and bread.

That was not what I wanted to do. The meeting had excited me about helping again. Black market work was ordinary work, a trading of life for rice and fish.

Then I remembered the starvelings. Of course. Food was the new commodity. The Germans used it to break this country. We could use it to break the Germans.

Stavros said nothing, neutered in this company. A list of black market sellers and buyers appeared on the table in front of me. I was given ten minutes to remember the names and places. The sheet was never to leave that table.

After I had done it, they rose and announced it was now time to have some fun. The four of us went like two couples on a night out. Proteus and Nikotsara with their loudness and laughs washing off my hesitations. I soon laughed too, and took Stavros' hand. I was gay, gay as we left the building, gay as we passed Germans. Gay as we passed starvelings. We were for a moment way above the life we were in. In the worst of times anything is possible.

The people at the trolley-bus stop must have been queuing for a long time, the line was so long. When Nikotsara and Proteus came through, the head of the queue made way to let us get the first seats before the crush for the rest. After ten minutes or so the bus let us off at a road I had never seen before, a road empty of invaders and full of loudening music and voices of abandon. In a courtyard, the shouts of men came from around a home-built roulette table. They were all laughing, the winners and the losers. The women must have been their wives, the way they dressed in frumpy clothes over their ordinary bodies. These wives laughed too. It was the game that mattered, not the money.

Others were talking or eating. Some sat, arms around each other, enjoying watching.

A man danced alone in the middle, hopping and jumping, slapping his heel to the music of two earnest-faced bouzouki players. When the music stopped the dancer flipped himself over in a triumphal finish, his arms open in a demand for applause.

After him came a woman with a ribbon. Large she was, large, tall and her fat made her all the more sensual, for there were few fat people in Athens. We admired her for keeping her womanhood, for still being as our mothers were in the good times. In the quiet of adulation, her dance started. It was a dance of feet moving back and forth slowly, and as it quickened, her big breasts swayed with her wide hips. There was lust in that courtyard, the most natural of all, lust for a barefoot woman with rough feet and hands raised in ecstasy. Enjoying a woman being a woman.

A man yelped and joined her, taking hold of the loose end of the ribbon. He aped her steps, and for a minute they circled the little dance space, slowly. More people joined them, arms on shoulders, hands holding hands. People yelled, people overarched and fell and flipped back to overarch once again.

I was grabbed by a man with a smile bigger than his face, and I was on the end, dancing for the first time since Sydney, since the Greek Club.

The song stopped, and I held onto his hand, wanting to go on with it. The music started again, and the big woman offered me the lead.

I began a move to the left in a start to a simple dance, side step side, close. Then back again, close. My feet were gliding like I didn't have to think. The others were following my movements, watching my feet, learning how to do Mother Hadjidaki's dance. The music quickened. I pulled the line around the courtyard so fast that hands were torn from hands and shoulders, but they always seemed to find each other again and the line moved faster. People were laughing. There was a lot of laughing.

When the players stopped, they put their instruments down, pretending not to hear the crowd's compliments. They went to the big table on the side of the courtyard, where a group of women had been laying food. Someone yelled out that it was impossible to stop musicians playing except when food was served, and everybody laughed again.

The host, the man with the big smile, asked if I was enjoying myself.

I said it had been a long time since I had seen so many smiles in Athens.

He shrugged. People need to laugh, he said. Especially people who could be dead tomorrow. If the Germans raided this party, they would have the backbone of the Athens branch of EAM. He broke off to yell at a child to stop throwing the okra.

Stavros was there amongst it, drinking Ouzos with Proteus, and all handsome again, as he was when he was the man I kissed. There was something in the way he never looked at me, he may have been repulsed by my white hair or the times. He just never looked at me as he once did.

It finished when the people sucked the party dry, determined to live before they had to go back to the Athens where people were dying.

Darwin, Australia

Nell is proud of the painting, though it is really just a print of a painting. Not that anyone would believe it is a real Van Gogh, or is it a Renoir, because the signature is mostly cut off. She found it leaning against a wall in the old junk shop in Cavenagh Street, covered in dust, with an old Chevrolet radiator propped against it.

It will, of course, have to be left behind. It's just too big. One suitcase. That was all they'd let her have. One case per person. One case for everything in a life.

Knock, knock. A funny pattern. Jean's pattern. Da da la la la. la LA.

Jean and Tina have been up from Sydney visiting Nell for a few weeks, and they've been caught up in the evacuation too. Nell is glad they're here.

Jean scoops five teaspoons of tea into the pot. She always makes it too strong.

I know it must be hard to leave your husband, she says. You know it won't be for long though, dear. It's just not safe. If the Japanese do come over... well you know. Your home will still be here.

Yes, Nell says. The baby needs a home.

Baby. Jean yelps and runs around the table to squeeze her.

Nell says she thinks it's a baby. She's way overdue, but hasn't gone to a doctor yet. She isn't really sure.

I'm happy for you, love. Someone for Jimmy to play with eh?

The home is why Nell wants to stay, heat and all. A baby needs a home and two parents. Like it never was for her. But of course she will leave Darwin along with all the other women and children and old people. This is another home that just isn't possible. In three days they will all be on a boat back south.

A Dark Kingdom of Boxes

(December 1941)

Olga

Today was my first trade and it almost killed me. Twice it almost killed me.

I had gone to an ordinary house, a square squat home of plaster and old wood. A woman who was obscenely fat for these times led me through a room where other women were stitching and sewing. The fat woman pulled aside a curtain to a passage that ended at a white stone wall. She banged a ditty on it. The wall moved and I was in a dark kingdom of boxes, with a short man in grandfather's sandals moving between them.

He read my list like an imbecile, as if my clear handwriting was impossible to work out. Cigarettes, he read out. Yes, but only Turkish. Sugar. Very expensive. Dried figs. Yes. Dark blue shirts. We are making some now. Not ready yet. Maybe another week. No, don't look like that. I know you can't get them anywhere else, so don't play the tragic character with me. Just get your money ready. Flour. Hmmm. There is another buyer wanting all my flour. He wants to pay top price. You will have to beat him. Dried

250

fish. Hard to get. The Germans have become very strict on the waterfront. They take most of the catch now but we have some. Paper, pens, yes, yes, the usual things.

He almost threw the list back to me, saying he hoped I had plenty of drachma with me because prices had changed.

He took a drink from a small coffee cup without offering me any. His bargaining lies had not riled me, but his simple rudeness did.

The man made the costing before putting together any of the goods. They could have been bad quality, or underweight, I could never know. He wanted the money first, and I would have to take luck on whether I got my worth. The group had budgeted for two thousand drachs.

The man handed me the bill, protesting that he had kept it low, and was taking the food out of his own family's mouth. He said this as he stuffed a perfectly ripe peach into it. The bill said four thousand five hundred drachs.

No, I said.

The man smiled, confused. This was no marketplace. There was no bargaining here.

I told him I would be paying him two thousand. I then went through the room, pushing my hand into boxes of dried fruit and fish.

He strode after me, telling me I could get out.

Oh, yes. I said I would get out if he wanted, but he could expect a call from the German command. If this food did not go to Greeks, the Germans would have it. People have died for this money. Two thousand would give him a big profit for after the war. Take it or lose it all.

He smiled, assuming a joke, before seeing I was making no joke. I knew that over my shoulder a boy stood with a piece of something. The man thought for a moment, then signalled the boy away. He knew I had people outside. He took my money, and told me never to return.

My three helpers were shown in, and loaded the supplies into three cars. With a wink to the fat man, I left his house.

I am not the kind who forgets things. There is a lot to remember: passwords, addresses, prices, things I am not allowed to put on paper. My head does go funny sometimes, like there is a cloud between me and what I have to know. It happened tonight after I left the little fat man's house as I was sitting in the front seat of the lead car on our way to the first drop off. The address, the street, was gone. My head was empty of it.

The driver asked for the directions. I could only say to keep going.

This was a big night, a lot of product, and there were the other two cars following us. Through an occupied city.

We drove on and I looked for clues that were not in the buildings or the closed-down shops or the faces of the hopeless.

The driver asked me again as we came to a T-intersection. Left or right. I could not remember. God.

My hands were wet and I was pressed into my seat. I had not taken a breath for a long time.

Then, as a miracle, the address came to me.

I told the driver to turn the car around, and we went back down the road we had just come up, passing the other cars in the convoy.

We had three large blocks to back track. With every street we crossed and every car I saw, I sickened, more sure we would be stopped.

The driver had noticed. Was I all right? Side on glances.

Yes of course, I told him. I was just making sure we weren't being followed. I said it just gruff enough to make him believe me.

Close to the exchange I walked down a lane to the fourteenth tall fence paling and tapped, two soft, one hard. An invisible gate was opened, and I went into a messy unkempt allotment behind a house.

A man whose face I never saw led me through the yard into a kitchen, to another man, large and shaded. His coat was tatty.

Hello miss. You have some things for me, he asked in German-accented Greek.

A German. I would be selling to a German. A player milking Greeks, buying their hidden food for his own little black market. And there was I in that ridiculous moment, selling to the enemy to get money for food or weapons to fight that same enemy. He too must have known.

Yes, out the front, I said as directly as he had asked.

A swarm of children were already all over the box on the road, with my men leaning against their cars, laughing. Greeks forget everything to laugh. They should have been stopping these children.

The big man stayed inside the house. He had heard the noise, and asked what had happened. Was something wrong?

I pulled the box into the gate, then along to the front door, telling the German that nothing was wrong, it was just some children pecking at the box. One last jerk brought it inside. I kicked the door shut.

He glared and threatened that if he was found out, I would die, just like that, with a snap of his fingers. The sweep of his arms opened his coat long enough for me to see the shiny belt of an officer.

I went cold. His rage would be enough to shoot me on the spot. He could then tell his superiors that he had uncovered an underground network. My drivers could be caught. He would be a hero in the Reich.

I was betting my life he wanted the supplies more.

His mouth moved, saying something silent. He knelt at the box and pulled out the top carton, smelling around its edges.

Sehr gut. American.

It was a good thing the Turks were good at faking cigarettes.

Arrangements, he pronounced, would continue as before. He told me to get out. Now.

I did not care for this man or his manners. I, the patriot working for Greek lives. He was the invader without honour. The man trying to make money from the vanquished. He had no right.

You have no right, I said.

He had started turning away.

What?

I had said it and now my head was spinning.

You... have... no... right... to talk to me like... that.

I imagined his hand feeling his pistol.

He smiled at me slightly. I thought it was like a smile of regret, but I could have been wrong about that. He pointed to the front door, more in the way of directions than demand.

I had gone two steps when I heard him, regretful and soft.

I am an honourable man.

Please, do not seek my forgiveness you officer of the shiny belt. You who use our resistance of liberation to make money for yourself. I'm sure you are thinking only of your children. I'm sure you didn't want to come to Greece. I'm sure you have pangs of guilt for taking food from the starving. I'm sure you see no other way.

Just don't tell me you are honourable. A nod or smile from me will never give you the honour you seek.

I smoked in the car, and shook. I had seen into a man's soul. For the first time I felt beyond death. It could come at any second. Now. Around the corner. Anywhere, as it should have come in that dark front room minutes ago. It will come fast, and whether or not I fear its coming will have nothing to do with it.

Moree, Australia

Jean and Nell walk and sweat terribly. In this heat walking is the only way of keeping little Jimmy quiet. Nell is feeling her own baby too.

Does it change you much Jean? Having the baby.

How, love?

Does it make you grow up?

Yes, love. It makes you grow up.

Why did my mum go, Jean?

Jean fans herself with one of Michael's handkerchiefs. Michael wouldn't tell her why Olga had left. He was never rude about it. He'd just change the subject, or find an emergency he had to run to.

Your mother had her reasons, I'm sure. One day you might know those things.

I will never leave my children.

Nell's voice is the hardest Jean had ever heard it.

I'm sure you won't, Nellie.

Our mother let us down.

Look love. Everyone has reasons for what they do.

What she did had no honour. Please don't try to make it all so reasonable.

Jean is glad that at last Nell is getting it out. Nell had never talked about her mother. Of all the girls she took her mother's leaving the hardest. Tina was too young when it happened. Freda has always been her father's girl. Nellie was old enough to know and to not understand.

But despite Jean's hopes, Nellie says no more about it. They walk home in the heat, without another word passing.

Olga

Darling Nellie, do you know what keeps me alive? It's knowing that you are far away from all this. From Germans with shiny belts, from good women who have nothing to eat, from death on the streets.

All this bad can also bring out the good. Today I saw a Greek man being beaten by a German soldier in a street, in front of everyone. I don't know what it was about, whether it was just some bullying or a payback for some offence. People had stopped, daring to look, something they wouldn't have done in the weeks before I went to jail. Then an old man walked up to the German and slapped his face. The German's mouth dropped open and his hand went for his gun, but the old man stood strong in front of him and put his hand over the soldier's holster.

You should be ashamed of yourself, he said to the German. You may occupy our country but you must treat us as people. This man, whatever he did, does not deserve this kind of humiliation. Stop this. Stop this now.

It surprised me, and I think everyone around, that the German nodded and walked off, leaving the old man and the beaten man, who had now forgotten his bruises and was watching with shining eyes.

I am sure it was luck that the soldier was a man of conscience, but that was something the old man could not have known. He put his life before another Greek's loss of dignity. I somehow feel that today I saw a turning point.

The Porcelain Cat

(December 1941 – January 1942)

Olga

A week ago Demerest sent a message asking me to come back as his housekeeper again.

I couldn't go for a few days, I had too many orders to fill in too many places. When I did get to the American embassy, my timing was lousy. The perfect office had lost its order and calm. The desk girls were crying together. The switchboard operator had gone from her corner and its lights were all flickering and not being answered. Demerest passed through in angry strides. He was red all the way down his neck.

There in the waiting room, in front of Greeks and Americans he broke down.

The stupid bastards, the fuckers. How dare they? How could they?

The Japanese had bombed one of the biggest American naval bases, Pearl Harbour, which is somewhere in the Pacific Ocean. The U.S. is now in the war, and its embassy in Athens is closing down.

First the British, then the French, now the Americans. Again here was I, the second-hand child of diplomats once more.

It's hard not to feel like bad luck.

Moree, Australia

Tina runs to the house and bursts into the kitchen to make the precious announcement.

Jean, Nellie. America's on our side. They're in the war. We're gonna win. We're gonna win.

Jean smiles and says they know already. It's been on the wireless.

Tina marches around the room.

We're gonna win, we're gonna win. Now mum can come home.

Nellie sees the slight gasp on Jean's mouth, and tries to stop the talk.

Tina, you know that mum's passed away.

Tina stops in her swirl and leaves the room. She is always being told her mother is dead, and each time is like a fresh slap. What she doesn't tell the others is that despite what any piece of paper says, she, like Nicky, knows her mum is alive.

Olga

This morning I bought a porcelain cat, a poor old thing that had lost its shine, grey from dirty fingers and dust. But it brightens the mantle so, this Christmas present from me to me.

Three letters came today. The first was an enveloped note from the German Command. There would be further gas and wood restrictions from two days ago. Anyone using more than the allowed amount would be arrested.

The second letter was for the French ambassador.

The third had stamps on it and the coloured, striped rim of overseas mail. It had been scribbled on by the Italian embassy, Greek external affairs, home affairs. It had been torn open many times, and each time a generous someone had decided to pass it on, to let it try to find me. The last diversion was from the German administration. Somebody in there cared enough to look up records and see my name in the deeds list.

There was no return address on the back of the envelope, but it had to be from Australia. Your father would know not to put Australia on the envelope.

Afterwards I threw it to the cliffs, and regretted doing it almost as soon as it had fluttered away. The memory of its words stays in my head.

Dearest Olga, it started.

I thought you were dead. There was no word from you to my letters, no answer to my queries, no sign you ever lived. For five years I hoped that you somehow lived still, but five years has a power to dash hope, and it did. Not for Nicky, he always believed you alive, long after I had lost hope. Then your little postcard arrived, too late for my hopes. I need to tell you that the government declared you dead only months before your card arrived. I am sorry.

Can you really think me dead my girl? You were one I always thought would have faith. You and Nicky. He and I knew each other so well, right from his birth. We would catch each other's eye, think each other's thought. After his deafness it got even stronger. Of course he would know I was alive. I feel he is with me now as I write, at my shoulder, his hand on my neck, letting me know that no bond is broken; he is my son, and I am his mother. I wish you had the same faith my girl. Your father also writes here of things being too late? Of course, he has made a new life with that Jean or someone else, he maybe even married one of them. It is no more than I could expect. He is a man with a man's needs. He was never one to look after himself.

Nellie is in Darwin. It was Mick Parrelis' idea. She is working in his coffee shop, the Resting Place.

This is a stupid thing to do. You hate the heat, daughter. You live in the furthest part of the world from me, and now you live in the furthest part of the furthest part.

The trip has been good for her. She has become engaged to a Darwin boy, Stephen Kafcaloudes, the son of a builder. He is a good-looking boy and is very fit, but a little happy-go-lucky. I gave her the choice and she said yes. The date is set for September.

September. Three months ago. Life changes without me knowing. My darling, you are too young to marry. I hope you have not sold yourself short. You never knew your own worth.

I am enclosing a money order for you. I hope you can use it to live on in Greece.

Michael Stambolis

He sends money so I will not come back and spoil his new life, while my death has been neatly decided by an official stamping a piece of paper. If this official knew I had been working for the British secret service, trained by spies to be a spy, with a clearance from the highest authorities to save and to kill, he would not be so quick to stamp me out of this life. Mother Hadjidaki warned me that men will take your life, and I never dared think that it could happen in this way. Your father must have known I wouldn't give up so easily. Or maybe it was he who gave up too easily.

Of course the money order which was supposed to keep me in Greece was gone, money he could not afford, sent in a vain hope, and probably now cashed out and in the pocket of some snivelling Greek clerk or German corporal.

I threw my purse across the room and into the little porcelain cat, which dropped from the mantle and gave out a crying crack. A white severed head rolled across the floor.

I cried for the cat, for the people who used to own it and love it, and my little Nicky and Tina who will not be swayed by the faithlessness of others.

I will not die so easily, daughter, and we will meet again.

The three o'clock change of wind came and rattled the window, telling me it was time to go to the city to trade again.

How easy it was to leave my regrets with my broken cat.

I had been standing in the dirt of the Pendeli Square for half an hour waiting for the bus. My white shoes, the only good pair I had, were getting sprinkled with road dust. A boy and a girl, fifteen or sixteen years old, were waiting too. The girl was flirting, the boy was too shy to know what to do. The girl asked about his schoolwork, his favourite subject. He rubbed his thighs in a poor try to look like he didn't care. History, he guessed. Really? She loved history. So which era was his favourite? Ancient? Modern? Oh, he didn't know. The First World War. We beat the Germans, he said, sneering at the quiet German half-track next to me.

No, she thought the Ancient times were the best. Nobility, leaders, plays. Which were his favourite playwrights?

I felt for the boy. Boys don't know plays. They know only games and trifles. He mumbled something.

My favourite is Aristophanes, the girl said, hoping. You know. He wrote about the women who stopped their husbands going off to war.

Yes, well, he started crossly. No-one is stopping me fighting the Germans. Nobody. I will kill them.

The girl, flustered, said Lysistrata was only a comedy. A famous Greek comedy.

Yes, well. I am not going to be stopped. I am going to kill them all.

The girl was sullen now. She said they had done nothing to him.

You talk stupid. They invaded us. Why don't you go kiss them?

The girl walked a few yards away, leaving the boy wondering what had just happened.

I am not naive. Young love is not the joyous thing of the moving pictures. I never knew such a love. Neither did Ellie, that little Alexandria street walker who taught me so much. But when it happens, no miscreant treading heavily where he doesn't belong has a right to destroy it with his careless footsteps.

The bus was forty minutes late. This was the end of the route, the place where it turns and goes back to Athens, but the people down the hill had caught the bus to ride the extra ten minutes in the wrong direction so they would have a seat for the long trip into the city. The idea had spread and the bus was full. I had to squeeze and stand. The boy and girl stood apart, her eyes trying to see his as he faced sulkily away.

There was an excitement among the passengers. I tried to hear what women were whispering. I heard Nikotsara's name.

I asked someone. Had Nikotsara done something?

The news was too exciting for caution. Nikotsara has been arrested, a woman said with the thrill of gossip.

Nikotsara caught? The strong woman who held the threads of the group together by daring anyone to rend them. The woman who was not a woman, the woman you could not imagine making love, or being a mother or being a daughter. She was now in an unfair room, with her eyes being blackened, her sex being used against her, beaten down. A woman who knows more than anyone else about the escape lines, the battle plans, the black marketeers, the food suppliers. Her arrest could be all our deaths, for no-one could be as strong as the Nikotsara legend purports.

I had to hide before the Gestapo came searching for the black marketeer woman from Pendeli. I reached for the stop cord, gripping it tight, making the bell ding.

But then I let go of the cord. I called out an apology to the driver who had braked hard to stop at the corner. I would go on to the city.

The seller in Omonios said it was true Nikotsara had been arrested, just that morning.

Cigarettes. Motor Oil. I think I have everything you need. Nikotsara will never talk. Would twenty boxes do? Not much coming in right now. Nikotsara's tough. Look at these paintings. Originals. With all that money, and all that risk, you should buy something for yourself or your family. Nikotsara would die first. She had better die first, or we are all dead.

I was followed from the store, my footsteps echoed on the pavement. It could have just been someone else walking the same way. No, the other person was walking lightly, and trying to step in time with me, to disguise. It was hard at first to tell how far behind he was. If I walked faster, it would have looked suspicious. I turned at the next corner and ran on before he could come around and see I had run. This only made the follower's steps become undisguised and urgent. Soon he would be close again.

There was a door. It was big and unknown to me, but the only one. Further on were factories and empty lots.

I knocked on that door. Still and waiting, I could judge the distance to the steps behind. Fifty yards. Someone had to be home. Thirty yards. The curtain moved.

My desperation made me beg. Please. I am being followed by a man. I am alone. Please open the door.

Ten yards. The door opened a crack.

Please…

The man was almost to me.

The door was flung open, and a peasant woman offered the biggest of smiles and said they had been waiting for me.

I fell in the door as the man's coat brushed my purse, and he continued on without losing a step.

The door opened to one bleak room filled with a family of gentle people. Two young women, four or five children, sitting quietly on a sofa, and some young men on the floor. Only an old woman had the dignity of her own chair.

The woman who answered the door stayed looking out the curtain till she was sure the man had passed well by.

Underground work? she asked.

Had I been pushed towards this house on purpose? Could these people have been working with the Germans? A look at the dismal family and their honest faces and I knew they were good people.

Yes. I was doing some black market trading for the movement.

There was relief. Good, she said, asking me to eat with them. She said she wouldn't take food from the children, but I was welcome to have half of hers.

I sat on the arm of the sofa, the chicken broth balanced on my knees. A little sallow boy pulled on my skirt, and opened his fist to show a dead cricket. The other children played around me, each wanting me to like them the most.

One of the men told me of brave cousin Stathos who was shot on the spot after shouting an insult at German officers. The old woman wailed instantly, and another said she'd do anything for the movement. She could sew and cook. Her husband, he could run messages.

The man nodded, flashing his eyes over my chest. His wife saw it and flew at him and slapped his face. The woman then covered the red face with kisses, clashing her passions.

I have given up trying to sleep tonight. I've been full of the women in that house, that child with the cricket, and of those women back in Averoff, crying for children they had not seen for months. On this night I would trade the rest of my life to have someone: my children, a friend, a lover. Someone.

Minutes in Wartime

(January – March 1942)

Olga

Again I waited in the Pendeli Square for the first bus, standing where those children loved and fought yesterday. It was six-thirty, I was alone, without even a German, only the half-track that's been here for as long as I can remember.

Other people soon came, one by one, also to get the first bus. Together we waited around the half-track and breathed out the steam of the very cold morning. A man tapped out a rhythm on its fender. A woman adjusted her make-up in its windscreen.

We said nothing. Words seem less necessary now. We know what the other thinks, what we hate, what we wish. Still, silence sits ill in a country of talkers.

There was no reason to go into the city on this, the last day before my new routine. Tomorrow there will be two hours teaching the Greek finance minister's children, then to a civil servant's brood, and on to my afternoon assignments.

Ahead of me in the line for a matinee film, some screwpot American comedy I had no interest in seeing, there was a woman who resembled the one who saved me yesterday, the woman in the little house. It was not her, of course, but it reminded me.

I bought flowers from a starving woman on the street. She had probably stolen them, and my few drachs would be food to her. I walked to the house from yesterday, feeling good for my good deeds.

The big front door that had saved me yesterday was open. Inside were no women, no children. Alone on the sofa was the same old man from last night. He grabbed my hand, the heaving of his caved-in back his only other movement.

You from yesterday. How are you girl? I wish I could offer you some food. But they took everything you see. They took them away, even the children. It was quick. I was in the toilet. They didn't check the toilet.

The old man kept apologising. To me. The one who had led them to this house. Because of my cowardice, these lovely, honest people were suffering.

I ran to the central police station and pushed past the Italian soldiers smoking out front.

Two Greek men were sitting behind the counter, smiling at something funny one of them had said. I remembered one of them from the day I had been brought in all those months ago.

Hey you. My family. Where the hell is my family?

It stopped the smiles. One of them stood, in deference to a woman's anger perhaps. He said there had been many people...

My family, I said. They were brought in last night. Two women, three men, and a lot of children.

The sitting man whispered something to him.

Yes, them. They are in the room down the hall. Go home.

I was already down the hall, pulling on doors.

The first room was empty.

The second had its door closed. I opened it to see a man standing over a terrified peasant. The interrogator, which could have been German or Greek, turned, surprised. I shut the door and moved on.

None of the guards had followed me, men not brave enough to stop an angry Greek woman.

Three doors down was the family. The woman seated at a table, the men standing against the far wall.

I grabbed the woman's arm and led her out. The others ran out with us, the children first.

We'll be killed, the woman said.

I grabbed tighter and told her not to think. Just come.

The desk men moved to let us pass. Please go back, they begged. It is worth your lives.

We kept going, out the door, past the Italian guard, who helplessly asked for the release papers.

I went up to the guard, and with my nose to his, told him not to be so stupid, he knew who would authorise such a large release. If he wanted to question it, he could go in and find out that silly officiousness never gets rewarded.

We turned the first corner, and like a duck leading her brood I led through back streets to the closest safe house I knew of. We climbed a fence and went through a hole in the wall, the children enjoying the frolic, the men following the women. Later they will be the heroes in their telling of the story.

The businessman sympathiser who owned the building snapped at me about the lack of notice, but he was always going to let them stay there. The family was given food and water, and locked away under the floorboards.

Now to the old man who was still in the family house. He would be in danger. I couldn't go there dressed the same way. The businessman gave me a skirt, blouse and cap.

The Germans were out already, searching, stopping people on the street of the police station. There was a different Italian in front of the building. Soldiers were on the other side of the road too. I would have to pass them. There was no other way.

Near the Central Police Station, Athens

The limping figure blocked the Germans' path. This person was afflicted through her whole being. It showed on her face. The woman was deranged, a subhuman, a mistake. They had no time to remember the master's song that these people had no right to breathe the air of the chosen ones. Instead, soldiers would remember the entreaties of their parents, to live and let live. So the Germans hitched their rifles, and divided, allowing the laughing, smirking hunchback with torn dress and dirty face through between them on her way to nowhere important.

Olga limped on, not changing the gait for a long time, dragging her right foot behind.

Olga

I reached the house, but not quick enough. The Germans were already there. From the end of the road I saw the old man and his bad back dragged out of the house and thrown into the car without respect. If I had been just a few minutes sooner, he would have been united with his family. Minutes in a war where seconds mean lifetimes.

I could almost reach across and pull him away. All this I have caused.

Stavros and Proteus came when I said it was an emergency. We sat knee to knee on some tin school chairs, the only other person in the room the guard at the door. It was fitting that the meeting place was dubbed the Stalag.

I asked about Nikotsara, and Proteus waved away the question. This was no time for gossip. What was so important, he wanted to know.

I told them about the family, the escape, and the old man. Was there anyone, a diplomat, anyone, who could get the old man released? I promised to do anything, would work harder and never sleep if they could help. When I finished the room felt empty. I had been shouting.

Proteus watched the side wall while he spoke slow and staccato.

You risk security by running into the police headquarters and smuggling out this group. You risk yourself and all you know, like that?

Stavros looked sickened by the story and tried to say something, stopped by a grunt from Proteus, and the clack of the old man's worry beads.

Proteus stared at the table for a long time.

He finally smiled, just a bit, and nodded. The words came out last and softly. He would see, he would see. If it spits in their eye, maybe we should.

Olga (a week later)

An odd couple, a fat loud woman, and a man in too-tight pants came to our car. The woman was bragging about her life, and the man was agreeing, and looked like he'd agree to anything, so long as he could keep looking down the saggy cleavage. A giggle and a shuffle, and the pair stumbled together up the street.

By this time the contact was already ten minutes late. Stavros said we should think about cancelling the mission. I refused to hear him. Two minutes later the contact came to the window, talking about a bicycle.

Two bicycle wheels meant two guards. Other things, fatness of tyres, number of spokes, they told us what he'd observed about the guards' movements.

Stavros started the car and slowly passed two cross streets, with me waving signals to cars waiting in those streets.

We stopped close to the compound, we got out and everyone went to their positions. Stavros counted to sixty. If the information was right, we would reach the front guard at the same time the other guard was just turning the back corner where the other group should be waiting for him.

I nuzzled into Stavros armpit just as we came up to the guard. Stavros played well, the way his arm gripped my waist as a lover. The sniggering guard went back to his box, half turning his back towards us.

We did what we had to do, and did it with no sound. His body was thrown into the passing car.

Two torch flashes came from the back of the compound, telling us the other team had done their work. We ran to the back, after I traced a cross on the dead German's chest.

There was no body back there. Greeks can hide anything, even a body in an open ground. One of the team had slouched a machine gun over his shoulder, a German machine gun, all that was left of their guard.

The first two in the team squeezed through a cut in the fence, and crawled lizard-like from thirty yards until they disappeared under the barracks building. The second pair then went in and ran to the side door. Stavros and I were last, taking the all-clear from the pair at the window. Stavros gave me a rifle which was older and heavier than the Lee Enfields the British used in my training. It was hard not to drag it on the ground.

I put my shoulder through the rifle's strap and knocked on the door, with the rest of the team hiding on each side. An irritated German voice answered. I told him in German I had food for the commandant, a cake from the Athens Command. After a long few seconds a rifle cocked, and a lock moved.

As soon as the door started to move, my men slammed it inwards, sending the commandant and his guard backwards. The team ran in around me and kicked at the guard before he could get control of his rifle. The commandant, sitting like a child, made no resistance and put his hands on the top of his head, smiling oddly. One of the Greeks ran in past him, returning a few seconds later. There were no more guards.

Stavros grabbed the German's sleeve and shook him. There must be more guards. They must be hiding.

No sir. No more, he said. Only prisoners in the sleeping quarter.

Some sleeping quarter it was, for there were no beds, just a few coats spread on the floor. The prisoners, thirty or so, were hopeless men who looked not to be wishing for freedom, but for death. I ordered them out, these sick, tired men.

They were slow or still, like birds being shown the freedom from the only cage they had ever known. The old man with the bent back was there. He didn't know me. What did I expect? A hug? I suppose I did.

I got cross at the group and said the Germans would shoot anyone who stayed behind, so make their decision. Slowly the rest got up, some grumbling, none thanking.

Just then I was pushed in the stomach by a young man with bulbous eyes and a big throat. I almost hit him with the butt of my rifle, but then I saw he wasn't looking at me, he wasn't looking at anything. His smile was a stupid one, his run a lurching gait.

Don't worry about him mother, an old man told me on the way through. He is simple.

But his eyes had an intelligence, even if his words and movements looked stupid. Then I realised why.

He pushed into Stavros, who was watching the commandant and the prostrate guard. Stavros pulled out his knife.

I screamed at him, and Stavros, on the point of thrusting, stopped.

I told him the boy was no threat. He had a balance problem because he was deaf.

It was a struggle to force the boy into the car. Inside he sat like he was told, even letting me take his hand. His arms were like bones, the skin on his jaw was stretched tight. He smelled of the dead.

Stavros didn't care about the boy. He was grumpy, chiding me for using his name in there.

I had. A stupid mistake I would never tolerate in someone else. Before I could ask, Stavros said it had been taken care of.

Two more German deaths, and because of me. I pulled the boy towards me, and put my arms around his bony body.

He didn't notice, and Stavros stayed angry. This should've been a night for celebration, not this.

Stavros came into my house with us and watched while I prepared coffee, which the boy hated, then tea, which he hated less. He liked my sugar water drink most of all and put his cup down for more. I gave him a knife and a fork to eat the 'horta' chicory greens with, and he used his fork all wrong. I figure he is about sixteen years of age. Like Nicky. Nicky with a pointed elfin face.

I made the boy a bed on the floor, but he wouldn't lie down. Sitting with his knees up to his chest, he would get sleepy and tilt over, then shock awake. Four hours I waited for the boy to sleep, with Stavros saying again and again the boy should be cut loose, he could take him and let out from the car near Glyfadia or somewhere. He'd survive.

My explanations were as much for myself as for Stavros. I said this boy was a good thing from the bad of the past few days, the family, the father, the police station, the man following me. This boy was something more than just me trying to fix mistakes. He was a gift.

That man who followed you, was this where it started, Stavros asked.

Yes, if not for that Gestapo man, then the family would not have been arrested. Of course it started with the Gestapo man.

It was no Gestapo officer, he said. It was me. I was the one following you the other night.

Relief can make you laugh, and I laughed. I hadn't dragged the Germans to their house, and my misunderstanding had saved a family and forced the rescue of a group of brittle old men. I was, frankly, delirious. I kissed him on the mouth and pushed him out. I didn't ask why he was following me. It didn't occur to me.

When I came back to the kitchen, the boy was in there, asleep against the warm stove.

Olga (two days later)

Stavros came back yesterday with more to tell me. That night was not the first time he had spied on me. How long, I asked. He flinched at my tone. Years, he said. He'd been spying on me for years, long before I was involved in the movement. He was the phantom at the bank and the back streets, his was the shadow that caught the edge of my eye in the market. Stavros said he had known your father way back in Castellorizo when they were boys, the two urchin leaders of a tiny island. But as Stavros wanted to take up scythe and rock for his island against the Turks and the Italians, your father could only see salvation in prosperity. Stavros become a policeman home guard and your father went to San Francisco to make his fortune. They never saw each other again, but they wrote, never allowing them-selves the damnation of a forgotten brother. It was in desperation that five years ago your father had written to Stavros, begging him to find me.

In the letter your father proudly bragged about my languages and my acting. My toughness. Stavros' shame was not, he said, that he had used the opportunity to grab me for his little group, but that he had never told your father he had found me.

Stavros told me all this expecting a fit of my famous temper. To be honest, I had been flattered by it. To be wanted by your father. I was flattered dumb.

Moree, Australia

The afternoon is another hot one and Nell is going for an ice cream. When she gets to the shop, people are crowded around its radio.

It's believed up to twenty Japanese planes were involved, and we are trying right now to confirm the numbers. The targets are understood to have been military installations, and ships in Darwin Harbour. Reports say many of the ships were destroyed. Some buildings in the town have been hit. The number of dead is twelve, but many more people are missing and rescue operations are starting. The military command has issued air raid alerts for Katherine and Cairns. Repeating: Japanese planes have attacked Darwin City in the Northern Territory. Death count twelve. More raids are expected. The mayor...

Nell tries to think where Steve is stationed. She did know, but can't remember. She puts her hands on her tummy, protecting the baby.

The other women in that milk bar are quiet, unusual for them. They all have husbands or brothers still in Darwin. Eventually they dwindle out, each alone.

Olga

Darwin is where my beautiful Nellie is. Please that she was evacuated. Please that she is safe. I damn this distance of my choosing. If I hadn't left, she would be in Sydney, safe. Instead she faces bombs and I live ringed by the hun. I have built a lie of a life in my little house with its cornices and gardens.

Proteus said nothing to me. This man of intuition knew what the Darwin news would have done to me. He hugged with those tree trunk arms and tried to telephone the Ultimo shop for me. The number was disconnected.

Proteus, Stavros, they all say Australia is too big to be properly invaded. Too big, too far away.

Of course these Greeks know nothing about Australia, but what they say is a comfort.

The Mark of Fear

(March – August 1942)

Olga

Life in wartime is a balance, a crude rendering of the law of physics. For every action, there is a reaction. Yet these invaders with their guns and their heavy boots can change such a law of the ages. Because for every German we kill, they murder ten Greeks. We kill soldiers carrying rifles; they kill the helpless they have plucked from streets, offices, shops and homes, people who have done nothing.

Try as I may, this skewed ledger of death beats us again and again. Today there was a public execution, a retaliation by the invaders for those we killed in the barracks breakout.

Stavros and I faced the five men and three women. The women and three younger men so terribly handsome and alive. You could see their defiance pulsing. The two old men were slumping, the bands around their wrists, and being held from behind by a German guard.

A German officer explained loudly that these people were to die because an atrocity had been committed against the occupation forces. Next time the shootings would be instant. No investigations, no waiting. Germans die, Greeks die. The same day. But today, this would be a lenient demonstration, a show of friendship. This time they would only kill two Greeks for every German. Four dead soldiers of the Reich, eight Greeks. It is not Germany killing these people. It is you.

The officer signalled to the four soldiers waiting in the shade with their automatic rifles. The squad marched mechanically up to the crowd, eye to eye with us, then turned about to face the condemned. The soldiers' faces had no decision in them. Their faces had nothing at all in them.

The officer half-bounced out of the way. A couple of commands, yapping commands, and the Germans holding the old men let go and came behind the officer. Strangely, the old men stayed standing. Two more yaps, and the condemned, all but the old ones, raised their arms and fists, yelling back loud and hard Long Live Greece. They fell after that horrible sharp charge of sound, leaving nothing but a crumpled mess of clothes and red, and quiet.

The crowd stayed after they were told to go. Two women rushed over to the fallen, brushing hair of one into a neatness, poking at a blood drop coming from the nose of another. One of the crowd left, and a second. There was nothing more here but to watch the anguish for mothers, sisters and daughters. The officer walked away too, snapping an order to the Greek men waiting on the truck to load the bodies like rubbish. They would do no such thing until the women had finished.

There are things that destroy me: the thought of someone breaking a little bird's wing and leaving it bleeding and dying; someone kicking a puppy not even weaned from its mother; the slap on the face of a child who has laughed at the wrong time.

Just so, I wanted to yell out that these were old men and pretty young women. Why could the crowd not just overrun the firing squad? Why could we not pick up stones and crush the heads of these perfect German officers and soldiers? They were close enough. Why could we not steal the rifles and run through the streets shooting at every German we saw till they were all dead?

I said none of these things just as we did none of those things. And I don't know why.

Olga (a week later)

I dream of one of the beauties shot in the square. I am standing over her, and I see she is still breathing. Then, as I watch, the other women move.

They are alive, I call out to those around me. No-one looks at the women. They are looking at me.

Just look at them, I say. They are alive. Look.

Then I wake, with a terrible feeling that I have left them to die because I couldn't do anything for them. And it was only me who was allowed to see; only I had been given that chance.

If they had lived, they could have been with their families, having their men visitors talk to them of marriage and children and long lives ahead. Their injuries now only something to thrill the grandchildren with in many years' time.

But if they had lived, then so too should the soldiers I have killed. The young soldiers under that hill. The Italian in the embassy. The Germans who died because I used Stavros' name.

I try to see the face of my son, yet all I see is my mute boy who I have also called Nicky. I can't remember what my own son looks like. I try and I try, but I can't see his face.

Pyrmont, Sydney

Tina and Freda palm a tennis ball against the back wall of the shop. Steve sits on the back step, smoking and offering advice between sips on a glass of ale.

The ball gets caught in the little olive tree again, and Freda rushes over and pulls the ball out without noticing that she also pulls off a branch of the gnarled and spindly tree, an ugly tree that clings to its little patch between where the rough cement paving ends and the sheet iron fence rusts into the ground. This is Olga's tree. After she left, Michael tried to pull it out, but it refused to move at all, the roots were so well set to the cement. He borrowed an axe to chop it out, but when he went to make the first swing at the little tree, clinging on in the littlest of dirt, he stopped. In that moment he didn't see its unlikeliness or its ugliness, instead he saw the beauty of its determination, quietly living without demanding anything. It hadn't been watered or fed in years, yet it lived. He went out the back gate and took some soil from under the sheet iron fence next door and laid it around the roots, his chest heaving and his eyes full with tears. That was the year the tree bore olives for him, little dry things like from northern Greece and only a few. Tough and bitter. Olga's tree never grew or bore fruit again, staying as just an ornament in the background, watching the children play in that tiny patch of a yard. Each year Michael would steal more dirt for it, each time giving a tear for its survival.

The night in Pyrmont is black. There is no moon and the only signs of life are the sounds of boats on Pyrmont Bay, a low hum and occasional clang of the night shift at the sugar works, and a clinking glass from the pub, the publican downing the ale he couldn't have during working hours.

With Steve downstairs on the couch, and Freda and Tina in the bedroom with her, just like in the old days, Nell falls asleep to these noises of the black night.

Get up, for God's sake, get up. You've got to get to the stairs.

Steve, with frightened eyes, is standing over Nell, shaking her shoulders roughly. Then he is over at Freda.

Get off me. What do you want?

We've been bombed. Couldn't you hear it? Sydney's been bombed.

Steve runs out of the room, desperate to tell, while Nell and Freda feel around in the dark, trying to find clothes.

Nell says maybe Steve had a dream, what with all the story telling he'd been doing. He might of spooked himself.

He's your husband, Freda accuses, tossing through jumpers in a drawer next to her bed. Does he have nightmares?

Nell finds her brassiere. She doesn't know. She hasn't had that many nights with him.

Michael switches on the light, making Freda throw her arms across her chest to hide her bosom.

Dad!

He says there is no time for nervous things now. He tells them to get their clothes on and do as Steve says.

After half an hour under the stairs they look to Steve, expecting him to be sheepish. He is having none of it.

I tell you, it was a bomb. Okay. I tell you what. If it wasn't a bomb, it was a big munition of some kind.

Michael has food to pick up from the market.

Yes, well maybe a boiler blew somewhere, mutters Freda.

No. I've been telling you. There's a difference.

Michael reaches for the door handle, saying that if they did bomb Sydney, then they only did it once. That's not much of an air raid. When he opens the door, the light is blinding from a day already started.

The markets are just as busy as always, with bowlegged Greeks and Italians selling in the same places they had been for thirty years or more. Olive is at her fish stall. She has her usual smile for him.

Olive. Tell me. Did you hear any loud noise last night?

Noise? Did you hear it? It was on the wireless. Some Japs they caught in the harbour. They were in submarines and some'ow slipped through the nets. They got off a torpedo first, it went into the shore somewhere, but no real damage. We got them but. Blew 'em to bits.

Olive breaks away to serve a customer. She throws her earnings in the rusty box and comes back to Michael.

Yer at Pyrmont eh Mick? Well we did'en hear anythin, and we're a lot closer at Surry Hill.

Well, no Olive, I didn't hear it. It was my son-in-law. He's down from Darwin on compassion leave, because my daughter, you know Nellie, she's going to have her baby soon.

The mention of a baby brings in the women. All congratulate the soon-to-be grandfather before telling tales of their own children. The market parents love their children and despair of them. The bomb is forgotten in the love of their own.

Olga

I thought I saw Ellie today. So much like her was the girl that I didn't think on the impossibility of it. I saw a fourteen year old girl, not the seasoned woman that Ellie would have been now. This girl stood as Ellie stood, with the body of a boy and the eye of a woman. Even the dress was the same as on that first day, flaming red and flat chested. Ellie, I said, almost called, to this waif. Ellie. It's me Olga. She flickered interest for a moment, then understanding I was not to be a customer, she sniggered and turned away. Ellie would not have turned away. Ellie could have turned away from me the child on that first day but she didn't.

I used to sit safe in my window and watch the street, barely bearing the happiness of so many children who could dare to play where there was no wall to protect them. It was a year after that importer man touched me, and for that year the window was as far as I could go into the world. I had not spoken since that man, but I could see out. Mother Hadjidaki had a woman come in to teach me the things the other girls were learning in the school, but it was in the window in the afternoons that I learned the lessons. I saw how people would choose to flare and bluster and lose arguments. I saw mothers threaten to drown their children for talking too much, then kiss them with passionate love. I saw the cruelty of children to the street dogs who would then follow them home for more of the same. In all this I almost didn't see the girl who appeared on the corner one afternoon, a girl with skinny legs with scabs on them. This girl wasn't scared of the streets. Men talked to her and she passed off with them. I began to watch for her, hoping that she would come back whole, and she always would, her so young face covered with fresh colours.

When she first saw me she smiled without thought and I ran from the window seat scared of her and not knowing why. The next afternoon she was there again with the smile that had scared me. Over days I began to crave that smile and I would go back to my window just for it, and it would always be there for me. She took to standing by my window and talking to herself, to me, saying the petty things women tell each other but that no woman had said to me. I was ten, she was fourteen and twenty years older. I spoke my first words in a year through that window to this girl, words not nearly grand enough for such a moment. I asked her if she would like a cup of tea. No she said, beaming, but she'd like a scotch. Mother Hadjidaki had no such scotch so I passed through a slopped glass of ouzo and she seemed happy with that. At night Mother Hadjidaki, pleased at my new voice, would tell me not to speak to Ellie, that rubbish, she would do me no good. Mother Hadjidaki and I argued a lot after that, and it was one morning, storming out of the house in tears, that I ran into Ellie there on the outside before I knew how far I had gone. She squatted and kissed my eyes and asked what was wrong. It stopped my crying for my tears had never been kissed before.

I took to being with her every day straight after lessons when Mother Hadjidaki couldn't know where I was. I would swing on the electric pole and we would tell each other things quickly. Before her men friends would come and take her away.

She had wanted to be a theaterina, an actress, and show the audience all the things about their lives, with them forced to sit and watch hour after hour. Then at the end, have these people clap and cheer at the lesson they have been given.

Some director told her she was not good enough, and she believed him, so she stood on cold street corners waiting for men.

One day she took me up into her little room of no more than a wardrobe, a mirror and a big bed. No-one else had been allowed here apart from her play friends.

The next day I followed Ellie and one of her men back to that room. The man walked a little bit ahead of her all the way but Ellie didn't race to catch up. She strolled, her hips moving slowly as a woman's. Good for you girl, I thought.

After they had gone inside Ellie's house, I needed to find some way to stay with them.

Around the back of her house there was a landing, old and rotten and covered in bird and rat droppings, a porch made for a sun that had long been built out.

I climbed the wire fence to get to the landing. It creaked and moved but it got me to Ellie's little window, a fixed cracked pane, dirty and opaque, letting through only a yellow light from inside. I licked my hand and wiped a corner, clearing it enough to see movement. But I couldn't understand it. I licked my other hand and made the corner bigger. The movement I had seen wasn't deep inside the room, it was next to the window. Ellie was standing against the back of the door, only a little away. The man was bouncing his chest at her, his pants down at his ankles, his hairy legs pushing back and forth, his head wrapped on her neck. I couldn't see Ellie's face, but it seemed she was laughing, her hands around his head. He cried out, sounding through the glass like some beefy animal.

The man pulled away and washed his face in the little basin.

Ellie had stayed against the wall, her legs still apart, just as he had left her. She was watching the man walk around the room and then he had her back against the wall pushing at her again.

I ran, crunching over the cracking decking, falling, crying, aching and wheezing till I got to my home. Mother Hadjidaki came as close to slapping me as she ever had, before her eyes saw mine and she backed away in some kind of fright and told me to wash.

It was a month later, after many days of deciding to go then thinking better of it, that I went to Ellie. It was morning. I knew Ellie never went out before midday.

She smiled and said she missed me, ever since that night on the landing.

Of course I heard you, she said. We heard the racket you made running along outside. I looked out the front window and saw you waddling along the street.

Why did you let him do that to you.

To eat, she snapped.

Mother Hadjidaki had said Ellie was rubbish. I wished Ellie would say something that would make it all right again, but no such thing was said.

So, you are… a moll.

She laughed and told me not to be so American. That wonderful laugh unfroze my fingers to sip Ellie's tea.

So. So. So how are you able to do it then? It looks like it hurts.

It's not that hard, Ellie said, still smiling as she lit her third cigarette. She would imagine she was somewhere else, or that he was someone else, a god just come back from battle.

Find your god in your imagination, she said as a seasoned woman.

It seems that once I got over my problem I became the opposite, stupidly impulsive. The girls who had known of my late muteness and teased me about it would wear bloody noses and stamped toes. I was a troublemaker, a difficult one who would end up in no good, their mothers told Mother Hadjidaki, who would never punish me, too pleased she was I had spirit at last. When she complained to me it was because I had been so obvious. Come now, she would coo and tut, was there a need to do it in front of the mothers? As if the sin was not in the doing, but in the being seen. If I was to take revenge, at least do it so no parent can come and abuse. I must learn to bide my time. Wait for the moment.

Olga

Peccadillo Watch they called it. Just look. Watch the new German commander. A surveillance job. Do nothing more. See if he had a fatal rhythm or a peccadillo, anything we could use.

As I watched the command headquarters for his comings and goings, a very good-looking German officer walked out of the building and spoke to the guards. He was different to the other officers. He wasn't stiff. He laughed easily. The guards relaxed with him, their elbows bending just a little. He slapped a shoulder here, and laughed a little there, perhaps enjoying this spring summer day with me.

His was a face I knew as well as my own, but I could not remember from where. From across the square I searched his face, and for a moment his eyes looked to mine, and what I saw were eyes that expected to be looked into, eyes that had been searched many times by many women.

My gaze was broken by a wail from down the square. At first the guards did not hear it, or they ignored. Then, as she cried more, they tried to see. The officer looked up too. I still could not remember who he was, but I did not want him to get involved with this.

It was a fat young woman with a cheap flowery dress and broken down shoes. She was standing over a dead man, as a mynah over its dead mate.

I had just meant to walk past and whisper for her to walk on, but she turned to me sharply.

Why is it happening, she shouted. Why is he dead?

I fought to pull her away from the body. At the cost of a few scratches I was able to get her around a corner, away from the good-looking officer.

There was no fighting left in her then. I needed to go back to my post, but without me she was just as likely to go back to the dead man. My German commander and his peccadilloes would have to wait. I took her to the church where I hoped she might calm down. We lit candles and sat in the back, and I of all people became her mother confessor.

Part by part, minute by minute, she spoke. She started by saying she was a singer with the Athens Opera. Then she froze, looking into the candle flame. Minutes. She spoke again as if there had been no pause. Yesterday, she told me, eyes never meeting mine, she had to sing for her director a sad role about a woman who lost her husband. The director told her she had no feeling for the part, and if she didn't do better she would be cut. This morning she knew she would be no better, but she went anyway, resigned to the sacking. Just one street corner from the Opera, she almost fell over the dead man. He was very young and very pretty. His eyes were open. Deep black eyes. She used this dead man to make herself feel sad. Not for him or his mother, but for herself, so she could sing the role better. The Director was pleased, and she felt a joy. Laughing for the luck of the world she walked home the way she had come, and the dead man was still there, his beautiful dead eyes now white from the heat.

I couldn't be appalled by this girl's confession. People survive, some by killing, some by not seeing. I hugged her and said there was enough suffering already, without worrying about guilt.

She dabbed her eyes with the frill on her wrist and told me her name. Maria Kalogeropoulos. But she said she was using the name Maria Callas on the stage. A lovely girl, a little torn though. I think she will suffer in her life.

Olga (the next day)

I woke up very quickly this morning with the face of that handsome German officer, a face of my dreams, a face I have seen every night.

I had to know. With the first bus I was back at the German headquarters, and I walked to and fro, looking into the doorway when I could. The guards ignored me. Staring was a Greek pastime now. There was nothing strange in it.

Noon came and went. I ate nothing, I drank nothing, my eyes flashed with the light, my legs cramped, but I didn't feel it until later.

Then, at two o'clock, the handsome officer came to the door. He slapped the guard on the back. You could see the guard wanted to smile back, but was bound to be solemn.

The officer strolled up the road alone in his shiny shoes and beautifully pressed uniform. I followed, watching his promenading walk and the way he would look in the shop windows at himself, flattening his eyebrows. Yes, he was good looking, and at peace with his life. I could see him living to be an old man, with grandsons who would crave his advice and beg his stories.

He went into the Plaka, rubbing his hand against the old stone of the buildings as he walked. An architect perhaps, or an arts teacher. He seemed to love this place.

No-one was on the streets, no Greeks or Italians, not even other Germans, it being sleep time. A few tavernas were open, and were empty but for waiters lounging.

The handsome officer turned into one of the thin lanes towards one of the older cafés, the one run by the old Cretan and his mother. This officer knew his Athens.

I took off my shoes and ran up behind him and thrust my knife deep into his back. He turned like he had been rudely pushed. He asked me, in a not unfriendly way, what was wrong. I pulled the knife out and stabbed in his front, under his breastbone. He looked down at the knife handle and his face asked why was this necessary.

I told him this was because he had raped me.

He looked like he could not remember any rape and that this was all silly. Then he died.

I ran to the safe house in the next street. Costas saw the blood over my arms. He told me to get inside and wash myself, then go home. He would take care of it.

Pyrmont, Sydney

Michael touches Freda's face. In sleep it is gentle, far gentler than it is awake. Her top lip sticks out and belongs to the mouth of a baby. Right from the first day her lip stuck out in sleep.

He leans across her and kisses her lip, just the top lip, and smells her breath. It is different now. The milkiness has gone. It is a woman he smells.

You are a fool, he says to himself. She is a woman now; soon she too shall marry and love a man, as a woman must. Soon she will be the one to watch the breathing of a baby. She is the age that her mother was when he went for her.

And he grieves; for it is as certain as birth that one must lose their innocence. He also grieves that the time for sitting on his girls' beds at midnight has gone forever.

Olga

Was it a cowardly thing I did, to kill this man?

I have known people who live in their cowardice without regret. These people absorb their failings and seem to be content. They have a mark though, the mark of a person who has done hurt to others through fear, and when they have done hurt to others through fear, they are condemned to do it more than once. They are marked.

Am I so marked?

Be Kind

(August – December 1942)

Olga

As we have become harder, the Germans have become harder. They have been squeezing us, closing harbours, blocking roads, stopping our ways out. They are not a bright people, but they keep their eyes open.

Everyone helps. Well no, not everyone. Some people revel in war. They enjoy the chaos. Small people who see a new way with the invaders, people you see on the arm of a soldier, smiling defiance. Funny thing about them, they smile but they never look happy.

These people are the few. The ledger is on our side. Politician and doorman; priest and gravedigger, we have all kinds with us, and we need them all. A gravedigger can dispose of bodies, because no-one knows the ways of the dead like a gravedigger. Priests know the ways of the living because in their confessions they hear all the ways that people do wrong, and they learn of humanity in the dark corners of their parish.

This is information an underground must have, and for months now branches of the group have been recruiting priests. Today my priest was Father John, who some time ago did us some favours from within his ordinary church tucked away on a corner near Monastiraki. This church is reputed to have tunnels underneath that only the priest knows. These tunnels, so the story says, lead to the palace and to so many other places that no single person could know them all. I am to speak to Father John and find out if these tunnels exist, and whether he'd let us use them as smuggling routes. With more Germans on the streets every week, the world under the ground is becoming our only refuge.

Sitting on a box across from the church, I massaged that varicose vein that came when I was pregnant with Christopher. As people and patrols passed by me, young women and the children, it struck me that only six years ago, when I first came back to Athens, I sat in this very square, and I felt the youngest there. Now I am old with my varicose vein.

Inside the church's corridor, a young frocked man heard my request. If the Germans had already reached an understanding with Father John or this underling, then I was in danger, so I kept a foot in the outside door as I spoke. Inelegant, but so is arrest.

He smiled and offered his hand. Yes. The father would see me.

The long frock and the lantern led me down steps and through twists and turns in a stone corridor that became colder and colder until it ended with stone on three sides. He left me, taking the light with him. Just as I had been lamenting how fast life had been in the square, here in this hole in the ground my minutes alone were so slow they agonised.

When faint footsteps came, they were not from the passage I had walked down, but from behind the other side of the stone wall. It slid forward, bringing light with it.

With the light came Father John. I knew him from his picture in the newspaper.

Come this way, he demanded, pointing through the new passage.

It had a musty smell like old damp rags. This way, this way, he kept saying, pointing as he walked. There, that little side tunnel is the one to the parliament building. It is very old and very forgotten, that one there.

This man of God could have been a labourer in the way he walked so definitely along the slippery steps. He was reputed to have been a secret counsel of Metaxas. Since Metaxas' death and the invasion he has become one of those lesser men of previous glory. This church was his only ground now, and he used his ground well, refusing proper absolution to the enemy, every day daring and challenging the invaders in ways impossible to prove, such as passing on information to the resistance in his sermons.

These tunnels were what we needed. They went to many parts of the city, and if we didn't know of them, the Germans certainly wouldn't.

You can start tomorrow, he demanded.

Proteus had warned me the priest would be impatient, but one man's impatience mattered little in the lives and deaths of a resistance. We needed approval from the head committee.

The priest flared on hearing this, swearing in the gutter talk of any fish market.

I told him I would recommend immediate approval. He grumbled away down the corridor about stupid bureaucracies, forcing me to stumble after him to find my way out.

Olga (six weeks later)

The operation started the next day and I have had nothing to do with it. This is proper protocol. No member involved in one part of an operation is allowed to be involved once their function is done. I wondered for weeks about those cold tunnels and the smell of rags, even dreaming of them and Father John. He was leading a group of prisoners through tunnels half filled with water. It rises, yet Father John keeps wading, as the prisoners drift away behind him. Finally, he climbs out of the water wearing a Nazi uniform.

Mother Hadjidaki told me never to ignore my dreams. They speak to me of me, of my deepest fears, she would say. Listen to your dreams, they are talking to you.

So I went back to the church and waited to see Father John. I don't know what I was looking for, his eye, his brow, I knew a glance would tell me if he was true. What I saw instead were three German officers coming out of his door, laughing. Father John came out after them, laughing with them.

It took me some time, and four breaks of protocol to find Stavros. He was on assignment at an interpreters' table in the parliament building, listening to sullen politicians and shouting Nazis. I faked my way to his table and whispered what I saw. He told me to be at a certain empty lot in the Plaka in an hour.

At the lot he grabbed my hand and led me through its maze of streets, lanes and low balconies, through the smells of cats and cooking, of people trying to forget. We stopped at the shadowed end of a lane, a sudden rock face in front of us. He moved a stone in the corner. It swung out easily.

I scraped into the undercliff on hands and knees, followed by Stavros who pulled the rock back in place, making it black dark. He pushed my bottom to start me crawling on the dirt, my hair scraping rock above me, my elbows touching the sides, black around us. We crawled for a minute, till a relieving thin light came through from in front.

Stop, he whispered. He had to give a password.

By now the tunnel was wide enough for us to be side by side.

Oichy. Ena Birra Paracolou, he yelled.

A rock moved to show a huge round cavern made of old blocks of stone. About thirty men with white faces and legs were kicking something that looked like a football. Rows of blankets were lined against the walls, a rifle next to each one. A thin shaft of light, only a few inches across, was coming in through the top.

Stavros left me at the entrance while he spoke to one of the Greeks. The Greek man looked angry and snapped at him. The British kept playing, but their eyes stayed on the two men, until the Greek came to me, no longer angry.

I'm sorry, he said. I didn't know who you were.

Then he turned to the rest. Men, this is Artemis.

They came to me, grabbing at my hands, shaking them and patting.

One said I had rescued him from a German prison near the mountains. I had forgotten. It was weeks ago. Another said he had fallen in love with me during our six hour walk down Sofias into the city. I had forgotten that too.

You may be tough, dear daughter, but you can be broken. Not by pain, but you can be broken by just a little niceness. It was all I could do not to cry.

Stavros saved my face by taking me out of there. We went out another way, through a drainage plate at the top of a sheer cliff in the hillside. We had to jump down to the grass below to get off it. He led me to a café.

The cave was known to few before the war. It has markings that suggest the Turks built it to use as a powder store and there are lines on the wall to show it was once a reservoir. It is not on any record or map. Father John had discovered it as a child when he fell through the roof. It became his little secret from the other boys. It was he who suggested using it as a hiding place for escapers.

The waiter brought us tin mugs of thin coffee, without sugar or smiles.

Stavros said the Germans trusted the priest. He pretends to be their friend, that's all, and risks his life every minute. If he was a traitor, those British would be dead now.

With a smile and a clap on the shoulder he went over to talk to someone else, leaving me alone with the hot cup and a warm memory of men in a hole in the ground.

Sydney

Michael's truck rattles over the corrugations to the Pyrmont Bridge, and strains up through the city to the Harbour Bridge.

The only times he had been to Balmoral were when the girls were small and he took them for a swim off the headland on hot Sundays. He had never been to a Balmoral house before; they weren't the sort of places people like Michael go to.

He pulls up the truck outside the neat brick building and the perfectly cut lawn and rosebushes. Clean, everything is clean. It makes him feel a ragged old man, shuffling up to that shiny front door. Even if he is in his best shoes.

Nell almost falls into his arms. She always has been pale, but never this pale. He squeezes her tight and can feel her bones. Such a change in only a few weeks.

I got your note. What is it? Tell me. Has something happened to Steve...

Steve is still at the barracks, she says. They won't let him stay with me here.

He looks around helpless.

But he's your husband. Write to them. You have a baby that needs her father.

Nell cries then. Michael has never seen a child of his cry in desperation.

Come back to the shop my darling.

But they both know the gap between them. She is a married woman with a baby.

I'll be fine. I just needed to see you. It's just a bit lonely here, that's all. I shouldn't have bothered you.

There is so little he could insist upon. He asks if she would like to have lunch down on the beach, just fish and chips, like they used to when she was little.

Nell is hungry, but doesn't want to go to these places of memory. She makes an excuse that Sylvia has just gotten off to sleep. So he sits on the very clean lounge seat, talking on about Jimmy and Nicky and Tina until it is decent to start to leave. He hugs her goodbye, and slips five pounds into her blouse pocket.

She feels it, and says no, she doesn't need anything. But she ends up keeping it, guilty despite her hunger.

When Sylvia wakes, Nell puts her best coat and bonnet on and takes her down the clean and cold hall. The woman had just given her a back door latch key, saying she doesn't want her brother being disturbed by the baby, so it would be better if she came in and out the back way.

The queue at the butcher winds out the door even though there isn't any meat in the window. Sylvia is the only baby in the line, but no-one looks or touches her chin or asks how old she is. All the women stare ahead, or look over their shoulder, making sure no-one is trying to jump ahead of them.

The butcher bellows that there are only a few cuts left, no T-bones, no fillets, no kidneys, only hearts and shanks. The clamour becomes more palpable, they edge closer, fighting for the bits they would have sneered at a year ago, trying to assure themselves that the last half hour has not been a waste.

Nell leaves without trying. She wouldn't get anything; she just wasn't pushy enough.

She goes to the grocer. The milk has gone. Tinned milk, the man says, that's all they have. It won't be there tomorrer. Four shillings, lady. Try getting it anywhere else.

With a bag strap eating into her wrist, and Sylvia screaming for food, Nell walks through the streets where no-one cares whether she or her baby lives or dies.

Olga

Daughter, I expect you are enjoying marriage now. It can be a very good thing for a young woman. It can give you a place within you for yourself. I am hoping though, that you always remember who you are and where you come from, and never let any man take that from you. I hope please that you wait to have children, not like me. I had you too young. I was only seventeen.

Your husband must be taking up most of your time, all the cleaning, cooking, shopping and finding time to be together. But do find time to find art in your life. Violin, please keep up your violin. You were so very good at it.

I have just sent you a message through a friend. He was an Australian soldier trapped here, and I had helped him get onto the route out. As we parted he said that if there was anything I could do for him, just say it. I said my usual answer, to just keep alive and get home safely, but as he walked towards the final contact I ran after him and asked him that if he made it back to Australia to come and see you and put all this nonsense about me being dead to rest.

I know though he first has to get out of Greece, into Britain, and then back home. He knew and I knew it was a long shot.

Olga (two months later)

My house is full with boys, resistance trainees of fifteen or sixteen years of age, who know much about starvation and death, but nothing of war. I am having to be a mother hen to mothered boys, who mess the house and demand food, who are noisy and tease my Nicky about his goitre and his funny walk. It is all I can do to not slap down these children who are hurting my boy.

This morning the boys went into the valley to play football. Their belongings have spilled everywhere from their rucksacks. Thick socks and comic books. Mother-made underwear and slingshots. Marbles of many colours for play or flinging. I fingered these marbles, rolling them on my palm.

A smell of cats came from a bundle in the corner, from a blanket hidden and wet through, from someone who had wet his bed. A boy too young to be spending nights away from his mother, but now expected to fight for his country.

I soaked the blanket, rubbed it and soaked it again, and stretched it in front of the stove fire. I must have it in the rucksack before they come back. I will probably have to do it every day. I must remember.

Olga (a week later)

I should have known how it would end from how it started. They groaned when I gave them the school uniforms to wear. One boy, with a purple birthmark over most of his face, challenged me to make him wear it, and the others stopped dressing, watching to see who would be the winner here. My slap was hard and knocked him down through the boys behind him. Quicker now the others pulled their pale thin bodies into their uniforms. The purple faced boy crawled to the back of the group and without word or scowl, dressed too.

Our bus got through most roadblocks north easily. The Germans had put the Italians in charge of them, and the Italians told the Greek soldiers to do the job. The Greeks, with no-one to bully, made no effort to lift themselves from their chairs to inspect a lousy bus, giving us just a head jerk or a wave through.

The boys in their school uniforms had become schoolboys again, teasing, punching, laughing and playing hand games. The chant of a child somewhere was taken on by the others to become a chorus. Even the driver, a frontier fighter who chides the flabby weak, was laughing with them through the rudest versions of old farmers' songs... ditties about pigs and farmers daughters. They expected me to be shocked, but it was they who were surprised when I sang along with them.

The bus turned off the main road into a country that had dried and died, where foot-long tufts of grasses sprang in brown bunches, grass that should have become milk, but here goats had long been killed for food.

At the compound of old stone farm sheds, a Greek man in mountain clothes jumped on the bus and introduced himself as their sergeant. They were to call him sergeant.

They stumbled into each other in their rush to get off the bus at his order. This Greek started on them straight away, angry and tough, yelling and belittling one who had been doing nothing. The birthmark boy.

I walked away from them, remembering the hurt of my first training session, and not wanting to see it done to others.

Flashes and the thunder. Things smashed into me and past me like a wind. I lay in the hot and in the cold. Two, three people ran past me and over me. A boot kicked my shoulder, dirt sprayed on my face. A boy stumbling. The smell of fireworks, of animals, of hay, of rhubarb, of dirty bodies. I needed to go to the toilet. My side hurt. Was someone crying?

The sergeant was lifting my arm. He was screaming for a bandage. He pinched my hand.

Listen to me. Listen to me. You have shrapnel in your arm. If it cuts your main artery it will kill you. Just lie still, he called out, running away.

I tried to lift to my elbows, and the effort pulled on my arm. There was no hurt, but the elbow didn't want to bend. I rolled instead to a crouch and somehow followed the sergeant. The child with the purple birthmark was crying dirty tears. Boys were lying everywhere, thrashing, as bandages unrolled in the dust.

Bits of German uniforms were also in the dust. They were all that remained of a patrol that had stumbled onto the training group. Time enough to throw four grenades and to shoot a couple of the boys, before they were caught by another training group of boys coming back from a patrol exercise.

The sergeant was busy with two German officers with hands behind their heads. A captain and a major who were experienced enough to know to surrender before being killed. They knew the Convention that says they should be treated humanely and given food and respect. They could not know of the resistance rule that says there can be no survivors, and no bodies for retributions.

I saw the sergeant walk slowly towards the two Germans, giving them every chance to look defiant or throw insults.

They did neither. The German captain was shaking just a little. His major had his head down, ready for whatever.

The sergeant looked at them in the face as he fired, keeping their expressions forever, accepting it for doing the dishonourable.

He ordered his men to dispose of the bodies in the usual way. Strip them, cut off their fingers, then bury them deep within the bloodied dirt. Wipe the graves with herb grass to try to kill the smell.

This cleaning and burying took two hours. The sergeant sent the German rifles and ammunition with his orderly to the mountain fighters, leaving as the only signs of the attack the pock-marked walls of the house and the smell of death, two things that could not be covered by dirt and bushes.

Lie down, the sergeant demanded of me, but there was too much to see: the unravelling of children; the dismembering of bodies; the stringy matted dog running around the courtyard, sniffing at bits and recoiling. I knew I should have been lying down. I knew I should not have been looking at the death. There was no purpose in it. I wasn't helping, but I needed to see. This was not part of my life. An inch or two from death I may have come, but all this death seemed as far away from me as the moon.

The driver was flitting around his bus, polishing windows and chrome, thanking the Lord the shrapnel didn't hit it. After the survivors got in the bus again he warned and tutted when bloody clothes and dressings brushed against his upholstery, and he would run to clean it off. The sergeant came down the aisle last, pressing an army water can to the lips of each of the hurt ones. I grabbed the can and drank as much as I could before he could snatch it back.

The exhaust smell and shake came through the floor. I breathed in the dirty taste and tried to imagine this was just a ride in the country. The bus jumped and swayed, pushing my chest into my head, then stretching it away again. Every time the bus went over a jump a sharp jar went up my arm and woke me. I would sleep again, then wake. The fifth or sixth time, the sergeant's face was close to mine.

There's a big new roadblock ahead. Do you want to stay on the bus?

The bus was empty except for us. The wounded had been dropped off at the home of a sympathetic pharmacist, the worst were taken to a hospital. I hadn't been left with them because of who I was. They were scared that in my delirium I might say something dangerous, so I was kept on the bus for the trip back to Athens, with a twelve year old next to me to watch that I did not bleed too much. Now, here at the roadblock the rest of the boys were ordered off to make their own way to Athens through the hills. The Greek driver had left with them, more afraid of the Germans than of what could happen to his bus.

The sergeant asked again. Did I want to stay on the bus and take the risk?

My thirst was a killing one now, more than any of the pain. Home. Home. My cat and my ceiling rose. I needed home and water.

To hell with the road block, I said. Get me home.

He helped me to cram under the big back seat, in the very corner, and covered me with a blanket. I heard him working the gear stick and the motor snapping to the gearbox. Soon there was the bark of a German voice, and someone banging on the bus door. The German voice demanded a ride to the city for seven of his men and their equipment.

I must have fainted then.

I woke with a sharp pain in my groin. Something was hitting me there, a foot, a boot, the heel of a boot swinging back and forth. And something smelling of oil and wood was against my nose. A rifle butt.

Senses came quickly, and I stopped the urge to reach out and grab that boot. Each press made me want to piss. I wanted to reach up the rifle butt and squeeze the trigger, blowing off the soldier's head.

I would not blow off his head. I would bear it and do nothing.

The commander of the first camp all those years ago, all those two years ago, said to control yourself to stillness was a control indeed. Easy said when there's a spider on your nose. Don't think there is a spider on your nose. There is nothing there, you must know that. Or you lose girl. It's a game you see. See the other side? They are not very good, but you can still lose to them. They can't see in the dark, so stay in the shadows. They can't hear silence, so be quiet. To be quiet is to live. Forget all the fancy crawls and the ropes. If you cannot master…

The boot moved away to yapping commands and the jolt of stomping. Then the freshness that always comes when bodies have cleared.

I moved my eye up to the window. The bus was in a place I had never seen. Half-tracks, staff cars, lots of German soldiers. All around us, ignoring us. Inside a big courtyard, like a monastery.

The bus jolted again and passed a lowly soldier acting as a traffic policeman, one arm pointing ahead, the other waving the bus through the activity. There were faces around the bus, the faces of soldiers who gradually were replaced by the faces of emaciated Athenians. We were out. The sergeant drove for a long time past people waiting uselessly at bus stops all along the road to the hills, then up past the staff cars in the Pendeli square.

Nicky touched my wound. He rubbed around it, hurting me and healing me. He soaked it with a flannel and stuck on some garden herbs with the authority of an aged doctor.

He pinched behind my calf. There was a burn there, a smooth one where a bullet had taken the varicose vein right off and left the tiny nick. A surgeon could not have done a better job. I went to bed happier. I know I am vain. It is a petty right.

When I woke this morning the sharp pain in my arm had become just a throb. I unwound the bandage to find only a deep blue patch and barely a sign of the cut. Nicky.

Nicky never looked at the wound again. He knew it would heal. Twen-ay he said in English Twen-ay. My reminder. The twenty-eighth, today was the twenty-eighth. A pickup? A contact? A rescue? My head was full of destroyed children and the boy with a purple birthmark. Their clothes were still all over my floor. I would have to get them away from here. If the Germans came back...

I remembered. It was not an assignment. EAM was planning a big operation for today. All operatives who had served jail time were to make sure they were seen in Athens on the twenty-eighth. From midday to eight o'clock. Be seen. Be seen clearly.

I forced myself up, and took an hour to dress. The wounds were dry, but the body weak.

At the Greek central police station in Athens I filed a reimbursement form for what was stolen from my home while I was in jail. I stood over the man while he stamped the paper and filed the official copy in a drawer that would never be opened again. Then I went to the German command office to present my carbon to someone in authority.

I was told to wait. That was fine. I waited an hour and rested, before reminding the Greek secretary I was here.

Yes. Just wait, they said. So I waited. After another hour I was called into an office.

A man stood on a chair trying to reach a high mahogany bookshelf. He was so short that the chair was hardly any help at all.

Yes. What is it, he snapped in Greek with a German accent.

I told him I had a claim against the German state for goods stolen from my house while I was unjustly jailed in 1941.

He asked what I was jailed for.

I said I had never been told. I was in Averoff for six months and never told.

He jumped down with a nice volume in his hand. He smelled of stale cigarettes and coffee. Rubbishy smell too. Was it a fart in the room? There was alcohol somewhere in the cocktail.

His bulby eyes might have been kindly, or may just have been made that way. They say the kindest looking people can be the cruellest. He took my paper and dropped it onto an in-tray on his desk. I thanked him for listening to me, especially as no-one listens to a Greek woman alone in Athens.

As I reached the door he whispered that he might be able to help. If I wanted.

I had to wait in the ante-office for some time before he came out with a fresh shirt and suit and announced that we were going to a jazz club. It was only around the corner, but he thought it was safer to drive. Greeks were getting stupid. Some idiot might try something.

I didn't think I was dressed for an evening out, but he thought I looked fine. If he noticed the bulge of the bandage under my sleeve he said nothing.

The club was in the old night club district near Omonios. The feel of the old days was still there with an enthusiastic doorman, but we were reminded of the menace of the new by two German guards just inside the door.

I didn't know there were night places like this any more. Red lights and lots of cigarette smoke and an orchestra playing American songs. Waiters glided past with trays of fancy cocktails. Men, many in Nazi uniforms, were eating fast the food of the rich, steaks, ribs, between unappreciated swallows of French wine. All the officers had a woman, Greek tramps who drank as much as they could while they could. Until they were dumped they would go on pretending to care about drips on their men's chins, while wearing clothes and jewellery of the dead. Heads are turned easily in days of war.

Here, you'll like this, my man said to me as the waiter poured the champagne. He betted out aloud that it had been a while since I had champagne. He was very pleased with himself. He touched my hand.

I almost pulled away from his fat hand. There was a ring he didn't try to hide, a fat band almost as fat as the finger, and grown in, in the way of a man who would never leave his wife. These fat fingers were groping over mine now. But his eyes were only for the other officers in the room. He leaned over to me with a cigarette breath, telling me I was the pearl of the room. See? They were jealous.

It was a clumsy compliment. I could only say that an old woman with white hair could make no-one jealous.

No, he said, not at all offended, my hair was silver, not white. It was movie star hair. It made me look like Carole Lombard. I was a platinum blonde.

Platinum blonde? My fat man wanted games of lies and romance. He laughed when I asked him to dance. No, I can't, he said, almost giggling.

I got to my feet, still weak, very sore. Come, my little man.

He let me pull him upright and over to the floor. He jiggled, only a little at first, conscious of himself, willed into believing my smiles and encouragement as I moved myself around him. His bent elbows and flaccid knees gyrated. He was at once grotesque and endearing.

When we went back to our seats, he was beaming. He left me with my fish entree and went to another table where he was cheered by some SS officers.

My alibi would have been set by eight o'clock. None of the Greek waiters was wearing a watch. I asked a German soldier the time.

It is a quarter after eight, miss. And you dance very well.

Pendeli, near Athens

It is the next morning and she is still full of the night. Not the dancing or the stolen champagne, but the fooling of the Germans. There was at least one General there last night that the underground did not know was in Greece.

She takes Nicky down to the taverna in the Square for someone else to make some breakfast. His face is still on a poster on its wall, but it is faded by the steam of the kitchen, and she can't keep the boy locked away anymore.

Nicholas, who owns the taverna is smiling. He never smiles. The Germans sitting at one of his tables see nothing strange in his happiness because they don't know him. After they leave, Nicholas announces, with a raised retsina, that last night the EAM blew the Gorgopotamos Bridge.

The Gorgopotamos bridge is the rail line, the supply route between Athens and Thessaloniki. Blowing it forces the invaders to either drive in supplies through the middle of the country, or ship them. They will round up anyone who has been suspected before. Her alibi of the Generals of the Reich has saved her.

Despite all the retributions that will come, the smell of death and the famine, Greeks will be smiling today.

Olga (The next day)

My group was getting restless. We had been staying still on the pebbles, the ants and the cold for four hours until we heard the rumble, then the sudden loud noise of a convoy.

The front truck came around the hill in front of us in a spatter of dust and went across our view, and then a German staff car stopped directly in front of us, across the valley a hundred yards away. A man in uniform got out. In the twilight, clouds had come across the moon's beams, and it was hard to see who the man was, or what rank. He stood majestically, looking around as if admiring the hills, his hands on his hips. He made the figure of a compact man, slim and tidy in a tight long coat. He was an officer, at least, obviously the highest rank in the car because the others waited without a complaint. He lit a cigarette and waited.

He was there to trap us, and we were expecting him. He had come because I had fed information to my little German man. That this convoy had come proved he believed me. Now it was time to give the Germans something so they would continue to believe.

I signalled for the birdcall. One of my people made the coo which went across the hills.

The answer was a deliberately loud metallic clink that came from the rail line down in the valley, then another and a third.

The officer heard them and ran, waving for his men to go into the field. The German soldiers stumbled out of their truck, a couple tripping, pinging their water bottles.

The clinking in the valley stopped. By the time the soldiers got to that part of the rail line, and they found an unseated rail, but no resistance members. That group was well away by then. As rehearsed.

My two groups gathered down the valley, the support group and the saboteurs. I congratulated them on a good mission. The Germans would now believe they had stumbled onto a sabotage mission. They would believe our planted information. The mission was a success.

Let's shoot them all, one of the group said as we prepared to leave. Pick them off. Easy prey.

I could see the others were like hyena picking up a scent, thinking, We Can Do This. Easy Prey.

I went among them and picked up their rucksacks. No, no easy prey tonight, I said. Our mission is not done until we get back.

To hell with the mission, said the instigator.

Easy prey, said another, and the words became a mantra, as these operatives became what they really were, wives, mothers, sons and uncles, angry and vengeful, with their own memories of violations and intrusions. These people were never soldiers. They were just people who but for a war would be peeling potatoes or digging up roads.

There is no easy prey in this war, I said. To shoot them down would show the Germans it had been a trap, so our undercover operative, our infiltrator in Athens would be found out and killed. They may be barbarians, but they are not stupid. No easy prey. Never easy prey.

Of course I didn't tell them I was that undercover operative. If they knew, they would just think I was a coward.

Which I might be.

I snatched the rifle from the closest one and they quieted.

The Little Things of Life

(December 1942 – June 1943)

Olga

I can't sleep. I seem to sleep less and less lately, as if there's
a splinter in the stomach of my mind that takes me back to
Alexandria, to times that your father says should be
forgotten. But I can't forget. We are what comes before. To
say you forget is to be a liar, and besides I don't want to
forget. I see my past in everywhere I go these days, I think
on things I had not remembered since I went to Australia. It
takes nothing to remind me: an old face I don't know but of
a type that has been everywhere in my life, or a building, or
a smell, or nothing at all. Tonight I woke from my bad sleep
with long dead words on my lips.

He has been shot. Help. He is dead.

My only words from my first time on stage. Going further back I can feel, holding Ellie's hand and skipping along
to the police hall to see the director for the audition. I feel
her combing my hair with her fingers and telling me to
keep my chin in the air and try to do what the man says.
She missed who knows how many of her men friends to
stay there all afternoon with me, just so she could hug me

for my success even though she had missed out on a role herself. Aren't you upset, I asked as we walked back the way we had come, and she didn't answer. I never thought on her silence, never for nearly thirty years. My mind wants to forget that ill silence of hers, remembering only the joys of that day and how pleased Mother Hadjidaki was for me, and how on the evening of the performance she fussed herself up and sat in the front row next to Ellie, not realising who she was.

Ellie was taken away barely three weeks later, on Christmas day, dragged into a police car like a street cur, a rapist, a murderer, a disease, with women spitting at where she had been. In those last seconds of our time she offered me no words of love, no farewells. Be kind, was all she said, as the policeman pulled her to the car and let her head bang on the door as he pushed her in. The sharp roughness of her captors caused her to drop her bag. The spitting women jumped on it and took what they liked, leaving only a carcass. I ran after the car, wanting to give a last word of kindness to my friend, but the car got further away no matter how hard I ran. I dream of it sometimes. The harder I run, the further away she always gets.

Later, in that first heartbreak of my life, I remember standing over Ellie's empty bag as it lay in the Alexandrian dust, its flowers still bright and hopeful. It has travelled the world with me. It survived the Germans in my house. It will go to my grave with me.

Olga (three days later)

Hands were across a table, joyful, respectful hands holding mine. Thin and old hands belonging to people of wet eyes.

Proteus had made me sit next to him for this meeting. In Nikotsara's chair.

Artemis, he said, broke into the Nazi command. She will be able to get their news, and pass information back to them, wrong information.

The council clapped this brave Artemis. This spying was bold. Sophisticated. Very French. Greeks don't like the French but admire their sophistication.

Proteus took a sip from the glass of ouzo that was always by his right hand. He asked me to give my report.

Yes, I started, I have made contact with a Nazi officer. I told Franz...

God, I really didn't mean to use his name like that.

...him, this man... really just works in administration. I have been able to get some things, and I have passed on some misinformation. We know they believed me from last week's mission with the rail line north of Kifissia.

At the end of the meeting a guard poured some ouzo into little glasses and put them down in front of each of us, spilling a little in that rough Greek way. Proteus patted the guard's arm, and said life you could waste, but ouzo was another thing. This was when they reached for my hands.

Later, as we milled, a pock-skinned man sidled to me and tried to make conversation. His cigarette was sticking between fingers of the arm resting along my back. Yellowed teeth jutted as fangs beneath slightly oriental eyes and horns of eyebrows that some wife should have clipped.

Proteus turned and put his arm around me too and roared laughter. His arm led me away from this strange man with the subtle firmness of a tango dancer.

Did the pocked man ask me about my contact? At my nod Proteus signalled to a bodyguard to run out of the room. It was only then I saw that the pocked man had gone.

The room cleared as a dream on waking. Seconds later there was a banging on the stairs outside, and the awful sound of a howl. The pocked man was thrown in the door, his knees landing heavily on the marble. Proteus came forward and kicked hard. I heard the crack of a fragile bone.

Proteus was barking questions. The pocked man was crying, swearing on his mother's grave. Proteus straddled him then, threatening a blow which would kill.

Elsie Stavropoulos, the pocked man cried at last, edging down from Proteus' ham fist. She had threatened to tell the Germans he was a spy.

The shot happened before I saw Proteus had a gun. It was a quiet shot, fired through a cloth he was carrying, and had been carrying since the meeting. The pocked man fell and rolled, his eyes open and empty.

Proteus stepped away. The two bodyguards were already moving and cleaning.

Death, dear daughter. They tell us death is not the worst thing that can happen. But it can be, when all that seems to be around you is death. You see death in everything and you forget about life. You learn to care about nothing but seeing your next breakfast, and in that way death wins by leaving no room for life. You become someone who tries to fix bad with bad. But I know death is not the worst. Can it be worse than being in a hole where it is always night? Can it be worse than where a mother sees her children die? Or when a mother makes herself dead to her children?

Pendeli, near Athens

Stavros calls her a slut for being with the German. A word spat with spittle, a blade as sharp as a knife to go into her heart.

He stands over her and she doesn't care whether he believes or not. She stands to him and whispers, quietly, so quietly that the words are almost not there.

He leans closer to hear, and she says the words again, just as quiet as a breath.

They are eye to eye, and he loses his wrath.

Tell me, he asks, softly at last.

I straighten his tie.

Stavros shakes his head. His tie?

His tie. I go to his city apartment, and eat with him. He holds my hand, he pretends I am his wife. I straighten his tie and tell him where he missed a spot shaving. I clean up while he does his papers and talks on the telephone. I listen, I hear. It is my job. As I said to you, I am not fucking with the man.

Stavros jumps at her and grabs her face in his hands. She lets him kiss her.

Some hours later when she wakes on the rug, he has gone. She washes and goes to bed. In the morning it is as if he had never been there.

Olga

Daughter, it is Christmas, the time when we used to talk, just you and me. Do you remember that we would find a porch or a step and tell each other a secret? It is Christmas, and it is time to tell what happened on that last night.

The day before I left you, your father called me into the lounge room. He had the table set up like a ritual. A cup of tea, a pen, a piece of paper.

He told me to sign the paper.

Said with the nervous smile he usually had for the police or health inspector.

Just sign it. Right there. At the bottom.

My pen tip was on the paper. It was making a blotch. I was frozen but the blotch lived, widening in a beautiful perfect circle. The words jumped up from the sheet.

Callan Park.

He stared at my blotch, his head the closest to mine it had been in four years. He too saw the words. He must have. Callan Park.

The asylum, Michael? Am I as bad as all that?

You tried to kill them.

I didn't mean to. I didn't mean to. The keys were in my hand, but I didn't mean to. Do what you want, but don't take me from my children. Not my children.

My heart was bursting, yet my voice was dead and I couldn't give it any passion. I had no breath to breathe.

He kissed my ear, our first kiss in so long. It was as tender a kiss as I had dreamt of as a child, soft and shy, a first kiss. But this was a goodbye kiss, a Judas' kiss, and he was gone. Gone gambling or drinking or seeing his woman. At that moment I knew it didn't matter whether I signed that piece of paper. My life was not mine. It hadn't been for many years. Somewhere in five children, a death, a new country, somewhere in all that. And here my husband was telling me I was mad.

I could take my choice, a poor paltry choice. To be either a woman of pity in an asylum or a woman of shame who ran from her family.

It was the moment I decided I would be a woman of shame.

Pyrmont, Sydney

It is the dream of his every night. He stands outside Long Bay Jail watching. Far up the wall, maybe a hundred feet up the wall, is a small window with bars. Through the bars he sees one black eye, accusing and pleading. The bars disappear and Olga tries to squeeze through, but the window is too small. She gets an arm through it and then her other arm. They stretch the window wider until she can get her body half out. Michael tries to tell her that she is too high. She will fall. She can't see because she is looking only at him. She pulls herself out.

He wakes to be in Jean's arms, she is stroking his hair with a cold flannel she keeps by the bed all the time. He can never remember his dream, but it is the same one and he has woken in the same sweat every night for six years.

Sleep my darling, Jean hums to him. You are a good man.

Olga

It has been three months since I have written. My last note was a last note. I could write no more. The story was told. Then two weeks ago something happened that made me know my hell may not be the worst hell on earth. There are deeper hells.

EAM sent me to Salonika over a rumour about the Greek Jews there. We all had heard stories of the Jews being made to wear yellow stars, like in Poland back at the beginning of the war, and of dozens of Jews disappearing. Proteus wanted me to find out what was happening.

It took more than a day to get there. The train kept being stopped for searches. My papers were seen at least twenty times by Germans whose ranks got more senior the closer I got to Salonika.

When I stepped off the train I faced the saddest crowd of Greeks I had ever seen. They were behind barriers and German guards, and I assumed for a minute the crowd was there to greet passengers, but there was only me. And they did not have the countenance of greeting.

Many had the 'Cocardia', those yellow stars, the mark of the Jew. It made them look like herd animals, and their faces showed that this was how they now felt about themselves.

A family came through the gate towards me, a rich looking Greek family without yellow stars, carrying clumps of cases. The mother was being grabbed by people. Perhaps by touching her the crowd was sharing her escape from the German zone. Near her a woman was pleading with a German guard who ignored her as completely as it was possible to do.

At the barrier a soldier snapped for my papers and stared at my face. He said 'Evraios' and touched my nose. I used my best German to say, no, I was not Jewish. I just had that kind of a nose. He gave me a sweeping wave through to the gate in a mock gallantry and the crowd parted for me, looking at me with a resentment that I had wasted myself coming into this place where so many were trying to get out.

The threat was everywhere. The Germans were open in their staring and their challenges. A growl of 'move on' would see proud old men shuffle quicker. Cafés had either

Greeks or Germans, never both. In Athens, Italian soldiers would talk to Greeks. Sometimes an Italian soldier was to be seen sitting at his post strumming a guitar, playing songs to the women passing by. But there is no such springtime in Salonika. Jews have a curfew; buses and trains are out of bounds to them; they can't even use a telephone.

I was not allowed in the Jewish sector, the 'ghetto', and was glad. I only want to see Greeks that are proud. That place would have no pride. I am sure they would not want a tourist there either.

The local EAM controller, a man who never told me his name, a nervous, flurrying man, said it was hopeless. There was no chance of stopping the transports out of Salonika. The Jews were to be rounded up any day and sent in cattle trains to the north somewhere.

He was not the sort who would stop a train if the train needed stopping. He would not think to pull a pin from an axle, or drop bolts into an engine or remove rails. He said it was different in Salonika, it had the two types of Germans. The believers, who will fight to the death for their Hitler, and the frightened ones, who will fight to the death to keep alive. The first would kill with a righteous smile; the second with a look over their shoulder.

That night I followed his little map to the station. There were the cattle cars, just as he told me. Dirty and empty, all facing the same way. Long lines of cattle cars, far more than could ever be needed for the stock of this country. I counted the patrols, trying to work out the interval and number, but they were cleverer here than in the south. There was no regularity. Sometimes they would pass the yards at five minutes, sometimes at two, unpredictable.

I sent a note to Proteus, double-coded.

The shipments are leaving as we thought. Big shipments.

And…

Impossible to cancel order here.

This last line was the hardest to write. We do impossibles every day. Maybe Proteus will see that the shipping could be stopped somewhere else. I doubted it.

I worked as fast as I could with the local EAM to get people moved, but I just didn't know Salonika well enough and the Germans were too many. We smuggled some people out of the ghettos, but only a few. In the hurry of our work, we didn't even keep the numbers. Twelve might have been saved, or fifteen, no more than twenty. When the first cattle car was being loaded, there were hundreds and hundreds being told to go to the train station. Old men and young men, women and babies, all with their combed hair and their good clothes and their belongings, neatly packed, kept safely close by them. They walked with their chins raised. I could see it all from the railway office where I had been given a ticketer's job as a cover. I could see the people being told to leave their bags on the ground. I could see them asking for care to be taken with their bags. I could see those guards who prodded at the people occasionally just a little hard with the tip of the bayonet or butt of their rifle. I could see the proud shoulders stoop when they saw the cattle cars were for them.

Finally, I could see them, with no protection at all, being taken to a place they could not know.

Proteus called me back to Athens to report. Through the station's gate I walked with my privilege train pass and ticket, passing through those families who I knew by then would never be allowed to catch my train.

Olga

The pain of those faces has haunted me asleep as it has haunted me awake. It's the hopefulness of the women at the barrier dreaming that those guards will raise their arms and let them through to continue their lives as they should be lived. It was the face of a little girl having her childhood interrupted to feel a fear that no child should feel. My God, isn't life hard enough without a child having to wear that look that haunts me so, and makes me glad even now to have left them like a coward. I could not bear that look of people no longer living. I had run. I now know I ran, oh yes, ever so elegantly and efficiently to write a report and to debrief Proteus, but it was still running away. For there was nothing I could do. To stay, to fight, would be to be honourable. But to stay and not being able to fight was more than I could bear.

No matter how far I run, the gods chase me, for now it seems, the time has come for the Jews here in Athens.

Proteus has confirmed the Germans were getting ready to round them up.

Now we will fight. We, who were so horrified by the cattle trains of the north. Athens is our ground. We know the train lines. We know the valleys the trains will have to pass. The invaders may stand their guards on the roofs of the carriages, but I would stand with the snipers and pick them off. I had a chance to do something to clear the faces of the cattle car children from my dreams, the faces I could have saved if I had been a better worker, a better woman.

It is not to be.

I am not to work on the Salonika train plan. Proteus assigned me instead to a scheme to try to make a new route out of Athens. This time, instead of going east towards Palestine, we go west to France. Then we go onto the Mira escape route through Spain. The boat is set to leave in a few days, and I am to lead the first run. There will be no rehearsals. On this maiden run there will be four French citizens and the two British officers. And me.

I fought against it. Without scouting, this would go wrong. A new route, even if carefully thought out, has problems that will only be found in the doing of it. Here are six foreigners taken from one occupied country into another occupied country.

You must go, Proteus said.

The Jews, I said, I want to help.

You are on the list.

I could not think for a minute. The list.

The list. Death list.

The SS assassination list found on the body of a Greek traitor. Half the list had already been killed, and killed well. Quickly. I had seen the list. I was not on it.

Proteus said I was now. An informant told him there was a new list.

I had no fear of a list. Like everyone else in the underground, the Germans wished us dead. The difference here is that they now know my name.

How long have I got?

He said it was a requirement of a methodical people that they be methodical in all things. Greek intelligence found that the Germans always did their lists from top to bottom. I was in the middle. Unless they changed their methods, I had enough time to tend to my affairs. Three days perhaps.

Three days to farewell a life barely begun. My Nicky. How could I farewell my new Nicky?

Proteus pulled a photo out of his top pocket and, with his fingertips, pushed it along the table to me. Two children and their mother, whose head had been torn off the picture. A boy of three or four was trying to hide from the camera behind the folds of dress around his headless mother's legs. There was a little girl too, all solemn, and my God she looked just like you, daughter, the same eyes, the same way of looking.

It was Proteus' family. He hadn't seen them for six months. His son, his daughter, they could be alive or dead. On the street. Could be dead. Being in EAM was no guarantee of anything anymore.

I pushed the photo back, and it was effort for him to stuff it in his wallet. It wanted to stay in the light.

He said I had family in Australia. Think of them.

I got up so quickly, my chair flew back against the wall, and I screamed.

You bastard. Do not dare...

The door flung open and two guards ran in, one with a pistol, the other with a rifle, both pointed at me.

Proteus waved them out. They glared at me all the way back through the door.

I was nearly killed. My work, my past all meant nothing. The war first, the people second. Nikotsara had never been mentioned again in this room after she was shot.

Proteus gripped my forearms, rubbing his hands up and down.

Please take these people to France. Make the contact for them, then go onto Britain with the rest. This war will be over for you. You will be leaving as a hero, and taking a parting shot. These men are so important that they could shorten our part of the war. Every day less in this war, and fifty children live. Another fifty children for the ledger.

My answer came so easily that I surprised myself. Yes, yes, all right.

As I was leaving, he said he thought I might want to know that it was my fat German administrator who gave the underground the death list. He had made contact with Proteus somehow and warned him to get me out of the country.

Pyrmont, Sydney

The man doesn't know Pyrmont at all. He had stopped over in Sydney a few times for air training, but it is night and Sydney shops all look the same at night. Olga said it was along Harris Street somewhere, ask someone where the Stambolis fish shop is. The only problem is that there is no-one about tonight except some rough kids who laugh at his uniform and a drunk who calls him dick-licker.

Through the glass he could make out a counter and a deep fryer, so he knocks. He knocks for a long time, and is finally about to leave when a woman's face comes to the other side of the glass. She is plump, red haired, with a woken-up look.

Is this Michael Stambolis's house?

It's the middle of the night. We've got babies here. Come back in the morning, she says, still not awake.

Please miss. I can't come back. I have to go to Melbourne first thing. I have a message for a Nellie. It's from her mother.

Oh…

And she is gone.

Nell stayed curled in the tiny bed, wrapped around little Sylvia.

Jean sits on the edge.

Don't you want to know about your mother? She must be alive…

I don't want to know. Please Jean. Just let him go.

Jean lets go of her hand. Nellie often got scared now. She was a nervous shy girl who, with the war, was growing into a fearful woman.

Well, do you want me to take a message?

No. Just tell him I'm not here.

This time Jean opens the door a little to the man.

I'm sorry. She's not home.

They both know it's a sad lie.

Well, can I tell you then…

No, no I don't think so. Things between mothers and children aren't for others. Besides I'm the wrong one to tell.

He thinks for a moment of breaking in and shaking her and searching for this Nellie, but he can't overcome the manners he has carried for a lifetime.

He simply says 'I see,' and moves on.

Afterwards he was sure he heard a 'thanks' behind him as he walked away angry. Thanks for what? Thanks for trying? He had tried to honour the promise to this woman in Athens. Still, his promise kept him going. It got him home.

Olga

I told the woman his name was Nicky. Nicky Mavromati. The same address as me. Pendeli.

She wrote it down roughly without caring why I was transferring my house and land to this child. It was too hot for her to care. The fan had stopped working. Like so many things in Greece these days, when it broke, it stayed broken.

I asked if this was all I needed to do. The impatient 'yes' was given to me along with a cheap paper which looked worthless, something I could have forged myself.

The bank was a disappointment. Only six hundred drachma in my account. I had taken money out too easily, and now I was left with only this. When the Germans took my house, and stole my chairs and bookcases, they also took, without knowing, all my money, thousands of drachma jammed in its springs.

Six hundred drachs. For a life. I took them, and in the polished toilet of the bank building I split the six hundred into four groups, two went into my brassiere, the other two into the toes of my shoes.

As the old bus pulled me up the Pendeli hill for the last time, I didn't care about the guards and the rifles any more. If some stinking coward Nazi wanted to shoot me for being a woman on the streets in this heat, then he could. There would be no hiding today. None of them even looked at me, and strangely, I felt a shame for my ill-will.

From outside my gate I watched Nicky's shadows move across the top floor window of the house which was not mine any more. God, how I love to watch him.

He was painting. He had mixed the colour of lavender flowers from clays. A man of colours is the most beautiful of men.

I pushed the money into his hands and he understood. He let it fall. I wish he had been angry and given me a reason to walk away from just another selfish man. No. He just stood like he always stood, except that the colour in him died.

Every bit of me wanted to pull the hair back off his forehead, to kiss his eyes and his tears and promise never to leave him. I loved him with food instead, the best meal I had in me. After I go he will eat from our garden. The six hundred drachma might never be touched. It didn't matter either way.

I took my few little things, some clothes, my diary, and left the house and left my Nicky, not knowing how I was able to do it.

Germans were in the square, and I walked past them, carrying the suitcase with the diary they would love to have. If they knew.

As the trees scraped the side of the bus I thought of everyone who would be left here. There was Maria, the opera singer who would always survive. Drago, who surprised me by overcoming his greed and helplessness. There was Stavros, who was only in this because they went too far. He was like so many other Greeks, ordinary people who had lived by plying their ploughs and had never thought about doing another man an injury. They are all good people who have been forced to fight until they win or die. This dry land was either too hot or too cold, but worth dying for. This was their war that had been made my war.

Anna jerked with a real surprise and looked, at that moment, very happy to see me.

We stood in the door, both wanting to say a lot.

I was jailed for six months.

Yes. I know.

I think I know who put me in to the Germans.

Anna nodded vacantly. You must want to kill them.

No. That is not the way anymore. I will let them be.

Anna's hand went some of the way towards me. Did they treat me well in jail?

It was a jail.

Yes.

I said I lost my hair colour in there. I loosened my scarf and let the white mane fall.

My God, sister. That's terrible. Anna looked like she had been punched.

I quite like it actually.

Come in and see mother. She would be happy to see you. It has been a long time.

Anna, what happened to Christopher? Why did he die?

Christopher. Do you still grudge against me for that?

What happened?

It wasn't me, sister.

What happened?

And there, in a doorway she told me what killed my baby, what ended my youth, what destroyed my marriage, my mind and my motherhood. It was Anna's sister, Xenia, the retarded one who threw herself into the front of a bus not long after. Anna found her with baby Christopher, but too late. She was feeding him cogs from an old sewing machine, little wheels that just fitted in his mouth. If it had been just one, then his little tummy might have passed it, but she kept feeding him, mothering him, trying to do what she saw other women do every day, feeding their young. But wouldn't the doctors know, I said, feeling that helplessness again. They never knew, she said, because she insisted there be no autopsy. Every day for thirteen years Anna had to live with knowing she could have saved him if she had only told me what she had seen. But she was scared, and so my baby lay dying while I tried every colic remedy I could find. Fear is meant to protect you. Every minute I see where fear only kills.

I thanked her. I said I had needed to know before…

Before what, she asked with some alarm.

As I left, Anna threw her hand out again and touched me, barely, and said she was sorry.

Pyrmont, Sydney

Michael set up the table in the back yard of the shop with lots of silly little things on it: ribbons, balloons, party hats home-made by a missus from across the road, and little crackers someone had found forgotten in a wardrobe.

Soon twenty or so people fill the yard, men from the pub, market people, wives from all around, sitting or standing, toasting Sylvia's first birthday, while Nellie bounces her and encourages her to smile for all these people who had come to say Happy Birthday. Sylvia is a good baby. She laughs for them.

Word has got around about the party. Mr. Bullock from the pub has brought some under-the-counter meat. Mrs Simpson the grocer turned up with some of her husband's pickles. Even the police haven't asked Michael for their butter this week. That is their contribution.

Toasts and cheers. No-one is forgotten. Nell is complimented as a beautiful mother; Michael, as a doting grandfather. Then Jean surprises everyone by proposing a drink to Olga, who made this beautiful family.

Nell watches all the people take this drink, even those who were jealous of Olga when she was here and hated her even more for leaving. These ordinary people with their hates and their loves, standing with their scrubbed scratched glasses full of ale and shandy, their long trousers that might be just a little too short, all of them standing together to make a wish that may or may not make anything happen. For at this moment these people are bound, of a mind in this cement yard with an occasional feather blowing from the tubs; in this cement yard where for years a man has bloodied himself with chicken entrails for his family; in this cement yard of an olive tree that no-one but him sees anymore.

Baby Sylvia cries then and Nellie must go upstairs to feed her, something that will wait for no reverie. Nellie gathers the baby, and feels a calmness she has never felt before. She knows it will not be there in the morning. But that's okay. She has all she needs, and one night is all right to feel at peace in this world.

Olga

It is my last night in Greece and I spend it here, alone, in a halfway house. I will leave this diary here with Ioannis. After the war is over he will mail it to me in London or Sydney. If anything happens to me he will destroy it, for only I will choose who will read this, and when.

And I might die. Days on a boat through enemy sea lanes, then through a patrolled port and another occupied country. It will be a miracle. I know it and Proteus knows it.

I have just gone outside for a last evening walk in my Plaka. I went to the café I liked the most. It was closed down when the Germans first invaded. It is open again now. The owner just couldn't stay away. I know that kind of love.

His coffee was bad, but I didn't care. It was made of Greek coffee and Greek water, and that's enough.

The café is near where I killed that officer for revenge. I have killed, I have saved, and hated and loved. Regrets? I don't know. I have nightmares, and that might be the same thing. I have won love. Nicky. Please, he must eat enough.

Somebody at the next table, a man, was swearing because he was losing at cards. Another man lit a foul smelling cigarette and drew it in deeply and thoughtfully. I breathed it in too, and took comfort in the bitterness.

The little things of life are still here, my daughter, and I know they always will be.

Postscript

Olga's team made it to England. One of them had information that helped crack the German codes.

In England Olga learned of Michael's marriage to Jean, and her later diaries show this was the reason she decided against returning to Australia at that time. We know the British authorities took advantage of her decision and set new jobs for her, including accompanying another agent back to France. She stayed in Paris, working with the French Resistance. In 1944, with news of the disappearance of Stavros, she risked a return to Greece to find him.

Little is known of Olga's whereabouts for the next year. Her diaries for this period are lost, if indeed they ever existed. But it is known that in 1946 she started work as an interpreter for the British King's Regiment in Athens, and later for the Americans. She finally decided to return to Australia in 1952.

Olga never saw Michael Stambolis again. He died while she was on the boat to Australia.

Acknowledgements

Although Someone Else's War is based on the true story of Olga Stambolis, writing it as a novel was a task that would not have been possible without the support and help of many people: Annette Barlow (Allen & Unwin), and Kirsten Abbott (Penguin) who pushed me into making this book better; Sandy Wagner, who was with me for so much of the journey; Anna Kannava, who was so frank; Gary Young, with his encouragement when I needed it most; Margie Gillett for finding the many typos, suggesting the chapter titles, and for calling me Shakespeare; Julie Ramsden for her artwork for the book's website www.someoneelseswar.info. Thanks too to Dan Mavric for his layout ideas and endless multimedia help; and Graeme Fettling and Gerry McKechnie from Network Sound and Vision for the site's video.

Many other people helped in the gathering of facts, especially Nick Manning, who was there in Greece and must've only just missed crossing paths with Olga many times during the war. Thanks to the Athens War Museum for bringing the war to life for me, and the British war records office in Dyfed, Wales for their help in the impossible search for information about Olga's wartime activities in an occupied country.

A special thanks goes to Jon Lord, a man of great heart who, without a moment's hesitation, generously allowed me to use the words from his most personal of songs.

As always, thank you Jac, for your love, honesty and understanding, and for your music.

To Nellie, Tina, Freda and Nicky, who carried the legacy of Olga with grace and told me so much of what is in this book. Of course there is the beautiful Jean, the only grandmother I ever knew, and my grandfather Michael, who I only knew through his daughter's stories.

And to Olga, who I felt at my shoulder on so many of the late evenings. I hope the diaries were as you would have written them. I will always be grateful that through this book we have become acquainted.